Christopher Baker

Chris enjoyed a successful career in the printing industry, spanning 30 years and taking him all over the world.

More recently Chris returned to his lifelong passion of astronomy by creating an art business based upon his astrophotography. Now his photographs of deep space can be found in homes and offices across the globe.

In 2017 Chris was commissioned to write a book based on his images of space. 'Photographing the Deep Sky' was published by White Owl Books in May 2018.

Chris's first novel, 'The Girl Who Sewed Parachutes' was published in 2020.

Chris and his wife Fiona divide their time between homes in Hertfordshire and Devon. He is inspired to write during long walks and cycle rides in the Chilterns and on Dartmoor.

They have two grown up sons, Alistair and Tim who both live with their partners in London.

Chris's space art can be found at www.galaxyonglass.com

Also by Christopher Baker

Non-Fiction

Photographing The Deep Sky - A Journey Through Space and Time

Fiction

The Girl Who Sewed Parachutes

THE SHORT LIFE OF AMY RIDLEY

BY CHRISTOPHER BAKER

The right of Christopher Baker to be identified as the Author of the Work has been asserted by him in accordance with the Copyrights, Design and Patents Act 1988

Copyright © 2023 Christopher Baker

All rights reserved.

ISBN: 9798866873913

For

my grandchildren

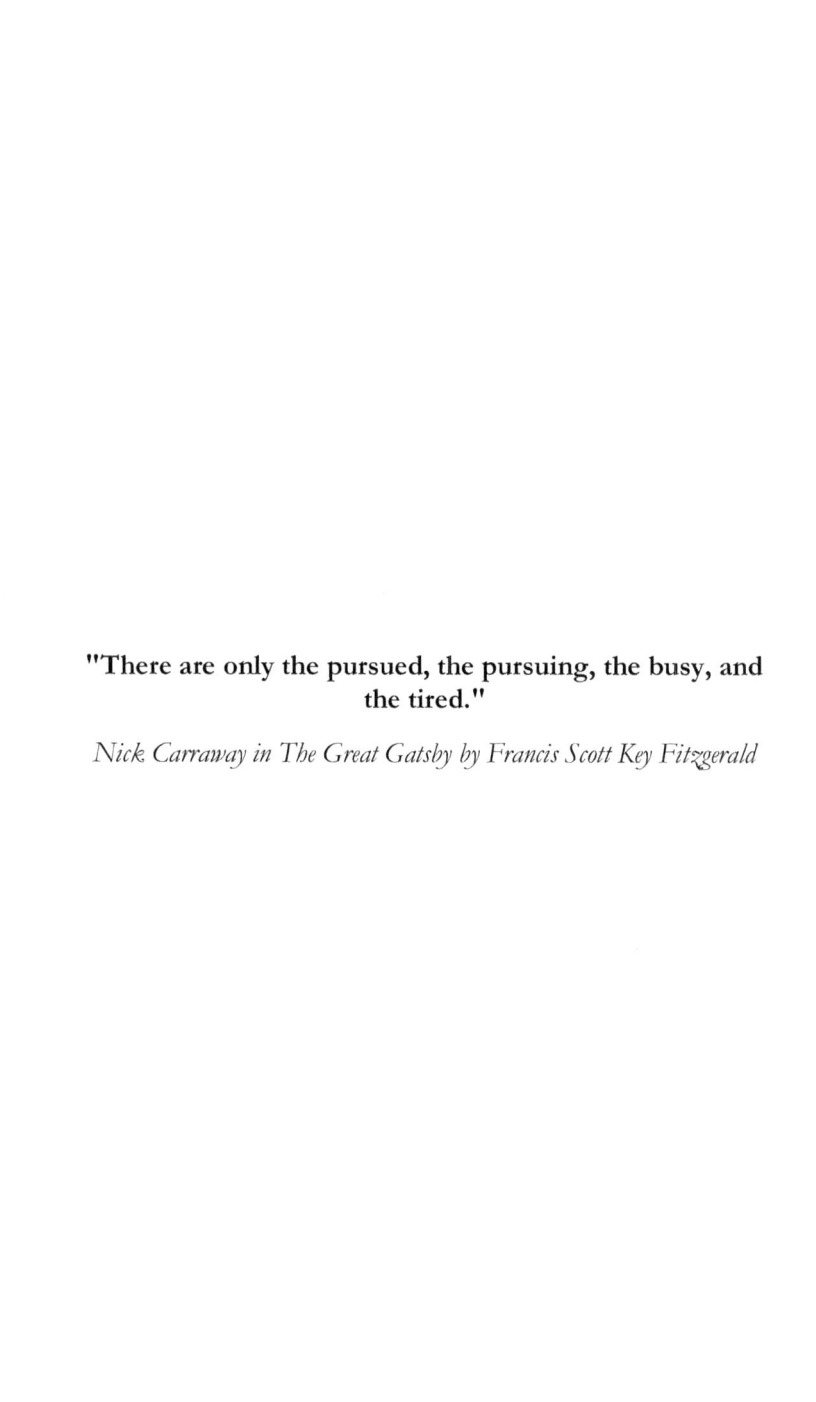

"There are only the pursued, the pursuing, the busy, and the tired."

Nick Carraway in The Great Gatsby by Francis Scott Key Fitzgerald

AMY

PROLOGUE

February 1995.

I'm sitting under the Witch's Tree, my back against the solid oak trunk; my legs bent, arms wrapped around my knees. The grassy dampness is seeping through my jeans. I've gathered my coat tightly around me and pulled up my scarf to keep the biting wind from chilling me and cutting short this time for contemplation.

Before I sat down, I had to look up, crane my neck to see where the high branch had been. I even walked around and around the tree, childlike as if in a maypole dance, one arm slowly dragging behind me, fingers tracing the rough surface of the bark.

It smells and looks so different on a day like this: winter has cruelly stripped the trees of their foliage, the dripping branches gnarled against the grey featureless sky.

So much of that afternoon back in the summer two years ago flashes through my mind. How it happened in a split second. The loud crack echoing through the wood, the sound returning again and again as if to punish me. The guttural scream. His eyes meeting mine as I watch him fall. I recall with a shudder the deafening silence that followed: that loud nothing-noise is thumping in my skull right now: as if I were back there in the moment. But I wonder if my mind conjures up scenes to fill in blanks left by the trauma.

Now everything is in place. Here I am, eighteen years old, ready to do what I know I must: end the life of Amy Ridley.

AMY

CHAPTER 1

August 1991 14 years old

Amy was half awake when her bedroom door burst open and her six-year-old brother Billy scampered in, full of beans and ready to play. He was wearing his blue glow-in-the-dark-space-dog pyjamas and his ginger hair stuck straight-up, defying the laws of gravity. She pulled the duvet over her head and groaned. "What is it?" she asked from under the cover, trying her best to sound stern. He was holding his bike helmet which only meant one thing.

"Ammy! I know you are under there." He pulled the cover back and leant close, his face inches from hers. "It's bike time!" She loved the way he called her Ammy rather than Amy; it wouldn't be right coming from anyone else.

Daylight shone through the curtains, flooding the room. She remembered the day Mum had taken her shopping for the curtain material. "You can have any pattern you want," she'd said. Back home Mum had taught her how to use the sewing machine and they'd laughed at her attempts to sew in a straight line. She could see the wonky hem to this day.

"What time is it?"

Billy skipped over to her desk, picked up her digital alarm clock and announced it was six o'clock.

"It's too early, come over here," she said patting the duvet. She'd not heard Dad pottering about yet and didn't want to wake him.

Billy replaced the clock, took a few strides, and leapt onto the bed. Quickly he snuggled in beside her and she could feel the warmth of his body. "We'll go later I promise," she said as she pulled him close.

He put his head on her shoulder. "We can go to the woods, and you can climb the Witch's Tree and read your boring books."

From the age of ten she'd been keen on climbing trees. Now as a fourteen year old, she'd still go to the woods, climb up to a branch, and sit thinking, reading, or watching the birds. It was her safe place where she felt free to read and think what she liked. The fact that her friends Tamsin and Rachel preferred the woods as cover for their smoking habit only helped; she'd hate it if they wanted to join her.

"The what tree?" she asked.

"You know, the one you always climb, by the open bit and the riverbank."

"You mean the oak tree by the water." She pulled away to look at him. "Why do you call it the Witch's Tree? I've never heard that before," she quizzed.

"What are those?" he said, putting the end of a finger on her cheek and pushing in the flesh.

"Don't!" said Amy, moving his hand away. "They're spots and stop asking about them, it's not kind."

"Will you always have them?"

"No. Billy, stop it," she said as she shuffled to sit upright. She looked down at him. "Anyway, what's with the witches?"

"Don't be silly, there aren't any witches!" He rolled onto his side resting his head on his hand looking up at her. "You look like a witch when you're sitting on that branch with your legs dangling down each side; like on a broomstick."

"You're in big trouble!" she said as she dug her fingers into his ribs.

"That tickles! Stop it!" he giggled as he struggled from her grasp and shuffled under the covers. "No more tickling!" She laid down next to him and within minutes he was asleep with one arm across her face. She gently repositioned it and was soon asleep herself. Amy was awoken by a tapping on her bedroom door. "May I come in?" Before she could answer Dad popped his head round. "Morning!"

"You're supposed to wait for an answer before you come in."

"Sorry, you're right," he replied. "Seen Billy? He's not in his room."

Amy pointed to the duvet cover and her dad winked. "Oh, I'd better go and hunt for him," he said loudly. As the door closed Billy pulled back the duvet laughing, his cheeks red from the warmth.

"Shh! He'll hear you!"

Suddenly the door opened. "Gottcha!"

"Ah!" Billy cried as he threw his arms around Amy.

"If you want to hide from me, you'll have to do better than that!"

Billy's face crumpled. "You cheated!"

"I don't think so!" said Dad smiling. "Right, it's breakfast in thirty minutes. Then the three of us are going on a trip."

****

Billy was attacking an overflowing bowl of cereal as Amy entered the kitchen and poured herself a glass of orange juice. She felt more at ease when it was just three of them. Although it didn't have to be her, Billy and Dad, as it could be her, Billy and Mum. More and more her parents seemed to argue about stuff. Sometimes at night she would hear them trying to argue softly. She would creep out onto the landing and sit on the top stair, listening. Dad occasionally slept in the spare room, but never for long. Despite these incidents, Amy knew that if she was asked, do you live in a nice family, and if *she* was loved, she would surely say yes. It horrified her to think Dad or Mum might not be around.

"Where are we going, Dad?" Amy asked.

"Mum called last night saying she won't be home tonight after all, it'll be tomorrow afternoon instead, so I thought as the forecast is good, we'd go to the seaside."

"Oh wow!" exclaimed Billy.

Amy sighed. She looked like a rake in a swimsuit and imagined overhearing boys on the beach laughing at her shapeless figure. "Where?" she asked.

"Brancaster, it's on the north Norfolk coast."

"I know where Brancaster is," she replied. "It's a haven for bird watchers." She thought for a moment, adding, "At certain times of the year you can see Avocet's, Bitterns, Black-headed gulls, loads. I read up on it."

Dad was about to take a mouthful of cereal but stopped, spoon in mid-air and smiled. "Amy Ridley, you know too much for a fourteen-year-old."

Amy blushed. "Whatever."

"Before we had you, Mum and I often went at weekends."

"Where is Mum?" interrupted Billy.

"I've already told you, she's in Norwich at an exhibition. Anyway, we'll leave in about an hour," added Dad. He stood up with the empty bowl in hand. "Bring a friend if you want, Amy."

Amy blushed again, sensing he'd noted her disappointment at the seaside idea. "I'll phone Rachel." Five minutes later, Amy called up the stairs to Dad, "She's coming!"

****

"Let's stop here," Dad suggested as he dropped the bags, wind breaks and the rest of the paraphernalia onto the sand. Amy could see the sweat running down the side of his face.

"You can bowl," said Billy handing a tennis ball to Amy and picking up the stumps. She smiled and ruffled his hair. It didn't take long to establish it was impossible to get Billy out. "That would have missed! No ball! Wide!"

"Teatime at the Oval." Amy caught Rachel's eye, adding, "Shall we go for a walk?" They wandered along the water's edge arm in arm, enjoying the chill of the sea on their feet. Amy was wearing shorts and a shirt tied round her midriff and Rachel was in her swimsuit.

Rachel stopped, pointing into the distance. "Let's go and watch those boys playing football." Amy felt her toes dig into the sand and hesitated before answering. "I think I may go looking for shells," she replied. "I'm making a bowl in pottery class and I'll use them to decorate it." Amy turned and looked out to sea, as if spotting something of interest. Turning back, she said, "it'll be a present for Mum as she missed out on today." She brushed imaginary sand from her arm as she glanced over at the boys.

"Whatever," replied Rachel.

Suddenly Amy bent down. "Look, here's one," she said, picking it up. She turned the delicate shell between her fingers, studying its intricate structure. "See the rainbow colours?"

Rachel leant over. "Nice," she replied before turning back in the direction of the football game. "I'll see you back at the towels," she added.

Amy stared at Rachel's figure as she walked away. They don't make clothes for garden rakes, she'd once whispered to herself as she'd stood in the shop flicking the shirts across the rail. She would go to great lengths to get out of having her photo taken too. Amy felt so different from her mother who was attractive. Amy would find herself staring at her mother and wondering how she was her daughter. And how Dad managed to even get a date with Mum in the first place? Perhaps he was good looking when he was young but then she couldn't imagine it. "See you later!" she called in Rachel's direction.

Amy made her way to the top of the beach walking parallel to the dunes. Now there was a gentle breeze which cooled her skin and rustled the grass sprinkled across the waves of dunes. She bent down and picked one of the spiky looking tufts, slowly turning it around between her fingers. Her mind drifted back to a class with Mrs Hanson, as she explained how the roots helped to keep the dunes stable. She tossed the stem to the floor and wiped her stained hands on her shorts.

As she looked up, she saw a woman, no more than thirty feet away, lying on her back with a wide brimmed sunhat covering her face. Maybe she was asleep or simply protecting herself from the sun. Next to her was a man holding a book above his head reading. The woman's legs were resting across his.

Amy moved a few paces to the left and walked closer, so another family was partly obscuring her view. If she leaned to one side, she could still see the couple but now she couldn't easily be spotted. She sat down, hugging her knees to her chest, watching. Amy was transfixed but wasn't sure why. It was as if she was trying to remember a dream; the harder she tried to recall the details, the more a veil was drawn over her thoughts. She fixed her gaze on a tote bag with candy red stripes and bright red handles. She put her head to one side, then the other, as if it would offer alternative views whilst not taking her eyes off the woman. A few moments passed and she noticed a pair of beige flip-flops. She could see they had matted soles and gold-coloured straps. Amy shielded her eyes then slowly put on her sunglasses. Suddenly the woman moved her legs off the man and sat up, brushing sand from her thighs, then her feet. The woman's toenails were painted an unusual purple. An odd sensation spread out from the pit of Amy's stomach and she wondered if she was going to be sick. Then the man tossed his book onto the towel, sat up and put his arm around the woman's shoulder and they kissed. It was a long and passionate kiss. One between lovers. As they finished their embrace the woman began to turn her head, first to look out to sea and then gradually in her direction. Amy threw herself backwards onto the sand, rigid with fear. Her heart thumped loudly in her chest as her fingers dug into the sand, the tiny grains forcing themselves under her nails. She watched as a puffy cloud skidded across the sky and a seagull squawked as it swooped and dived overhead. Amy rehearsed what she would say if she came over, but it all sounded ridiculous. Minutes seemed like hours as she lay still, waiting, waiting. She could vaguely hear the couple chatting. Laughing. She suddenly felt dizzy as the thought pounded and whirled around in her head: how could her mother do this?

  Amy took one last look as she carefully moved away, then ran toward the sea. Her body shook and at one point she stopped and held her shaking hands out in front of her, palms down. Perhaps she had fallen asleep on the sand and dreamt it all? Perhaps she should go back and check? No, it was her. It was her.

  By the time she got back to the others, Rachel was lying on a towel sunbathing. Amy could hear Boyzone playing loudly through Rachel's headphones. She slunk down on her own towel facing the other way, clutching a sodden paper handkerchief. She could see Dad and Billy kicking a football to each other, oblivious to how their worlds had changed.

Suddenly the music stopped and she heard Rachel sit up. "Where did you go? You didn't miss much by the way. Dumb boys as usual."

Rachel put her hand on Amy's shoulder and leant over. "You're crying, you okay?"

Amy tried to speak but couldn't.

"What's happened?" added Rachel as she cuddled close. Amy felt the warmth of Rachel's arm across her shoulders.

"Nothing," she managed.

"This is not nothing," said Rachel.

"I can't tell you. But don't worry about me. Don't say anything to my dad."

Rachael stayed close with her arm around Amy's waist, both of them lying there in silence. Soon Billy came bounding over, followed by Dad. "You okay, Amy?" Dad said standing in front of her. She moved her sun hat to cover her face.

"She's had a bit too much sun, Mr Ridley," said Rachel. Amy felt Rachel tighten her embrace.

"Oh dear. Amy, can you talk?"

She nodded, sniffed then mumbled. "I'm fine, it's not that bad. I'm just tired."

Dad put his hands on his hips. "I'll put the umbrella up, you drink lots of water and we'll see how you are in half an hour."

"I'll look after her Mr Ridley," added Rachel and gave her friend another squeeze.

****

"We'll get some crab sandwiches next time," said Dad as he slammed the boot shut. Nobody said anything and within minutes Billy was asleep, exhausted from all the games and swimming. Amy could sense Rachel looking at her, but she continued to stare out of the window, replaying every shocking moment of what she had witnessed.

As they approached the house, Amy was relieved to see that Mum's car wasn't in the drive. She dashed inside and went straight upstairs for a bath. Before long she heard Mum return. She strained to listen in case there was shouting from downstairs but heard nothing untoward. How would her mother react when she found out where they had been today? Soon there was a tap on the bathroom door.

"Dad says you had too much sun. Are you okay darling?"

Amy remained silent, staring at the surface of the water as she gently moved her hand from side to side.

"Amy?"

Amy moved her hair away from her face. "I'm okay," she replied.

"Are you burnt?"

"No."

"Just too much sun?"

She didn't say anything until she heard another gentle tap.

"I'm fine."

"Okay darling, I'll see you later."

Amy immediately switched on the radio, turning Alanis Morissette's *You Oughta Know* up to full volume. *"And I'm here….to remind you, of the mess you left…"* blared out loudly, temporarily drowning her thoughts. After a while she switched off the radio, giving herself some peace. Lying in the tepid water she agonised over what to do. She was half minded to confront her mother. She imagined a scene with her screaming at Mum. 'How could you love somebody else?!' 'What's Dad done wrong?!' 'You don't love us anymore!' But then what would happen? She couldn't think of anything worse than the family breaking up. Maybe Dad would leave? What about Billy? She couldn't bear the idea of not being with her brother. By the time she had dried herself she had vowed not to say a word to anyone. It was a secret she was going to have to carry.

Later her mother sat on the edge of Amy's bed. "Are you sure you are okay?" she asked. Amy pulled the duvet closer around her neck and kept her eyes tightly shut as she nodded.

"Is there anything you want to tell me?" her mother asked.

Amy shook her head.

"Alright. I'm exhausted and going to bed now too. Let's see how you are in the morning and try to get some sleep. Nighty night," she added as she stood up to leave. Once Amy was sure Mum had gone to bed, she got up, slipped into her dressing gown and slippers and went downstairs. She could hear the TV and knew Dad was still up. She made two teas and took them into the sitting room.

"Hello, you," smiled Dad, "lovely to see you up. Feeling better?"

Amy smiled as she handed him the tea and sat down. Dad switched off the TV, "thanks," he said holding up the mug, "to what do I owe this?" Amy rested her head on his shoulder. She could feel the tears welling up. "Thanks for taking us today," she snuffled.

"That's kind. I'm glad you enjoyed it, and I'm sorry, I should have taken more care of you."

"It's fine, Dad," she said wiping her eyes. "I should take care of myself. We all had a good time anyway." Amy wondered if Dad could feel her heart racing. They were silent for a moment until she asked. "Are you and Mum happy?"

Dad pulled away. "There's a question." He turned to look at her. "What's brought this on, may I ask?" Amy's throat felt dry and her palms clammy and for a second, she wished she'd never asked. She moved closer again with her head on his shoulder, not able to look him in the eye. "I....don't know. Nothing in particular, it's just sometimes……you seem to argue a lot."

"Amy. You don't need to worry about us." He ruffled her hair and was quiet for a moment before he sighed and said, "We do have our moments though. But then all couples have their ups and downs, Amy." He sat upright. "Maybe we are

going through a rough patch at the moment." He turned to
Amy, half smiling. "You're a perceptive young lady." She
watched as he clasped his hands together and looked down.
"We're both working hard. Then your mum has to be away
quite a bit, which is tough on our weekends. Life's so busy and
sometimes things get in the way of what's important. It's how
it is." He looked at her. "We'll get through it though. So, I
don't want you to go worrying yourself."

Amy put her arm around his chest and leant her head
on his shoulder. "I'd hate it if anything happened to us Dad,"
she said as she began to cry. "Our family… I couldn't take it."

He pulled her close. "Hey, hey shush. Nothing's going
to happen to us. I promise."

She knew then that Dad had no idea. Nor must he
ever find out from her. Nor could Mum ever know she knew
what had happened on Brancaster beach.

AMY

CHAPTER 2

It was Saturday morning, a week since the beach trip and Amy didn't want the day to begin. Her mother had called from outside her door more than once to 'get up, it's late' but she'd ignored her. It was almost midday before she appeared downstairs. Billy and Mum were playing a board game as she came into the dining room.

Her mother didn't look up as she rolled the dice and said, "About time."

Amy felt anger well-up in the pit of her stomach. "I'm tired," she replied, rolling her eyes.

"Try and cheer-up, you're like a wet weekend these days. Come and play with us, it might do you good."

Amy thought briefly and decided no, she really didn't want to spend time playing happy families. "I'm going out," she said, picking up her book, "I'll see you later."

"Where are you going?"

"To the park," she replied as she shut the door behind her.

"Don't be too long!"

In the centre of the field close to the school was a small play park for young children. Amy liked to come here from time to time to be alone. She'd sit on top of the elephant-shaped climbing frame and watch the children with their parents or read a book. Today she read for a while and then just sat there, feeling lonely, thinking back to last weekend. After a while she clambered down and lay on the grass with her hands behind her head, watching the sky as she had on the beach.

Suddenly she was aware of somebody close by. "Can I sit with you?" came a girl's voice. Taken by surprise, Amy was unsettled and briefly speechless. "Oh, err," she eventually stuttered as she sat up to look at her visitor. The girl was wearing smart jeans, pristine white trainers, and a floral-patterned shirt, similar to Amy's favourite. Amy could smell something sweet, similar to molten chocolate. Her hair was short, neat, and blond. She'd never seen a girl as pretty. "Okay," Amy added and patted the grass by her side. She watched the girl's every move as she effortlessly sat down crossed legged next to her.

The girl turned to Amy. "You looked sad, so I thought I'd see if you're alright." Amy tensed. What gave her that idea? "I didn't realise it showed." There was an awkward silence before the girl smiled. "It does," she replied, hesitating, then adding, "my name's Catherine, what's yours?"

Amy stared into her eyes. They were the deepest blue she had ever seen. "Amy. I live up there," she said pointing up the hill. "What about you?"

"Not far. The Old Town." Catherine's soft voice relaxed her. "I go to Nettledon. You?"

"Oh, that one," replied Amy. "I'm at Saint Mark's." Amy pictured the Nettledon pupils in their smart uniforms at the bus stop. She wished she'd gone, but Dad had said it was no better and wasn't worth the money. Amy knew full well they had more girls getting into Oxbridge. After a moment Amy replied, "sounds like you're posh."

Catherine gazed off into the distance. "Not really."

"How old are you?" asked Amy.

"Fifteen in November."

"I'm fifteen in a couple of weeks," replied Amy. All of a sudden Catherine put her hand on the small of Amy's back and gave it the slightest of rubs. This act from a stranger seemed right somehow and Amy wanted her to stay. They were silent for a moment, then she just came out with it, almost as if it were someone else speaking the words. "My mum's cheating on my dad."

"Is that why you looked sad?"

Amy nodded. "I couldn't take it if our family split up. I mean, I can't imagine things being different from how they are now." She thought for a moment, then added, "some of my friends' parents have split up and it's always a mess. A weekend here, another there, arguments, new partners you're supposed to like. It's a nightmare."

"Maybe it's just a fling and your dad will never be the wiser and they'll be happy again."

Her words lifted Amy's mood. "Could be," she replied. "Perhaps it won't end like I think it will."

Catherine sat closer. "Adults do crazy things to each other. You just have to get on with your own life. Do the things that make *you* happy."

Amy thought for a while, then lay back again, feeling the coolness of the grass through her shirt. She turned to Catherine. "What do *you* do when you're sad?"

Quick as a flash Catherine said, "I study extra hard. The more I study the better I do and the more it helps banish any sadness." She smiled. "It really helps me, anyway."

It was as if Catherine could read her mind, but more, she could understand her; sympathise; know what to say. Amy looked up at the sky and thought about it. Yes, that's what she'd do too: work extra hard. "Good idea," she replied. "Studying's fun for me."

Catherine lay down next to her. "Do you fancy meeting up sometime?" Then as if as an afterthought said, "most of my classmates board, so I'm a bit out of it."

Amy lay there wondering if she wanted a new friend. But then Catherine seemed different to the likes of Rachel and Tamsin. "Okay," she replied. "Come over and we can hang-out for the afternoon, listen to music and chat."

"Great," Catherine replied. She stood up and brushed grass from her jeans.

"Tomorrow?" asked Amy.

Catherine smiled. "Why not! Two o'clock?" She looked around then added, "I'd better go, my parents will be wondering where I've got to."

Amy watched her as she left, transfixed by the way she walked. She had poise and confidence. It had only been last week when Mum had said to her, 'you have a bit of a boyish gait young lady. You stride along; slow up a bit.' Amy had hidden away in her room for the rest of that evening.

When she got home her mother was in the kitchen. "Here," she said, handing Amy a T-towel, "make yourself useful." Amy took the towel and started drying up, carefully stacking the plates one by one on the side. Her mother turned to her and smiled. "Good to have you back," she said. Amy smiled too but not as a reaction to what her mother had said. She was thinking about Catherine.

"Something's chased those blues away," said her mother as she stroked her daughter's hair. Amy wondered if she should say anything. How could her mother think the blues would ever go away?

"I made a new friend."

"That's nice. Who?"

"Her name's Catherine. She lives in the Old Town."

"How did you two meet?"

"I was in the park. She just came up to me and started talking."

Her mother looked quizzically at her. "That's unusual, isn't it? Didn't think teenagers did that."

Amy smiled to herself and thought about answering but instead began putting the plates into the cupboard.

Mum touched Amy's arm. "I look forward to meeting her."

"Sometime," replied Amy as she crumpled-up the towel and dumped it on the draining board. "I need to tidy my room," she said as she hurriedly left.

"Amy!" called her mother.

"And catch-up on my homework," she called as she ran upstairs. Amy lay on her bed for a while, content that she had made a new friend; one that really understood her. They could be friends for a long time.

****

Amy immediately took Catherine up to her bedroom and soon they were lying on the bed chatting. Amy watched as Catherine got up and walked over to her desk. She joined her as Catherine picked up an exercise book and flicked through the pages. "Maths, it's my favourite subject," she said turning to Amy, "what about you?"

"I can't believe it. It's mine too, my dad's a maths teacher."

"That's cool. Does he help you?"

Amy thought for a moment. "Yes, sort of. He wants me to study it at uni."

"My parents say I can study whatever I want," added Catherine. "Physics is cool too."

Amy jumped as she heard her mother call. "You okay in there?"

"Please don't come in!"

"No, I wasn't going to," replied Mum. "Do you want a drink?"

Amy turned to Catherine then called out, "two Cokes please. Can you leave them outside the door?"

"Two? Okay," her mother called.

"Are you still upset about your parents?" Catherine whispered.

Amy lent against her desk and looked down as she fiddled with her hands. How did she feel? "Up until I caught out my Mum, I thought we were all good as a family. Since then, I've realised I've not seen things that are staring me in the face. Mum's the child in this house." Amy wiped her eyes with the back of her hand.

"Really?"

Amy sighed. "I don't know…"

"But you don't think it will last do you?"

"I just don't know." Amy could feel tears welling up. "After you and I chatted, I thought maybe you're right and it will blow over, things would be okay. They've been together long enough and maybe they're stuck in a rut, accepting what the other's like. It's not great but it would be totally worse if they split up." They were silent for a moment before Amy asked. "What about your family?"

Catherine smiled. "My parents seem really happy. I've got a younger brother and he's fun." She fell silent briefly and Amy watched her intensely, wondering what she was going to say next. "My parents treat each other with respect. Anyway, there's no chance they'd ever split up."

Amy wished with all her heart that her family could be the same. It had been, hadn't it? Then everything changed. Suddenly Catherine stood up, as if she needed to change the subject. She ran her hand along a row of books on the shelf, eventually picking out one titled, 'The Night Sky'. She turned to look at Amy. "I love the stars. I want to study astronomy at university and then one day maybe become an astronaut."

"Wow, that would be amazing." Suddenly Amy's mood lifted. "I've never thought about doing anything other than maths." Catherine came over and sat next to her still holding the book. "Hey, we could go out one evening, star gazing."

Amy smiled. "I'd love to be able to recognise more constellations."

They sat at Amy's desk and flicked through the book, reading about the constellations, and testing each other. Amy hadn't had so much fun in a long time and it took her mind away from her mother. After Catherine had gone, Amy was in the kitchen when her mother suddenly looked up from her magazine and asked, "Who was here?" Amy opened the fridge searching for something to eat. "Catherine," she answered without turning round. She picked out a pack of cheese. "She'll pop over again sometime. She likes astronomy, wants to be an astronaut one day."

"Sounds like an interesting girl," replied her mother as she flicked the pages. "Brainy like you."

Later Amy climbed into bed and curled up into a ball, warm in the knowledge she had found a real soulmate.

AMY

CHAPTER 3

November 1992

In the hallway, Amy put her coat on over her two jumpers and slipped on her woolly hat. She'd been given a telescope for her 16th birthday and had been out into the garden whenever she could. Suddenly her father called from the sitting room, "How long will you be?"

Amy sighed and stuck her head around the door. "It's only six o'clock Dad, I'm not five!"

"Don't talk to me like that. I'm asking, how long?"

"I don't know. Couple of hours?" She felt a flutter of excitement as she got two deckchairs out of the shed and set them up on the grass. Soon Catherine would be here and they'd lay back looking for shooting stars. Amy fetched two hot water bottles from the kitchen and placed them under the blankets on the deck chairs.

She smiled as Catherine appeared. "The Moon looks amazing!" said Catherine as they hugged. "And that's Saturn down there low in the west."

Amy looked off into the distance, her heart racing. "I know." She fiddled with the telescope to find the planet. "But I've never seen it through the telescope," she said, "you have a look, you can see the rings!" Amy sat in the deck chair looking up at the crystal sky, a hot water bottle on her tummy and the blanket tightly wrapped around her. Soon Billy came wandering out in his hat, coat and gloves and plonked himself down in the deckchair next to her.

"Five minutes, they said. "It's not fair." He looked at Amy. "Why are you laughing?"

"I'm not. I was just smiling. Anyway, do you want to look through the telescope or try and spot shooting stars?"

Billy pushed himself further down in the chair so he could look straight up. "Shooting stars."

Within ten minutes Dad had called him back in.

"I like your brother," said Catherine, pulling away from the telescope. "He's cute."

"I know. Come and sit here and we'll look up at the sky," she replied, patting the blanket left by Billy.

"That's Vega," said Catherine pointing to a bright star.

As Amy looked up she felt Catherine reach out and take her hand. Amy smiled and turned to her. "Don't forget to make a wish when you see a shooting star."

Suddenly she heard the back door opening. Her mother appeared by the door squinting into the darkness. "Amy," she called. "We need you to come in."

"Now?"

"Yes now."

Amy pushed herself out of the chair. "I'm busy," she called. Her mother went back inside slamming the back door.

"Sounds like you're in trouble," said Catherine.

Amy had the same feeling as when she'd had to read in assembly. "I can't think why," she replied.

"Weird! Anyway, I'd better get going. Can we do this again?"

Amy didn't answer at first as she struggled to think why Mum would be so cross. "Tomorrow if it's a clear night," she eventually replied.

Catherine smiled. "See you then. Hope you're not in the bad books!"

Amy went back to the telescope and stared through the lens at the beautiful rings of Saturn. Suddenly she felt someone beside her. "Oh God Dad, you made me jump!"

One hand was in a pocket jangling coins. "We need you inside," he said.

"Why are you both so cross tonight? What have I done?"

"We're not cross and you haven't done anything. We just need to talk to you and you're not helping."

Amy looked back through the eyepiece to adjust the focus. "That's better," she said.

Dad jangled the coins some more. "Amy, I don't want to keep having to ask. Just come inside please."

Amy stood back from the telescope. "Alright, alright. I need to pack this up first though. I'll be about ten minutes."

"Leave it until later."

"It might rain."

Dad looked up at the sky then back at Amy. "Two minutes," he said as he walked away.

She waited until he was inside and flopped into a deckchair. She felt angry that Mum had sent him on the errand to get her to come in. It made her want to stay out longer, although she knew it wasn't helping. Five minutes later she was in the kitchen and could hear them whispering in the next room. Amy stood still but they must have heard her as it abruptly went quiet. The thought of them sitting in silence at the dining room table made her feel uneasy. Before going in she filled a glass with water and glugged it down in one. As she placed the glass back on the worktop, she noticed her hand was shaking.

As Amy walked into the dining room she knew something wasn't right. Dad was sitting slightly sideways on the chair as if he'd hurriedly sat down or was about to jump up and Mum had a blank stare on her face and was holding a scrunched-up handkerchief. Nobody said a word as she walked around the table and pulled out a chair. Her first thought was that one of them or even Billy, was seriously ill. Please no. The clock on the sideboard ticked, ticked, filling the silence. Just as Mum was about to speak the clock began to strike, so she hesitated, the three of them not knowing where to look. Amy counted down the strikes from eight to one, each seeming to last an age. As the ringing died away, Mum reached across the table and put her hand on Amy's arm. "This is difficult," Mum began. "You may have noticed that Dad and I haven't been getting on so well recently."

Oh God, this is it thought Amy. Please no, no, it can't be. She looked from one to the other, Dad still looking down.

"We've been going through a difficult time, Amy, and…"

Amy's chair flew backwards, tipped over and crashed onto the floor. "You're getting divorced!" she cried, "just say it!!" Amy covered her face with her hands. "No! How could you?! Please no!"

Mum jumped up and ran round to Amy, picking up the chair and helping her sit back down. "Amy darling," she said putting her arms around her. "Let us explain."

Amy pushed her away. "Let go! It's all your fault!" She turned to Dad who sat passively, looking as if this was the last place he wanted to be.

"Amy, please!" begged her mother as she turned to Dad. "Say something, will you?!"

In the brief silence, Amy slowly sat down, her chest rapidly rising and falling. She wiped her eyes with the back of her sleeve. "You can't do this to us. It's not fair!"

Getting no response from Dad, Mum continued. "We're not getting divorced; we're just trying some time apart. And, there's nobody else involved."

Mum glared at Dad, finally initiating a response from him. "It's nobody's fault," he said calmly. "Believe me, we've tried and the fact is we've been growing apart."

"Dad! We're a family, how can you 'grow apart' from a family!?"

"No, I meant me and your mother." He shifted in his chair and coughed. "What I mean to say is, it's not Mum's fault. It's the both of us."

Amy turned and glared at Mum then looked back at Dad. Oh God he didn't know. She turned to her mother. "There is somebody. Don't pretend, I'm not a child!"

"Amy please! There is nobody else. It's not that."

Amy put her head on her arm, resting on the table and sobbed. Her chest tightened as she thought of the family breaking apart. Suddenly she felt her mother's arm around her shoulders. "Let go," she said. Amy sat up and looked at her father. "And you promised me!"

"Promised you what?" asked her mother.

"Dad promised me you'd never split up."

Mum turned to Dad. "What's this?" Dad shook his head and gave Mum a look of disdain, then turned to Amy. "I'm sorry, I really thought we could work things out."

Mum glared at Dad. "Have you been talking about us?"

"No of course not." He replied. He banged the table with the flat of his hand making them both jump. "Let's not argue," he said. "Please," he added in a softer tone.

Through her tears Amy looked at her mother. "Are you moving out?" Asking the question made her cry again. She wasn't sure how much longer she could sit there as her world crashed down around her.

"Oh Amy, no, of course not!" She saw Mum turn to Dad. "Are you going to say something?"

Dad sighed. "Look, I'm going to be moving out. We've found a flat close by, but I'll be popping in every weekend, Saturdays, and Sundays."

"I know what a weekend is, Dad."

Her mother put her hand on Dad's arm as if to stop him making it worse. "What your father is saying is that we will still be a family, even if he's not here all the time."

"I'm not stupid, Mum. That's not being a family." She looked at Dad. "Please don't do this! Surely you can work it out!" She turned to her mother, "Please!"

Dad got out his handkerchief and blew his nose and Mum looked at him as if to say, 'you're no help.'

As her sobbing subsided, Amy asked, "couldn't you try a bit longer?"

Mum bit her lip as Dad remained silent. Through her tears Amy said, "and we'll never go on holiday again." She wiped her tears away. "We love our holidays, don't we?" She shook her head as she cried. "I'll hardly ever see you, Dad. You say you'll visit but it won't last. Soon you'll both find new partners and they'll have kids and I won't be able to bear it," she sobbed.

Dad got out his handkerchief again and left the room blowing his nose. Mum leant across the table again and now Amy allowed her to touch her arm. Amy's lungs gasped for air and she thought she may be sick.

"We still love you. That will never change," said Mum. "We can still go on holidays."

Amy knew that was ridiculous. "I guess Billy doesn't know," she said. "When are you going to tell him?"

Mum sat back in her chair and put her hands behind her head. "We're not sure he needs to know yet." Mum put her palms on the table and stared at her hands as if studying her nails, then looked up at Amy. "We are going to say Dad is working away at a new school during the week and given he'll be home weekends; Billy's life won't change that much."

"More lies then."

"Amy, don't. It's difficult enough as it is."

"Lies, lies." Amy stood up. "I'm going to bed."

Her mother held out her hand. "Please Amy, let's talk. We'll work it out. We still love you dearly."

There was no sign of Dad as she went upstairs. Amy threw herself onto the bed and cuddled her pillow. Tomorrow she'd tell Catherine everything. Thank God for her, she thought. Later that night she sat at her desk in silence. Eventually she picked up a pencil and pushed the sharp end into the back of her hand, making a bright red mark. Then she scrawled in her diary:

Once upon a time there was a family – Mum, Dad, me and Billy. It was a happy family – we all loved each other, laughed, went on holidays, played silly games, my dad taught me maths and was sometimes embarrassing, Mum was smart and Billy was Billy. We had our own words for things, we looked after each other. There was an outside world and there was our world.

Then things changed and nobody was happy anymore: there was no family. Not like others have families.

If I ever have a family, not that that is likely the way I look, then I promise never to break it up. I'll always be with my husband. I'll not let <u>anything</u> come between us. My heart's been broken and I'll never do to my children what my mum and dad have done to us.

CATHERINE

CHAPTER 4

April 2018

Catherine put her arm through her husband's and pulled him closer. "Thank you - I love you so much." She leant against him as they walked across the sand. The beach stretched out as far as the eye could see. "This holiday was such a lovely surprise."

There was a chill in the April air, but the sun shone: warming her face. She closed her eyes, breathed deeply and scrunched her toes into the sand. As they walked on, she absorbed the smells and sounds: immersed herself in her joy for life.

John turned to Catherine, "it's only a weekend. And you deserve it." He was momentarily distracted. "Not too far, girls!" The six-year-old twins had run ahead towards the sea. It was their first visit to this beach and the Norfolk coastline. Chloe and Ruth turned briefly, then continued skipping hand-in-hand along the edge of the shallow water, laughing - lost in a world that only twins could share.

John stopped and held Catherine close. "You've been working so hard; I worry about you sometimes."

Catherine rested her head against his chest and put her arms around him, pulling him closer. "I know. But I'm okay. I have been neglectful but I'll make it up. I promise."

John pulled away and took her hands in his. "You don't need to. I'm so proud of you. Anyway, now you've made professor you'll be working even harder. I understand it and we're a team."

Was there a flicker of sadness in his eyes? She was reading too much into it. She did it all the time. You're being over-sensitive, he would say. Once he had hoped to make Head Teacher. But they had agreed, even before the twins were born, he would stay at home and she would work. Now in his early forties and still part-time, he would be lucky to make Head of Year. In contrast her career had been stellar by any measure. Masters at Oxford, PhD at Cambridge, Postdoc, Fellow, two years in the USA, then back to Cambridge, Associate Professor at thirty eight and now, at forty one, one of the youngest Professors at Cambridge. "And don't forget I squeezed in having twins aged thirty four," she would often add.

"I don't think it will mean more hours," she replied. But she knew that wasn't true. There'd be more invitations to speak, more international travel and a greater volume of departmental work. Then of course she'd throw herself back into her research. She couldn't wait. Suddenly she poked him in the ribs. "I'll race you to the girls!" And she was gone.

****

"Quiet!" Catherine called up the stairs. She paused in the hallway of their holiday cottage, listening. One whisper, two whispers then giggling. Catherine let the girls be and returned to the sitting room where John was kneeling, stoking the open fire. It crackled and spat as he laid another log across the flames.

"They're excited from the beach trip," she said, flopping onto the settee.

John looked around. "I know. They had such a wonderful day. You'd think they'd be out like a light."

Catherine picked up her glass of wine and took a gulp, enjoying the acidity hitting the back of her throat. "I think *I* will be out like a light! Not sure I'll make it through a film tonight after all. Shall we sit here awhile, enjoy the fire and wine, then go to bed?"

John sat next to her and kissed her on the cheek. "Yes professor."

She lay her head on his shoulder as the flames flickered in the fireplace. "I don't think I've ever been as happy as I am today."

He put his arm around her shoulder and pulled her closer. "Me neither. I love you so much Catherine. And our little family."

"I never want anything to spoil it - nothing means more to me."

John kissed her hair. It was still damp and smelt of unfamiliar shampoo. "I'm so excited about your new job. Tell me what you'll do in your first week."

Catherine sighed and held up her glass, gently swirling the wine so she could watch the flames through the ruby-red liquid. "Not so different from what I have been doing, really. I'm joining two new committees, but they don't start for a month or two." She looked into her glass and picked out a stray piece of cork. "I still have the same research group with Neil and Lucy. It's getting interesting and I think we'll have a paper within a few months, so I wouldn't want to lose them."

"What's the research?"

Catherine put her feet up on the coffee table and lent back, looking up at the ceiling. "Studying the atmospheres of distant planets." She handed him her glass. "You'd better top-up the prof's glass if you know what's good for you."

John picked up the bottle. "Don't forget the talk at school on Thursday morning. The entire sixth form will be there. The girls in particular will hang on your every word - wanting to know how you've made it to where you are in the male world of physics."

Catherine sighed. "It's fine, I haven't forgotten." For a while they watched the flames in silence.

"Do you remember when we first met?" John began.

She turned to him, smiled and snuggled up closer. "Of course!"

"And look how far we've come since those uni days. We were so young."

"We're old timers now!"

"Hardly. I've still got the picture in my head of that moment I first set eyes on you: Looking up from my work in the library and seeing you staring at me."

"Staring? I think I smiled when you caught my eye," she replied.

"Whatever, it made my heart leap. Then you gathered up your books, and with such confidence, came straight over and sat opposite me. I so remember being struck by your blond hair and smart clothes. Such a contrast to the other students, that was for sure. An all round sassy lady!"

"Ha! Do you remember me leaning forward and whispering, 'the guy next to me smells, can I sit here?' What a chat-up line!"

"It made me laugh, anyway!"

Catherine glanced at the back of her hand. "The truth is I'd noticed you a few times before as you worked away in the library. I think I already knew you were the one for me."

John smiled. "I'm glad we came away. Living in Grantchester is all well and good but being by the sea for a few days is special." He sighed. "We'll have to do it more often: give you a break from the pressures of work."

"Sure," she replied, then closed her eyes and leant back on the settee. "What shall we do tomorrow?"

"More beach?"

Catherine glanced out of the window. "Probably." She hesitated then said, "by the way, what made you choose here?"

John sipped his wine. "I'd heard it was beautiful and we needed somewhere relatively close." He turned to her, "Why?"

"No reason. Just wondered."

"You do like it though?"

Catherine squeezed his arm, "Of course. I love it!"

"So let's go back to that beach tomorrow."

Catherine ran her hands through her hair, "Tell you what, let's try a different one, Holkham Bay perhaps?"

"Oh okay. If you're sure."

"I'm sure."

"You're a funny fish, aren't you professor?"

"Maybe yes. Maybe no." She smiled as she stood up, then carefully positioned the guard in front of the fire and held out her hand. "Come on, let's go to bed."

CATHERINE

CHAPTER 5

April 2018

Lucy neatly shuffled the spreadsheets scattered across the desk, while Catherine saved the files on her laptop and shut it down. She carefully placed her pen on the laptop lid, ensuring it was parallel to the long side. They were in her cramped office in the Astrophysics Department in Cambridge. In contrast to most of her colleagues, her papers were neatly stacked on the corner of her desk, documents alphabetically stored in her filing cabinet and the box files and books carefully arranged on the bookshelf. The immaculate condition of their boss's office never ceased to amaze both Lucy and Neil and it still made them smile.

"Great progress," said Catherine, "and you're clear on what to do next?"

Lucy and Neil were two PhD students working on what Catherine considered the most exciting area of her research, the atmospheres of distant planets.

"Got it," replied Lucy looking at her watch. "You'll have it next week. I must go, I'm due at a seminar at ten fifteen. Didn't you say you had to leave by ten?"

"Oh God. Thanks." Catherine glanced at the wall clock – five past. "I'm due at my husband's school by ten thirty. I'm supposed to be inspiring the sixth form to do what we do."

Lucy turned as she left. "That won't be difficult: who wouldn't love it?! Hope the traffic's okay."

Catherine scooped her laptop and papers into her bag. "Sure thing. I'll be back after lunch." But the door had already closed.

As she drove through the school gates, she spotted John standing by the entrance with his hands in his pockets looking anxious. Jumping out of the car she glanced at her watch. "Damn," she whispered as she grabbed her laptop bag and slammed the car door.

"Thank God you're here," said John. "I was beginning to worry."

"I'm here now," replied Catherine. "It's been manic."

John turned to go in, "they are waiting in the hall," he added, curtly.

Catherine checked her watch again. Only seven minutes late. He didn't need to fuss, did he?

Late last night she and John had chatted about the talk.

"What do they want to hear?" She'd asked.

"Insight into your research, how you got to where you are, what you do in a day, why you love it. Why should they go to university? Sound about right?"

"You know them best."

John studied his hand as his fingers tapped the arm of the settee. "You seem anxious," he said. "Don't you want to do it?"

Catherine picked up a magazine and fanned the pages as if looking for a particular article. "Of course I do. I'm fine."

"What is it then?"

"Nothing." She tossed the magazine on the coffee table, stood up and went into the kitchen.

John followed her. "Okay, I'm sorry," he said as he put his hands around her waist. She had her back to him as she filled the kettle. "The students are looking forward to it."

She flicked the kettle switch. "I just prefer giving talks within my own world of academia. That's all."

John let go of her and reached for the mugs. "Why?"

Catherine put her hands on her hips. "I just do." She turned to face him. "Now will you give me some space? I haven't even got room to make the tea."

He stared at her, surprised by her animosity over something so small. Saying nothing, he went back into the sitting room and switched on the news. No tea appeared so eventually he went and made his own. Catherine was in the spare room tapping away on her laptop.

****

"...*which brings me to my own research.*" Catherine looked around at the children's faces to check she still had their attention. One boy at the end of a row was looking down at his phone. Apart from him she seemed to have them with her.

She'd talked about her university life and how she'd got to where she was; how exciting physics could be; how the cosmos was a frontier for humankind to conquer; how it was full of surprises, mystery and rewards. Now it was time to talk about her own work.

"I have several researchers, some based at Cambridge, some dotted around the world. The one thing they have in common is they are researching various aspects of planets and their formation. Now, when I say 'planets' I'm not talking about what we would normally think of as a planet: such as Mars, Earth, or Jupiter: those planets in our solar system. I'm talking about something quite different. To illustrate this, let me take you on a journey through space. I apologise if some of this is obvious, but we'll get there in the end, I promise."

A quick glance around, yes she still had them with her. She looked across at John and he smiled.

"Obviously we live on a rocky sphere: a planet we call earth and along with other planets, rocks, comets, dust and general detritus - we all orbit a star we call the Sun. This is what we call a planetary system, or in our case, the Solar System. Then our sun is one of tens of billions swirling around in our galaxy, the Milky Way.

And what's beyond that? Nothing much until you reach the next galaxy, then the next, then the next. That's why Edwin Hubble, who first discovered galaxies in the 1950s, called them 'islands in space.'

In 1995, two astronomers discovered a planet orbiting a star, other than our Sun. They called it an exo planet. So began a new journey of discovery, every bit as exciting as those 15th century sea-farers discovering new continents here on earth.

Here we are, twenty three years on and the journey of discovery continues. We have found thousands of planets orbiting other stars in our galaxy. But my team is not searching for exo planets. We are looking for gases in exo-planet atmospheres that could support life or better still, gases that could be a result of life being present, such as Oxygen and Methane. We also want to find evidence of water. As far as we know all life needs water.

In the coming decade I think astronomers will make these discoveries. Maybe it will be one of you here today who will be part of a team who achieves that goal. There's no reason why not – you too can be the new sea-farers of the twenty first century. I'll leave you with that thought. Thank you.

As the Head rose the pupils applauded. "Thank you, Professor. We have time for a couple of quick questions." She pointed to a boy in the front row. "Jake, yes."

"How did you become interested in astronomy?"

"*A good question!*" Catherine began. "*I think I was interested in the night sky from a very young age, but then when I was sixteen a friend of mine suggested using a telescope she had been given as a present to look at Saturn and Jupiter and from then on, I was hooked. It was as simple as that! So, if you ever get the chance, look up into the night sky; you might just be inspired too!*"

"One more question?" added the Head. "Yes Julie, what would you like to ask the Professor?"

"Do you believe in aliens?"

Catherine clasped her hands in front of her. "*It's a question I often get asked.*" She thought for a moment. "*It depends on what you mean by aliens. If you mean microbial life, then yes, I think we will find it. We are already seeing evidence that it once existed on our neighbouring planet, Mars, when it had more of an atmosphere and water on its surface. Then, intriguingly, some of the moons within the solar system, such as Europa, a moon of Jupiter, have underground oceans. In the coming decades these will be explored by new missions.*

As for complex life, that is still hard to say. It's a huge leap from microbial life forms to something like us. It needs specific and stable conditions over a long time period. There are most likely hundreds of billions of planets and moons in the universe. So it's probable that a proportion have, or have had, the right conditions and time for sophisticated life to develop. Whether their time-period will correspond to our time-period and both civilisations have the means to communicate and know where to look – well, they're completely different questions. As Arthur C Clarke said, 'Two possibilities exist: either we are alone in the Universe or we are not. Both are equally terrifying.'

The Head walked with Catherine to the staff room and as she entered John turned to her. "Catherine, this is Martin Mitchell, he's a science journalist at The Times Educational Supplement."

"I'm covering these talks run by Cambridgeshire South Academy and would appreciate a follow-up interview," he began.

Catherine looked across at John but got no response. Martin continued. "I'd like to explore some of your early life. How you got to where you are; what or who inspired you; what battles you had to fight; as part of a piece I'm doing. Mainly to get an inspirational message to a wider audience."

Catherine looked from one to another as they waited for her reply. "Err, I'm really busy right now: I've just taken on a professorship." She hesitated. "Travelling. You know. I'm not sure I could give you the time you need." She saw John look away, as if not wanting to be part of what he had started.

"I'll only need about an hour. I can get most of the information online – I simply want the human angle - more of your early years, you know – your influences."

"I'm in Copenhagen next week so I'm not sure when we can get together. Call me at the university later in the month." Catherine turned to the Head. "I apologise but I must be going. I'm due back for a seminar."

"No problem. Thank you so much for coming."

Catherine smiled, "It was my pleasure." She shook the Head's hand, smiled at John and left. There was a brief awkward silence until John said. "She's really busy with her new job." He put his hands in his trouser pockets. "I'll have a word. Leave it with me and I think we'll get it sorted. Can I have your card?" Martin pulled a card from his jacket pocket. "Here you go… and here's another for Catherine."

John studied the card. "Thanks. One of us will be in touch."

****

John was sitting on the floor with his back up against the bottom bunk as Catherine came into the girls' bedroom. The twins were snuggled under the duvet on the lower bed. He was reading 'Return to Hundred Acre Wood'…again.

"Mummy's home!" The girls pulled the duvet aside, jumped from the bunk and gave her a hug.

"Want to take over?" he asked.

"Yes, we want Mummy to read!"

John smiled at Catherine. "See you soon, dinner is nearly ready."

Catherine kicked off her shoes and took his place as the girls pulled the duvet around them. "Where were you up to?"

"Christopher Robin's coming!"

She picked up the book and gently stroked the worn cover. It had been John's as a child and it even smelt different to a modern book. In that moment she wished she had something like this from her own past to give to the girls.

"Come on, Mummy," pleaded Ruth.

She ruffled Ruth's hair and began. *'Who started it? Nobody knew. One moment there was the usual Forest babble: the wind in the trees, the crow of a cock, the cheerful water in the streams. Then came the Rumour: Christopher Robin is back!'*

After she had settled them down, she came into the sitting room. John looked up over his glasses. School books were scattered across the table as he ploughed through the marking. "I'll make some tea," he said as Catherine flopped into a chair. "How was the rest of your day?" he called from the kitchen. She didn't reply. John returned and handed her the mug. "Busy I guess? Your talk was perfect."

"It was no bother. Let's hope at least some of them will be inspired."

"Sure they will. Oh, and sorry about the journalist by the way. I didn't even know the Head had invited him and he collared me, insisting I introduce you."

"Don't worry, I shan't be meeting him." She blew on the surface of her tea.

"You being an orphan is quite a story though. It would add to the message of what can be achieved."

"Losing my parents in the accident. Nobody wanting me as a child. It's not something I want to dwell on now, or ever."

44

John put down his mug. "No, of course not, sorry. I'll head him off at the pass."

"Thanks."

"I didn't know you were going to Copenhagen next week, did I? We've not sorted the childcare. I could still get my parents I think."

"There's no need, it was a little white lie."

"You really don't want to meet him, do you?"

"No," she replied, "I don't. I really don't."

CATHERINE
CHAPTER 6
June 2018

"Morning," whispered Catherine, "Go back to sleep, it's only five thirty." She threw the duvet aside and crept softly into the girls' room. Ruth was asleep on the floor holding her teddy and Chloe was on the edge of her bed, one hand hanging over the side. She cradled Ruth and her blanket and gently laid her back on her bed. She sat for a while taking in their beauty, the delight of having a family and the excitement of her new job.

By eight she was at her desk, catching-up on emails and checking her diary. In the short time she had been professor, the volume of work had increased: the meetings; the research groups; conference requests; grant applications. She thought how she was loving every minute of it and how it was more of a vocation than a job.

Mid-afternoon Catherine walked back from the communal kitchen toward her office with a fresh coffee. As she approached her half-opened door, she could hear Neil and Lucy chatting, they'd arrived early for their meeting and must have gone straight in. They were whispering, but as she stood motionless outside her door, she could hear every word.

"She's obsessed more like," whispered Neil, "it's her whole life."

"I think she expects the same from us, as if we don't have a life," replied Lucy.

"Honestly, I've never worked so hard and it's never enough," added Neil. "Now she's a prof it'll only get worse."

"I'd not want to be under anybody else though, would you? I mean, we're learning so much and doing ground-breaking stuff."

"Guess we can't have it both ways."

Catherine quietly walked down the corridor and leant against the wall thinking. Was she obsessed? Did she work them too hard? Maybe, but what did they want? Simply to secure their PhDs or to be at the forefront, where she would lead them? They'd better step up she thought as she strode back to her office and pushed open the door.

"Afternoon! Everything okay?"

"I think so," replied Neil as he twiddled his pen around in his hand.

The afternoon raced by as they immersed themselves in the data, until eventually Catherine interrupted. "We have the departmental drinks at five thirty, we can't miss that."

On the dot Catherine had her glass of wine and had just joined a group of students when her phone pinged - a text from John. "Excuse me," she said and went out into the corridor. She placed her glass on the window ledge and called his mobile.

"Hi! Everything okay?"

"All good," replied John. "Just wondered what time you'll be home?"

"I'll leave around six."

"Great, you'll catch the girls; we're running a bit behind. They set up a sort of tent in the sitting room and brought their duvets down."

"We should go camping sometime!"

She could hear, 'Daddy!' in the background. "Maybe. See you later," he said.

"Top-up?" Asked Neil. Catherine held out her glass. Looking round she smiled as she saw Professor Stuart Morehouse. When Catherine first came to Cambridge, having finished her PhD at Oxford, she worked for the Prof as a Postdoc and as a Fellow. Later she had gone to America with John for two years and returned to Cambridge, eventually becoming an Associate Professor, again under Professor Morehouse. While she had been away, he had been awarded the Nobel prize for astrophysics, elevating him to head of department. It had partly been the opportunity to work under a Nobel prize winner that had tempted her back from the USA to Cambridge. He was tall, thin as a rake and always appeared with boundless energy and enthusiasm.

"How's it going?" he asked.

"Absolutely loving it," she began and gave him what she soon realised was too long an explanation. She circulated for a while then checking her watch, made for the door. Back in her office she grabbed her laptop bag and was about to leave when she had an idea. Catherine sat down, opened her computer, and retrieved a file. The sun shone through her window warming her back. Deep in thought she closed her blinds and sat down to continue, tapping away oblivious to the fact she'd put her phone on silent or that the evening was racing by.

At some point she glanced at her phone and saw it was eight thirty and she had six missed calls from John. "Damn it," she said, picking up her phone. "Sorry! Something important came up and I completely lost track of time."

"Where are you for god's sake? I've been calling."

"I'm in my office, I'm packing up now."

"See you whenever you decide to come home," he said, and the line went dead.

It was only a fifteen-minute drive from the Institute of Astronomy to home in Grantchester and as she passed the rugby club she saw a police car pull out from the car park in her direction. She instinctively braked: worried she may have been speeding. Before she knew it the car was right up behind her, headlights flashing and blue light spinning. Her mouth went dry as she slowed down. Catherine pulled into a lay-by and as she waited, she realised she was tightly gripping the steering wheel with both hands. Watching in the rear-view mirror she saw one of the two police officers get out and approach her car on the passenger side. She lowered the window.

The police officer leant forward, his head almost in the car. "Do you know why we stopped you?"

She shifted in her seat to better face him and clasped her shaking hands together. "No. I'm sure I wasn't speeding was I?"

"Your nearside brake light is out."

"Oh, I didn't know."

He ignored her reply. "What's your name?" he asked.

"Catherine Holmes."

"Can I see your licence?"

Catherine delved in her handbag, fumbling as she did so, dropping things onto the floor. He studied her license then handed it back. His intense stare immediately made her feel guilty.

"Where are you going?" He asked.

Catherine swallowed hard. "Home. I live in Grantchester and I'm on my way home from work at the Institute of Astronomy."

"I can smell alcohol. Have you been drinking?"

"Only a glass. We had a social after work. We do every Wednesday. We meet in the senior common room and discu…"

"I'd like you to step out of the car Ms Holmes and come with me. You need to take a breathalyser."

"But I've had virtually nothing, really." He ignored her and stood back from the car, waiting for her to get out. Catherine gingerly followed him to the police car where he asked her to sit in the back, before getting in beside her. Something about the crackling of the radios made her hands tremble. She wondered if they'd spot her state and conclude she was drunk. Her stomach knotted and her palms felt clammy as she blew into the device.

"Okay, let's take a look at this," he began, "It's on the edge. The right side fortunately." Catherine sat there, wide eyed, unable to speak. She had no idea how she could have faced going to a police station.

"What happens now?" she asked tentatively.

"You are free to go. Although, I would advise you to be more careful in the future Mrs Holmes. Any alcohol is dangerous once you are behind the wheel."

Catherine nodded. She ran her tongue over her dry lips and tasted blood.

"And you'll need to get that brake light fixed."

"I will. It must have just happened," she replied, immediately feeling silly for saying it. They must hear it every time. She wasn't surprised when he ignored her and said, "drive carefully."

"Thank you," she replied, trying not to sound too relieved.

Catherine concentrated as she walked back to her car. Was she walking in a straight line?

She sat in her car and watched as they did a tight U-turn and drove away. But she was in no fit state to drive and rested her head against the wheel. Her heart raced as she struggled to control her breathing.

"I'll go in a minute," she whispered to herself as she tilted back the car seat and lay back.

As she walked in the front door John called from the sitting room, "the girls won't settle, you sort them."

"I love the tent," she said as she joined him in the sitting room. The books for marking were strewn across the settee. He hardly looked up. She moved them aside and sat down. "Room for me?" she asked brightly.

He dropped a book into his lap. "What's going on?"

"What do you mean?"

"With you. Saying you'd be home shortly, then not appearing for ages." John opened a book and picked up his pen. "Clearly you love your work more than your family."

"Now that's not fair!"

"You say the words but let's face it you spend more time at work than at home and when you are here your mind is elsewhere."

"I'm sorry," she said putting her head on his shoulder. At that moment she made a note to tell Lucy about what she'd been working on that evening. It would save Lucy a lot of time.

"Are you?"

"Am I what?"

"Oh, for goodness' sake," he said standing up.

She looked up at him. "John please, sit down," she said patting the seat next to her. He reluctantly sat, leaving a space between them.

"Really, I am sorry about tonight," she replied, snuggling up closer. "It was thoughtless of me. In fact I don't need to go into work tomorrow, I can work from here. I'll take the girls to school and collect them. It'll be an easier day."

"Great." He looked down at the book and underlined a sentence, almost cutting through the page. "Dinner is in the oven," he said, then scribbled in the book, 4/10 and ringed it twice in red.

****

The next morning, alone in the kitchen, Catherine made herself a coffee, sat at the table and opened her laptop. But she couldn't concentrate and within minutes snapped it shut. Suddenly she started to cry and sat upright to wipe her eyes with the back of her hands. A fine line existed between true happiness and the darkness she had once known. The encounter with the police had reminded her how fragile the life she had built really was.

AMY

CHAPTER 7

January 1993

"This is so embarrassing," said Tamsin. "I so wish he wouldn't read the exam results out for everyone to hear." Amy, Rachel, and Tamsin were three rows back in class waiting for the mock GCSE maths and physics results. Mr Clarke, short, rotund, and in the main well liked, stood at the front of the class holding the papers.

Rachel leant across to Amy, "Why *does* he do it?" she whispered.

Mr Clarke glared in their direction. "Anything I can help you with?"

Tamsin giggled and blushed as she answered, "No sir."

"Good."

"You'll come top Amy," whispered Rachel.

"Maybe," she replied. "Or Jimmy."

"Nah," said Rachel.

Mr Clarke walked to the back of the class and as he did so Jimmy threw a screwed-up ball of paper in their direction hitting Amy on the back of her head. She didn't turn round or acknowledge the laughter from him and his friends.

"Okay here we go," said Mr Clarke. "The results of the maths paper first. Right, in reverse order: Janice, twenty three percent." Mr Clarke continued to read out the results and hand the papers back to each individual. "Rachel, forty two."

"Oh thank you sir," she said sarcastically.

A minute later there was a tap on Amy's shoulder and the boy behind passed her a piece of folded paper.

'*Amy you're a dyke.*' She screwed it into a tight ball as the anger welled-up.

"What was that?" asked Rachel.

"Nothing."

Before she could stop her, Rachel grabbed the paper and passed it to Tamsin who quickly unfolded it. They read it and turned to Amy who had covered her face, trying to hide her tears.

Tamsin turned around and stared at Jimmy who was smiling at her. "Twat," she mouthed.

"What's going on with you girls?" asked Mr Clarke.

"Nothing sir."

"Well keep your 'nothings' quiet."

Rachel put her hand on Amy's shoulder and leant close, "you alright?" she whispered.

Amy shook her head. "He's always doing this. Why me?"

"Right that's it!" boomed Mr Clarke. "Anymore talking and you leave the classroom!"

Amy blew her nose.

"Jimmy," said Mr Clarke, "Seventy five percent, just pipped again I'm afraid."

"Yeah, well I have a life."

"Now, now, we don't need that," said Mr Clarke as he walked over to Amy. He put her paper in front of her. "Eighty percent for Amy Ridley, top mark."

"Keeno!" called Jimmy.

"Enough! Now for the physics results."

Amy dug her nails into her hand, hoping the pain might distract her from bursting into tears.

****

"Have you ever been bullied?" Amy asked. She and Catherine were lying on her bed.

"Never," replied Catherine. "Have you?"

"Yes. There's this boy at school called Jimmy."

"How does he bully you?"

Amy sighed, not knowing where to begin. "In lots of ways."

"Have you told your Mum?"

"No way! She'd either tell me to grow-up or go to the school and complain and that would make it worse."

"I think teachers know how to handle it. I'm not so sure it would make it worse."

"I can't. He's been really devious and it's only recently he's made it obvious so that my friends know. He's horrible to me. I think I know how it started."

"Go on."

"A couple of years ago he asked me out on a date. To be honest it freaked me out. I'd never been out with a boy before and I just reacted badly saying 'no chance'. I guess he was embarrassed as he's not used to being turned down. After that, things went downhill." Amy hesitated then added, "today he passed a message around in class calling me a dyke. And he's started openly calling me names. And what makes it worse is he's clever, bright, and funny and everybody likes him, including the teachers. What can I do?"

"You should tell your mum."

Amy thought for a while. "No, it's not going to happen."

"Think about it."

"Maybe." They lay in silence, Amy hugging her pillow. She turned to face Catherine. "I haven't told anybody, so you must keep it secret. I like him in a funny sort of way. I think he knows it and that makes it worse. He messes with me."

"How so?"

"Well, a few weeks ago he asked if we could meet up."

"What?! Like on another date?"

"No not really, he said we could meet and…I don't know…. I guess I thought things were changing."

"What happened?"

"He said we should meet at the shopping centre one Sunday afternoon. He told me to wait outside Next at 3 o'clock, but he didn't show up. At one point I wondered if he had meant another shop. It was so stressful. Then I thought oh god maybe there's another Next, but I didn't dare leave, in case I missed him. He would have been so angry."

"What happened in the end?"

"Eventually I spotted him and his mates leaning over the railing of the floor above… laughing and pointing at me."

"Oh, Amy!"

"I haven't told anyone else." Suddenly a smile crept across Amy's face. "On the Monday, I confronted him. There's a quadrangle at school with benches and in the middle there's this central bench where he and his friends hang-out and nobody else can sit there. Unless invited. I went up to him and slapped him on the face. I can't believe I did it! The whole place went quiet."

"Oh my god, Amy! What did he do?"

"Nothing really. Just sat there looking shocked. I was shaking all over. But a teacher spotted us and we got hauled in front of the housemaster. We both said it was 'nothing' and wouldn't happen again, so I got away with it."

"Did he do anything after that?"

"Weirdly *he* apologised and said we should try and meet up again and he'd make it up to me."

"Do you believe him?"

"……… I don't know."

"Don't be crazy. He'll stand you up again."

"He apologised again today after the note. I saw him in the corridor, and he was like, 'don't hit me!' Then he said he was going to the roller disco on Wednesday and did I want to come."

"And you said 'no' I hope!"

Amy cuddled her pillow tighter. "I said I would think about it and maybe come along with a friend. He said, whatever you want."

"You're not going, are you?"

"I think he's nice at heart it's just that… I don't know."

"Come on Amy. He'll hurt you again."

"I probably won't go. I'm useless at skating. It'll be so embarrassing… and the whole place smells of Lynx and sweat."

"Amy!" called her mother from outside the door. "Teatime. You need to come down before it gets cold."

"I'll be there in a minute," she called. "You need to go. Thanks for listening," she said adding, "See you soon." Minutes later Catherine was gone and Amy put her pillow back in position and went downstairs.

"Why do you spend virtually every minute up there these days?" asked her mother.

"I don't."

"You do, you've started to spend most of the weekends in your room. I know you have to study and that's all very commendable but surely you should get out more. What happened to your friends Tamsin and Rachel, you hardly ever seem to meet up with them these days? They're welcome here you know."

"I see them every day at school. Anyway, I've got to study extra hard now."

The truth was, Jimmy had taken her aside at school and explained that Tamsin and Rachel talked about her behind her back and that they weren't real friends, and she should be careful. How could they do that? She knew she was spending more time with Catherine and less with her school friends. And avoiding the places they used to go to steer clear of them and of course Jimmy. Last time she saw him in the town he'd shouted across the street, 'hey Squidly!' Later he told the other boys he called her that because squids are flat and so is Amy. Plus, it rhymed with Ridley. She filled a whole page in her diary with the words: *'Squidly Ridley'*.

CATHERINE

CHAPTER 8

July 2018

"It's here, quick." John pointed to the sign as Catherine braked hard. "Bigbury five miles." She turned right onto a narrow lane.

"Are we nearly there?" asked Chloe. With all the stops it had taken them almost six hours from Grantchester to south Devon. Catherine looked in the rear mirror. The twins had books and toys strewn across the seats and each sucked on a lolly. John turned to look at them. "Ten minutes and we'll be there."

"Why do we keep stopping?" asked Ruth.

"Why are we going backwards?" added Chloe.

Catherine glanced in the mirror. "It's a narrow lane, everybody needs to make room for others to get past."

"Is there a beach?" asked Chloe.

"You know there is!" replied John. "We're staying on the beach. You'll be able to play there as much as you want."

"I'm going for a swim." said Chloe.

"Don't be silly," replied Ruth, "You hate the sea." And so it went on until they passed the golf club and swept down the hill toward the bay. Stretching out in front was the beautiful sands of Bigbury beach and beyond Burgh Island. There were tiny figures walking on the island's peak and crowds milling around the hotel and pub.

"You know that hotel inspired two Agatha Christie novels?" said John.

"I thought it was just 'Evil Under the Sun?'" replied Catherine.

"And 'Then There Were None' apparently."

They pulled into the beach car park. On the far side overlooking the beach was the entrance to the apartments. John went to the shop to sign the paperwork and collect the key while Catherine and the girls ran down the jetty onto the beach. At high tide the sea washes in from each side, creating the island. But now with the tide low, the sea shone and sparkled in the distance and a vast expanse of beach opened before them. Families played ball; surfers did their best in the light breeze; fathers blackened sausages on tiny barbeques, kids chased their dogs into the water.

Catherine watched as the girls ran hand-in-hand across the beach. She took a deep breath, taking in the sea air. She was relieved to be free from work for a week and was determined to immerse herself into the family holiday. She kicked off her shoes, picked them up and chased after the girls as they headed to the shoreline. "Wait for me!"

Come evening, with the girls asleep, Catherine and John lounged on the balcony overlooking the beach. The tide was in, cutting off Burgh Island. They sat in silence watching the snake of people climb the ladder of the sea tractor. Soon its engine rumbled and people waved as it trundled down the short stretch of the beach into the shallow sea, making its way to Burgh Island. Ten minutes later the passengers disembarked and walked the short distance to The Pilchard pub or made their way up the steep path to enjoy the fabulous views from the top. The sun was low and the small stretch of beach that remained was largely empty. Only a few sun-drenched stragglers remained along with tired children; wet dogs with wagging tails and trailing behind, weary looking grandparents.

"I thought the twins would be up all night after the day we've had, what with all that excitement," said Catherine as she sipped her wine.

John poured himself another glass. "The journey, the beach, the girls were out as soon as their little heads hit the pillow."

Catherine put her feet up on the balcony rail. She was dressed in her lounge trousers and sweatshirt, her hair still wet from the shower. While John had overseen the twins' bath-time, she had raced into the sea. "It seems no time since we were in Norfolk and I'd just started my new job. Here we are on holiday again."

John sighed. "We both need it, especially you. It's been manic."

"I love every minute of my job. But yes, I was ready for this. And I'm not checking my emails or phone for a week."

****

Catherine held the girls' hands as John carried all the paraphernalia they needed for the day out. It was a steep hill down from the grassy car park to Coastguards Beach. John fixed up the windbreak while Catherine laid out the towels and positioned the sunshade. The tide was going out and the shallow estuary water sparkled as it raced on its journey to the sea, shimmering on the horizon. The other side of the estuary was steeped by green hillsides, cows and sheep dotting the landscape. The girls splashed about at the water's edge and searched for crabs.

John grabbed his hat and sunglasses and put his arm around Catherine's waist. "I'll take the girls for a walk along the estuary to the sea. Why don't you stay here and soak up the sun in peace?"

Catherine lay back letting the sun warm her skin and her mind gently float away, thinking of nothing. Half an hour passed and she heard her phone buzz inside her handbag. She half sat up and wondered if it was John. But she could see them playing in the distance, collecting water in buckets and emptying them into a rock pool. She eased herself back down, determined not to check. As she lay there her mind raced through all the things it could be. Maybe Lucy needed an answer to something and it would only be quick? She sat up and went to open her bag for her phone, hesitated, and pulled out her book instead. She smiled to herself, thinking; they can wait.

Ten minutes later she heard the phone ping again, this time a text. She sat up, resisted again and lay down. Two minutes later it pinged again. Catherine placed her book on the sand and sat up. It could be John's parents and an emergency she thought. Seeing it was only a text from Lucy she dropped it back into her bag. Catherine lay down on her towel, moving her back to adjust the sand and looked up at the blue sky and puffy white clouds.

"Damn it," she whispered as she sat up: she couldn't resist. As she listened to the last message she saw the girls and John approaching, so threw her phone back in her bag. "Hi!" she called as she picked up her bag, put it over her shoulder and waved. "How about if I go back up the hill to the café, get some lunch and bring it back here?"

"Ah would you? Thanks," replied John. He sounded weary.

"Can I come too?" asked Ruth. "No, you stay here with Daddy and your sister," she replied, a little too firmly. Halfway up the hill she called Lucy.

"What's up?"

"Thank God you called. Wait," replied Lucy. "I'll put you on speaker, Neil is here too. Neil, shut the door, will you? We're in your office Catherine, we need privacy."

Catherine moved aside to let a family pass. "What on earth is going on?"

"Are you alone?" asked Neil.

"Well sort of," said Catherine. "I'm walking to a café. Everyone else is on the beach. Is that okay?"

"We just meant: can anyone hear us?"

"Okay, come on. Is this a wind-up?"

"No," replied Lucy. "You may want to be sitting down though."

"I can take it, whatever it is. Go ahead," she added, as she continued her walk up the hill. By the time she reached the top she was breathless. Not from the incline, but from the shock of what she had just been told.

CATHERINE

CHAPTER 9

July 2018

The café had once been a small schoolhouse and what had been the playground was now littered with tables and chairs, busy with diners on this sunny lunchtime. Smooth jazz gently played from speakers hanging in a tree. A queue of people snaked its way toward a serving hatch. Catherine joined the back of the line in a daze, her mind whirring. A 'checklist', that's what I need, she thought: a procedure to go through to get further observations. Who should she tell at the university and when? Not before she and her team had a higher level of certainty, that was for sure.

She suddenly realised the person in front had said something to her. "Oh sorry I was day-dreaming," said Catherine.

"I was just saying, 'what a beautiful day.'"

"Yes, gorgeous," replied Catherine. Without thinking she asked. "What's the date today? I've completely forgotten."

"Thursday the twenty sixth of July."

"Twenty eighteen," added the small girl holding the lady's hand.

"Thank you."

"Why do you want to know?" asked the little girl.

"Oh, well, good question," she replied. "I think it may turn out to be a date I'll always want to remember."

****

It was some time before she got back to the beach with sandwiches, crisps and drinks. "Sorry it was crazy busy." The girls were playing a game, immersed in their own world. John was lying on a towel reading his book. "What's the book?" she asked.

"Educated. Tara Westover. Not sure how anybody could have had such a dysfunctional childhood yet still function in later life. More than function actually, she wrote this," he added, holding up the book.

Catherine didn't reply.

"What's up?" he asked as he turned over a sandwich packet in his hands.

"Nothing." She looked away, staring at the horizon. "This is one of my favourite spots." She turned to face him. "I'd love to come back next year."

"I can tell when you've got something on your mind. And, there's something on your mind." He reached out his hand and stroked her arm. "What is it?"

"Nothing. The queue was long and I wanted to get back to you guys. I'm fine." Catherine brushed crumbs from her T shirt, slipped on her shades and laid back with her hands behind her head. A thousand thoughts raced through her mind.

She knew she had to phone them back tonight: there were so many things she'd thought of since the call.

Later back at the apartment Catherine cleared the plates away from the girls' tea. "Will you read them a story tonight? I'd love to go for a walk on the beach. Maybe have a swim like last night."

John looked up over his newspaper. "No problem. You do it. Maybe clear your head at the same time," he added, catching her eye. Catherine turned back to the sink to avoid further discussion.

"What shall it be tonight girls?" asked John.

"More Winnie The Pooh," came the reply.

Catherine dried her hands, went into their bedroom to retrieve her phone. She slipped into their bathroom to text Lucy: '3 way call 6:30'.

The tide was coming in fast and with only a few feet of sand uncovered, she ran from the mainland to Burgh Island. Before reaching the jetty she took off her shoes and splashed through the shallow fast flowing water. Later she'd have to get the sea tractor back. On the island a few people sat outside The Pilchard enjoying the dying embers in the shadow of the hotel. She was tempted to stop at the pub, get a large glass of wine and make the call overlooking the sea. But glancing round she could see there would be little privacy so pressed on with her plan to walk up the steep path.

She soon reached the top of the island and walked along a grassy path to what she had read was the remains of a small chapel. Close by was a bench which suited her perfectly, giving her a stunning vista and the privacy she needed. The three hundred and sixty degree view was magnificent and she made a note to bring the family here tomorrow. Across the bay was Bigbury and the block of apartments where they were staying. To the left, not far along the coast was Chalborough and the holiday park, the static homes littering the hillside. From there and as far as the eye could see was the beautiful green coastline. To the right was Bantham beach and in the distance she could just make out South Milton beach too. She took a deep breath. "Hi. You both there?"

"Yes," they replied. "Where are you?" asked Neil, "it sounds windy."

"You don't want to know," replied Catherine. "And it wouldn't be fair to tell you!"

"You're right. We're still in the uni and it's raining."

"Bad luck. Now run me through it all again."

For the next thirty minutes she quizzed them both on how they had arrived at the results. Then she asked, "Have you said anything to anybody?"

"No," they replied in unison.

"Including girlfriends? Boyfriends?"

"No."

"Good. It's critical we keep it that way. For now." Catherine checked her watch. "Listen, I have to go soon. Before I do, there are a couple of things you need to start working on before I see you on Monday."

Before leaving, she sat for a while, thinking through all that Neil and Lucy had said. On the one hand she felt immensely excited. On the other, she felt a dread. She did her best to put her negative thoughts aside and struggled up, realising she had been sitting badly. How could she act normally with this going on?

"That was a long walk. I couldn't see you. I was worried."

"I went to the top and round Burgh Island. I can't believe we've been here nearly a week and not been up there. It's stunning. Let's do it tomorrow."

"Perhaps you can take the girls in the morning. I've got my last surfing lesson at ten."

Catherine thought for a moment. "Lovely idea. I'll get them ice creams from the hatch next to The Pilchard, a bribe to get them up the hill."

"Done," he said. Then added, "It will help take your mind off whatever it is."

AMY

CHAPTER 10

March 1993

She woke with a jolt, immediately aware of the sweaty dampness of her nightdress and her thumping head. It was two thirty in the morning and Jimmy Evans was at the forefront of her mind. She worried about seeing him at school. What would he do next? Amy paced the room as if searching for an escape from this labyrinth of fear. But around each corner her imagination created more scenes of humiliation.

All week he had joked about her ruby red birthmark on the lower part of her neck. He said it was the size of a bad penny. It was all she could think about when she got dressed and covering it up didn't make it go away. She scratched at it, digging in her nails.

Amy sat on the edge of the bed with her head in her hands and sobbed. "Damn him, I can't take this," she whispered through her tears. Going to her desk, she opened the drawer, pushing things aside, until she found her small pencil sharpener. She turned it around between her fingers, carefully studying it. Then using her nail, she unscrewed and removed the blade, holding it in the palm of her shaking hand.

Each action was calculated and deliberate. First drawing back her chair; then carefully sitting down; adjusting her position; switching on the desk lamp, pointing it away to dim the light in her eyes.

She began by digging her thumb nail into her arm as if to mark the spot. Then taking the blade she drew it across the patch of red skin, just below the elbow, watching the blood oose out and trickle down her arm. It was like a drug, bringing instant relief from her worries. She deserved the pain, the marks that scarred her; the guilt and shame of what she was doing. She dug her nail into her other arm and cut herself again. She'd put salt in her wounds next time, just to make it sting more. Eventually she patted both cuts with a paper tissue and stared at the stains, faintly brown in the dull light. It was as if the stains contained her worries. By throwing the paper into the bin, it would take them away. But not for long. In one motion she pushed her chair back and leant forward, drawing the blade over the side of her thigh.

After a while, she went to the bathroom and carefully washed each injured patch, patting and drying each scar with toilet paper and covering them with plasters.

Back in bed, Amy tossed and turned, one minute cold the next too hot, as sleep eluded her and the night dragged on and on. There was no way she could go to school in the morning. She would study at home and easily keep up, even if she was off for a week. Amy decided she would 'have a bad tummy and headache.'

****

"It's been three days now Amy. You really should see a doctor and the school will want a note, too."

Amy sat up bleary-eyed and looked at her mother standing by her bed with her hands on her hips. No sympathy she thought. Just practicalities. Her mother was dressed for work, immaculate in her suit, with her hair cascading over one shoulder. In that moment Amy knew she would never be as attractive as her mother and that she would never want to dress like that. So formal, so, what? She wondered. For men, probably, she didn't know, only that her mother annoyed her in every way she could think of.

Amy pulled the right sleeve of her nightdress down just in case and looked up at her mother. "I'm feeling better, I'll be going in today, so you don't need to worry."

"Well, you'd better get a move on, it's late and I'll drop you off at the bus stop."

"Alright, let me get on then."

Billy sat in the back of the car not saying anything either. He had become so much quieter since Dad was around less. Amy still took him out on his bike and he had even started climbing trees with her. They lived in their own world away from their parents. Or was it the other way around?

"Drop me here," said Amy.

"That's not a bus stop," said Billy.

"It's fine, I need the fresh air," replied Amy. She watched as the car disappeared into the traffic and when she was confident they were out of sight, she turned and walked in the opposite direction.

As she entered the library her heart raced as she saw the librarian look up. "Hello Amy," she said in hushed tones, "No school today?"

Amy flushed, "No Mrs Storey, I've got a few study days, preparing for exams."

"This time of year? You must have them all the time. It's nice to see you again, anyway."

Amy nodded and smiled then made her way to a table at the back. She decided to work until mid-afternoon, then go home. There she would be, sitting at the kitchen table in her uniform, when her mother and Billy returned.

"How are you feeling?" asked her mother, dumping her keys and purse on the worktop. "You look much brighter."

Before she could answer Billy said, "Will you help me with my arithmetic?" She turned and smiled, ruffling his hair. "Of course, little man!"

Her mother poured herself a glass of wine. "So, school again tomorrow?"

Amy looked down at her study book, "Yup."

"Good. I'm glad you feel better. I'm going away this weekend with a friend. You'll both be staying with Dad."

"Does Dad know yet?"

"Of course he does."

"Where are you going?"

"I don't know, it's a surprise."

"Who are you going with?"

"Just a friend." She hesitated, finally adding, "a man friend." She sat down at the table opposite Amy and leant over and closed her notebook. Amy looked up at her mother. "You can meet him if you want, but I was thinking to wait a while longer."

"Best to wait," replied Amy and re-opened her book.

"Dad knows." Her mother added.

"Whatever."

"Don't be like that!"

"Like what?" replied Amy.

"You know, unpleasant."

Amy stood up and gathered her books. "It's not me who wrecked the family!" she said as she marched out. "Billy! I'll help you now if you want," she called.

****

Billy snuggled up to Amy as they watched the telly together in their father's flat.

"You two okay in there?" he called from the kitchen.

"Yeah," they answered in unison.

The flat was pokey, but she could see Dad had made it his own with his chess set permanently out and the pictures he'd once had in his study now decorating the sitting room walls. The place smelt of Dad. In some way that she couldn't articulate, it made her feel more at ease than she felt at home. She was jealous that Billy had stayed over countless times. The one time she did stay she'd asked Dad if she could move-in and he'd said 'no your mother needs you'. She really didn't understand why he'd said that until she thought about it later and realised it was another one of those adult lies and what he had really meant was 'I'm happy here without you'.

Amy eased Billy off her shoulder and wandered into the kitchen where Dad was making a salad.

"I'll order pizza soon," he said turning and smiling.

"Great." There was an awkward silence before she added, "Have you met Mum's boyfriend?"

He almost dropped the bowl as he stopped what he was doing and looked at her. "No, of course not. Have you?"

"No."

"Good because we agreed we wouldn't introduce a new partner until we had been together for at least six months and I think it's only been weeks with this one."

"There's been a few then?" asked Amy.

"I don't doubt."

"But they're going away together, and she's only just met him."

"They're adults Amy." He hesitated then added, "mind you, I wonder with your mother sometimes." He looked at her. "Sit down," he said pointing to a stool. "Want to talk?"

Reluctantly Amy sat. "Do you have a girlfriend, Dad?"

She watched him closely as he wiped his hands on a cloth, pulled out a stool and sat opposite her, his chin on his hands. "I do Amy, yes. We've been together for over six months so it would be nice if you could meet her." Amy allowed him to take her hand and he gave it a squeeze. "Her name's Janice, she's a headmistress living in Bristol."

"That's miles away," was all she could think of to say.

"We met at a conference," he replied as if anticipating her real question. "And I stay there, and she comes here. Some weekends."

"Oh." Amy felt her stomach tighten. She could see her parents were moving on, finding new lives, new happiness, but she was stuck in between: she was an inconvenience from their past. It took all her will to hold back the tears. "You loved each other once though, didn't you? I mean you got married."

He squeezed her hand again and now she could feel her eyes watering. "Of course. It was all a whirlwind. We were young. It happened so fast. It was fun and yes, we were in love. Both of us. But listen, your mother has always been a restless soul." He looked Amy straight in the eye. "Outwardly very engaging, friendly, fun, but there's a barrier which stops you getting too close." Suddenly he stood up. "Oh, I really shouldn't be talking to you like this about your mother: it's not fair."

Amy remained silent, waiting for him to continue.

"And well then there's me. I'm not exactly the most exciting person."

Amy wanted to say something nice but couldn't.

"So, in the end we simply drifted apart. It happens." He started to wash up a few cups with his back to her, Amy suspecting he may have tears in his eyes. "How are you doing anyway Amy?" he added without turning round.

"Okay. I'll smash the exams in June."

"I know. You're super intelligent. You take after me!" he said as he stared out of the window.

"Ha, ha," she replied. "I'll go and see what Billy's up to," she said getting up. Billy looked up as she walked in, "you've been crying." He immediately turned back to the television. "Look," he said pointing at the screen, "this is so funny, but you've missed the best bit."

Amy wondered if Dad had a pencil sharpener somewhere in the flat. She could do with it right now.

****

Amy knew something was up the moment she walked through the front door; the frosty atmosphere was palpable.

"How was your weekend?" she asked her mother. Her immediate thought was that something must have gone seriously wrong as without answering her mother said, "Billy, it's late, go up to your room and get ready for bed." She turned to Amy. "We need to talk."

"Tell me about this," she said handing Amy a letter. "And they called me this evening to make sure you hadn't intercepted it."

Amy took the letter – it was from the headmaster, wanting to know why she hadn't attended for three weeks. She'd called in twice pretending to be her mother, but it hadn't worked.

"And they want a meeting. You could be expelled you know."

Amy's hands shook as she put the letter down on the coffee table.

"Well?" Before she could answer her mother added, "think how this makes me look too. They must think I'm a neglectful mother. What have you been doing?"

"I'm bored."

"What do you mean 'you're bored?' That's no reason to bunk off school."

"I get more done by working on my own."

"That's ridiculous and you know it. Where have you been going, because you've put on your uniform every day to deceive me. Is there a boy involved?"

"No, Mum!" She swallowed hard; her mouth as dry as it could be. "I went to the library, so you don't need to worry."

"I certainly do need to worry. We've got a meeting this week with the Head, so you'd better have a stronger story than this one. Are you going to tell me what's behind this or not?"

"I've told you Mum, that's it - I'm bored by school, the teachers, my so-called friends. I hate it and I can pass my GCSEs without being there."

"That's not the way it works. Plus, I don't believe it. You are required to be at school and you're required to be honest with me, not go behind my back like this."

She couldn't help herself. "What, like you've been honest?" Suddenly, Amy ran out of the room, before she said more.

****

A few days later Amy met Catherine in the park. "That was *so* humiliating," she began. "I can't tell you how angry it's made me."

"What happened?" asked Catherine.

"Mum and I had a meeting with the Head and a so-called counsellor today. Nightmare. I *told* Mum not to arrive miles early. But guess what? She did of course and hung about in reception. It was inevitable that someone would see her, and sure enough Tamsin asked me later what Mum was doing at school."

"What did you tell her?"

"The truth, in the end. What could I do? She'd been quizzing me about why I'd been off school for such a long time."

"And what happened with the Head?" asked Catherine.

"Oh God I'm so cross I can hardly speak. He went through my attendance record and then asked what had been going on. He was all smiles and nice which made it so much worse. I think Mum was squirming as it was clear she had no idea what had been going on and it made her look neglectful."

"What did you say? I mean, it can't have been easy."

"I can't remember - it was a bit of a blur – but basically I said I'd had enough and that the lessons were for the slowest pupils and I got a lot more done away from class."

"Nothing about Jimmy?"

"Of course not! I didn't want to make it worse. Anyway, they quizzed me a lot, trying to uncover the real reason but they didn't get anywhere."

"Sounds hellish. What happened in the end?"

Amy jumped off the swing and stood facing Catherine with her hands on her hips. "You know what really got me angry? It was when the Head said I was on notice and anymore misdemeanours and I would be suspended - then he went on about how I'm the brightest pupil in the school and they didn't want me to miss the lessons or GCSEs blah blah. Oh, and the counsellor will meet me once a week and follow-up with my mum. That'll be fun."

"What about your mum, will she ground you?"

"Nah, she'll be fine. I can handle her well enough. She hasn't much time for me anyway. My anger is with Jimmy as he's the one causing all this and there he is, in the eyes of the school, a little angel and here I am close to being expelled. And because of him! It's so unfair! It makes me mad!"

Catherine clambered off the swing and put her arms around Amy and gave her a tight hug. After a moment they sat on the grass together and Amy started to cry. "I don't know what I'd do without you," she said wiping away the tears. "You're the only person who understands me. Please never leave."

Catherine gave her another hug. "I'm not going anywhere; we'll be friends for life."

Suddenly Amy heard a voice behind her and as she turned a woman approached holding the hand of a young boy. "Are you okay dear?" she asked. "It looked as if you were crying."

Amy felt foolish as she stood up, flustered. "Yes, I'm fine. Just got a bit sad about something that's all, but I'm okay…really."

Amy could see the woman wasn't convinced. "As long as you're sure."

"Thanks for asking." She smiled. "I'd better get home."

All the way she chatted to Catherine about how much she hated Jimmy and what he did to her. She could feel the anger well-up inside at the mention of his name. She ran through all the horrible things he'd said and done and what she'd do to him to get revenge. But she knew she never would. Not really. When she got to her room, she went straight to the desk drawer to retrieve her blade. She made a mental note to quit the netball team. She couldn't wear her sports kit without revealing the marks she'd made.

AMY

CHAPTER 11

It was Friday 23rd July, the first day of the summer holidays and even Amy felt the freedom from no more exams. She was sitting in her favourite spot, the lower branch in the Witch's Tree, reading The Pelican Brief. The dappled sunlight scattered green and yellow light through the branches, lifting her mood. She rested the book on her lap, leant against the trunk and breathed deeply, taking in the fresh summer air. She realised she hadn't thought about Jimmy for the entire time she'd been in the woods and imagined what it would be like if he didn't exist at all. How *good* that would be. She glanced at her watch: Tamsin and Rachel were coming over and she was late. Amy grabbed her jumper, threw her book to the ground and clambered down the tree. At the edge of the woods, she saw Mr Jones from two doors down walking his dog. "Hi Mr Jones," she called, lifting her book in her hand. He simply nodded, appearing preoccupied as he often did.

The three friends sat in Amy's garden. "We hardly see you," began Rachel.

"Exam study. Hope it pays off," said Amy.

"You've nailed them, don't pretend," said Tamsin.

Rachel touched Amy's arm. "What's with the bandage?"

Amy pulled her arm away. "I was out running in the woods, caught my arm on some brambles that's all."

"Didn't know you jogged," replied Tamsin. "Anyway, we wanted to know if you're coming to the party tomorrow night."

She looked from one to the other, not wanting to admit she had no idea what they were talking about.

"Don't say you've not been invited, everybody's going," added Rachel.

Amy's heart sank. "Not me."

"Jimmy's house," added Tamsin. "His older brother and sister will have their friends their too, so there'll be older boys."

Making it worse Tamsin added, "His parents are away. You've got to be there." She turned to Rachel. "She's coming, right?"

"Totally," replied Rachel.

"Not sure I want to. Not if I haven't been invited."

"Of course you want to!" replied Tamsin. "Anyway, there will be loads of gate crashers and you'll probably not be noticed."

"He'll notice me alright," replied Amy. She thought her face must be red she felt so angry.

Rachel smiled. "I'm sure he meant to invite you. Maybe he just thought he had - or assumed we'd tell you." There was a moment's silence until Rachel repeated, "you're totally coming."

"Yeah, it's final!" added Tamsin. "We'll come here around four. I've got a few bottles of Alcopos hidden at home, so I'll bring them and we can have a drink while we get ready."

They both looked for a reaction but seeing Amy's blank stare, Rachel added, "It's set then. See you Saturday!"

****

Her mother looked up from her book. "How will you be getting home?"

"Tamsin's mum is collecting us."

"What time?"

"Midnight."

"That's quite late."

"Is that an 'okay'?"

"I don't want you drinking."

"Have you ever known me to have too much to drink?"

Her mother shook her head. "You shouldn't be drinking at all! And don't forget I was once your age. Just be careful that's all: especially if there are older boys."

"Jimmy's parents will be there, so you don't need to worry."

"Okay, but I won't sleep until I hear you return."

"That'll be them," said Amy as she went to the front door.

"Quick!" Amy whispered as she grabbed the plastic shopping bag from Rachel. The bottles clinked in the bag as they ran upstairs. "I'll put them in here," she said opening the wardrobe. "In case Mum comes up." Both girls were carrying clothes under their arms ready to get changed.

"Let's drink them now!"

Tamsin put her hands on her hips. "You on a mission?"

"Aren't we all?" said Amy as she removed the tops. "Here, three Alcolas!"

She rolled onto the bed trying to keep the bottle upright and kicked her legs into the air, her shoes flying across the room. The brown fizzing liquid splashed onto her shirt as both girls jumped onto the bed next to her giggling.

"Are we going to have fun, or what?!" said Tamsin.

"Time we got ourselves ready," said Rachel as she took another swig. "It's gonna be wild!" She opened a bag, "I've brought all the make-up we need."

"You can't go dressed like that," said Tamsin, opening Amy's wardrobe. "You're always wearing old jeans and a T-shirt. You should wear something sexy tonight."

"Oy! That's my stuff," said Amy, as Tamsin threw clothes onto the bed.

Tamsin held up a dress. "You can't possibly wear this," she said, as she hung it back in the wardrobe. "When was the last time you bought any new clothes?"

Rachel got off the bed and put her arm around Amy's shoulder. "Come on Tamsin, give her a break."

Tamsin turned to them. "We've got to get her paired off tonight. Look, this one will have to do," she said holding up a dress Amy had bought but never worn.

"It shows off my non-breasts," said Amy.

"Don't be ridiculous," said Rachel. "I bet it looks lovely."

"You should wear it," confirmed Tamsin, taking it off the hanger.

"Whatever," replied Amy, placing it on the bed. At least it had long sleeves and would cover her scars.

"Hope you've got a push-up bra," added Tamsin.

Rachel held up a hand. "Okay enough Tamsin, she'll look great."

****

As they got close, they could hear the music from down the street, making Amy's tummy flutter. They quickly merged with others from school as they approached the house.

"God this is a bit different," said Rachel as they reached the drive. The house was surrounded on three sides by an old wall. The large gates opened on to a sweeping gravel drive with a row of huge lime trees to one side. The tear-drop shaped lawn had perfect stripes diagonally across, neatly circling the apple tree at the centre. They could hear music coming from behind a fence at the side and as they approached the front door, heard splashing and shouting. "God a pool as well!" exclaimed Tamsin. "They're rich."

Amy was relieved they had arrived en-masse as she thought this may give her cover. The last thing she wanted was for the three of them to arrive, knock on the door and to see Jimmy answer. Her heart was racing as they went through the open front door. She imagined Jimmy seeing her in the hall and saying, "what are you doing here?" She'd die.

Tamsin touched Amy's arm. "It'll be fine. It's us three or none of us."

An attractive girl met them in the hall. "Hey, are you Jimmy's friends?" she asked.

"Yes," Rachel replied, "School."

"I'm Tina, Jimmy's sister."

The girl looked at Amy quizzically. "Aren't you Amy?" she asked.

Amy felt herself blushing for the second time in five minutes. "Yes," she replied.

"Jimmy mentioned you," she said staring at Amy. There was a moment's silence before she added, "now take your jackets and dump them upstairs - first bedroom on the left and put those drinks in the kitchen and help yourself to whatever."

As they began to walk upstairs, she called after them, "Jimmy's in the garden somewhere. Or by the pool. Stoned most likely."

"How come you know her?" asked Rachel as they walked upstairs.

"I don't!" whispered Amy. She took a deep breath, worried she'd answered aggressively. "Don't forget I've known

Jimmy since I was five - at our first school, so no surprise she's heard of me." Amy changed the subject. "Wow this is a huge room," she said as they dumped their jackets on the bed. "Must be their parents'."

"Didn't know they were so well-off," added Rachel. She looked in a mirror and adjusted her dress. "I think Tina's seventeen and training to be an actor at some special school in London. Apparently, she's already been in a soap. According to Jimmy anyway."

"She looks amazing," added Amy.

"There are drugs," whispered Rachel.

"I know," replied Tamsin. "I could smell it as soon as we got into the drive. It's not for me."

"Nor me," replied Rachel.

"Never say never!" said Amy as they skipped down the stairs.

The kitchen was packed with party goers most of whom the girls didn't recognise. Every surface was covered with bottles; Hooper's Hooch, Smirnoff Ice. Amy had never seen anything like it. In the centre of the room was a large island with food laid out on the shiny black granite top.

"Here, take this," said Rachel handing Amy a bottle of Alcopops. "I'll mix up some blastaways next!" shouted Tamsin. "Yeah!" called Amy, although she had no idea what that was.

"Let's dance!" Said Rachel pointing toward the door. "It's Ace of Base!"

Amy looked up to see a boy with messy blond hair and her first impression was he must be three or four years older than her. "And what's your name?" he asked, smiling.

Her stomach flipped as she answered, "I'm Amy. I know Jimmy." She took a swig from her bottle and felt her hand shaking.

"I'm Gareth. I'm at Manchester uni with Jimmy's brother, Michael." He replied.

Tamsin touched Amy's arm, smiled, and said, "we'll see you later."

"Wait…" she replied but they were gone. She felt herself blushing again as she turned back to Gareth.

"Go if you want," he said and smiled. He had a kind face she thought.

"No, no… it's fine." Then she blurted out the first thing that came to mind. "What are you studying?"

"Physics," he replied, "same as Michael."

"That's what I'm thinking of doing." She took another swig from her bottle as he put his beer-can down on the counter and fizzed open another. "Maybe with astrophysics too as I love astronomy," she added.

He looked straight at her which made her giddy. "What A levels are you doing?"

God, she thought he probably thinks I'm in the upper sixth or something. She'd never had a boy take an interest in her like this let alone someone older. Her heart raced. She'd already decided what A levels she would begin in September. "Pure Maths, Applied Maths, Physics and Chemistry."

"Wow four, bit of a brain box then."

Her heart sank. She'd said the wrong thing, trying to impress. The noise was getting louder, so she had to shout. "Not really!"

Suddenly there was somebody at their side. "This is Michael," said Gareth. "Jimmy's brother."

He pointed to Amy, "and your name is?"

"Amy."

"Oh, yes. From school, right?" said Michael.

She could hardly speak so nodded instead, hoping she wasn't blushing again.

"I think Gareth and I are off to the garden for a smoke, if you'll excuse us," said Michael turning to his friend. Gareth put his hand on Michael's shoulder to steady himself and smiled a huge grin. "We are, my old friend. Maybe see you later? A dance perhaps?" said Michael as he turned to go. She watched them walk away and saw Michael laughing and whispering in his friend's ear. It's about me she thought. So embarrassing. And Michael has heard of me too. What on earth had Jimmy been saying? Her heart still raced as she leant back on the kitchen worktop. Next to her was a bottle of Smirnoff Ice, so she opened it and took a long swig. After a minute of feeling abandoned in the kitchen, she moved off in search of her friends.

The room was packed and the music loud as she pushed her way to the centre where her friends were dancing with others from school. Amy felt free from her cares and let herself go, immersed in the music; her body moving freely; not caring what anybody thought. She danced to Abba Esque, Rhythm Of A Dancer, Even Better Than The Real Thing,

Shake Your Head and Too Funky. "I love George Michael," she called, flinging her arms as the drum beat pulsated. Before long she felt giddy and gestured to her friends she was going outside. Leaving the room she grabbed the door handle, taking a breath as she worked out her route; through the dining room, past two groups of people and out into the garden through the patio doors. She blinked, yes they were open. Were they? Someone walked through the opening. Yes I can go, she thought and put one foot in front of the other, walking more quickly than she had planned and having to hold onto a bookshelf to avoid colliding with someone. The cool air filled her lungs, almost knocking her over. She staggered to the side and leant against the house for support, taking deep breaths. Amy scanned the garden: the people milling around in small groups, drinking, smoking, laughing; a couple kissing under a huge lime tree. No sign of Jimmy. Good. But then again, she thought, she'd like to see him. She was torn, as always. She loved his dark wavey hair, his brown eyes, his strong physique, his sharp mind and his sense of humour. But hated him so much more. Damn him! She thought. Then she wondered, would he dance with her? That older guy had been keen, so maybe Jimmy? Perhaps she looked better than she thought tonight. Tamsin and Rachel had helped do her hair. Before they left, she had kept going into the bathroom to look; she couldn't believe the transformation. Even her mother had said, "you look so grown up!"

"Here, have this." He handed her a glass. "It's water, you may need it." It was the boy she'd seen earlier. What was his name? She tried to remember as she took the glass. "Thanks."

"Gareth." He said as if reading her mind. "Ever tried this?" he said holding up what at first Amy thought was a cigarette." Of course, the smell, weed.

"No," she replied, "smells disgusting."

"Go on, try it," he said holding it closer to her face. "It won't hurt you."

"Nah."

"Really," he said waving it in front of her. "It'll make you feel great."

Amy waved it away. "How?" she asked.

"How will it make you feel? Well, chilled; at ease with life; relaxed; maybe it'll make you a bit chatty. I think it'll make you giggle!" he added, smiling.

"Okay hand it here," she said, "I'll have a drag." The smell made her feel nauseous as she put it to her mouth. She sucked and inhaled. The smoke burnt her lungs as she doubled up coughing. "Oh god!"

"Hey, take it easy," he said putting his arm around her shoulder. "Don't take so much in at once. There's no hurry."

"I don't feel anything," she said.

"Give it time," he said, "I'm going to the toilet, I'll be back in a mo." As he stepped away, he added, "don't go crazy with it!" She stared at him and thought what a lovely smile he had. She held the joint between her thumb and forefinger, examining it. What would Mum think, she wondered? She leant back against the house with one knee bent and her foot against the wall. She took a quick tentative puff and blew it out almost immediately. Rather than feeling calm her heart was racing, thumping in her chest. She took a longer drag, slowly drawing it into her lungs and holding it there, before blowing it upwards toward the moon which hung above her in the blue-dark sky.

One more, she thought and took a long drag, again holding it in her lungs for as long as she could bear.

"Hey steady on, leave some for me," said Gareth grabbing the joint from her hand. "How's it feel?"

Amy stared at the moon. "I've gotta go," she mumbled. Back in the house she danced with her friends hoping she would soon feel different but instead she felt increasingly angry that Jimmy hadn't invited her. She shouted at Tamsin, struggling to be heard over Jarvis Cocker in full flow with Common People. "Have you seen Jimmy?!" Tamsin simply shook her head. It irritated her so she left and went in search of him. She wandered around the garden pretending to be joining some friends. Through a small opening in the hedge she spotted the pool, the water glowing blue from the submerged light. It was half full of people in the shallow-end drinking and chatting. She saw him immediately, leaning against the side in deep conversation with a girl who had her back to her. He had one elbow on the patio holding a drink in what Amy thought was an obvious pose. Creep she thought. She stood there a while staring, her anger rising with each second that slowly ticked by. Suddenly there was a tug on her arm and she twisted round. "Rachel," she said.

"We were worried about you, disappearing all the time." Rachel grabbed Amy's arm, "you're required in the kitchen." They squeezed between people to find Tamsin mixing drinks. "This one's yours," she said handing Amy a large tumbler.

"What is it?"

"A blastaway! It'll refresh you," replied Tamsin as she handed the same to Rachel.

"Cheers!" called Tamsin. Amy chinked her glass with her friends and took a sip. "God that's strong. Tastes like Lilt. A bit minging! What is it?"

"Castaway and Diamond White cider!" replied Tamsin. "To us!" she said raising her glass again.

"The three Musketeers!" said Amy, her anger subsiding.

At that moment, Jimmy appeared at their side, now dressed but with his hair straggly and wet. "Having fun girls?" he asked as he put his drink down.

"It's wicked!" said Tamsin.

"Amazing," added Rachel.

Jimmy turned to Amy, "are you having fun?"

Amy tensed, "sure," she replied.

Jimmy grabbed her arm just above the elbow, "I need you for a minute," he said looking her straight in the eye. Amy's heart missed a beat. What was this about? He'd grabbed her tightly and it hurt. He turned to her friends, "you'll have to excuse us ladies, I won't be long," he said adding a cheeky smile.

"Whatever," replied Tamsin.

"That hurts!" called Amy as he guided her through the kitchen into the crowded hallway. "Excuse us!" he shouted as he pushed past, almost pulling Amy along behind him. At the front door he stopped and turned round facing her. "What are you doing here?!"

She felt as if she would be sick as her heart thumped and her mouth went dry. "What do you mean?"

"You *know* what I mean. Did I invite you?" His face was inches from hers and she could smell the marijuana on his breath making her feel she might retch.

The anger took over. "Fuck off Jimmy!"

"No, you fuck off," he said opening the front door.

"Why are you always so horrible to me?"

"I'm not. You just won't leave me alone, will you? You're obsessed!"

Amy felt dizzy as she leant against the wall. "What are you talking about? Don't be…"

"Hey, what the hell's going on?" said Tina.

Jimmy turned to his sister, "Amy's just leaving," he said.

She looked at Amy who had tears in her eyes and back at Jimmy. "Are you sure?"

Amy nodded. "I'd better go."

"You don't need to go. Jimmy, leave her alone and come back into the party."

He glared at his sister. "She's leaving."

Amy noticed the hallway had gone quiet as the others watched on. She saw at least four people she recognised from school. So humiliating, God she had to get out of there. "I'll get my coat," she said as she turned to go upstairs.

"Your choice," said Tina. Jimmy just stood there. "You're a piece of work sometimes," said Tina glaring at Jimmy. "Let it go. It's a party!"

At the top of the stairs, Amy heard Tina add, "I know she's irritating, but still."

Amy threw herself on the pile of coats in the darkened room and sobbed, her hands covering her face wet with tears. "I hate myself." Still crying, she began to grab the coats throwing them off the bed onto the floor, searching for her own. Suddenly the door opened behind her and she swivelled round. A shockwave bolted through her, ending with a flip of the stomach and a sick feeling deep inside. "Oh it's you. Don't worry, I'm going."

Jimmy said nothing as he slowly approached, his eyes wide and staring. He reached out and touched her arm. "I don't know what came over me. I didn't really mean it." He put his head slightly to one side as if pleading. "Do you believe me?"

Amy stared at him unable to comprehend how radically and fast his demeanour had changed. Then he took one step closer, put one hand around the back of her head and kissed her gently on the lips. She'd never experienced the sensation that now shot through her body. Before she could respond he leant forward again, putting his hand around the back of her head and caressing her hair as he kissed her full on the lips. Her mind raced and her heart thumped as she responded kissing him deeply and putting her hands around his waist, pulling him closer. She could feel him pressing against her and she began to shake.

He moved away. "Here," he said, taking hold of her hand as he sat on the bed. "Sit next to me."

She hesitated, a thousand thoughts flooding her mind. "Can I kiss you again?" he asked gently. She kissed him and they toppled over, without releasing their embrace. His tongue was in her mouth, and she grabbed him tightly, frantic. Then she felt his hand raising her dress and before she could respond his hand was inside her knickers, fumbling.

"No!" she gasped as she tried to move his hand away, but he was too strong and in one movement he ripped hard at her knickers, half pulling them down over her thighs. Amy wriggled and kicked but he was too strong and held her tight. "Stop it!" she screamed.

She felt him push and roll over, so he was sitting on top of her. Amy looked up and his eyes were wild, like an animal. He appeared triumphant as if he'd caught his prey. He moved his legs over her upper arms, so she was trapped and despite her kicking he turned and ripped her knickers off in one violent motion.

"Let me go, you…" But she couldn't finish her sentence as he clamped a hand over her mouth. She tried to shake her head but the pressure was too great and she couldn't escape as she breathed heavily through her nose.

"Mmmmmmmm" she cried through his sweaty hand. Now he moved his other hand behind him between her legs. She wriggled but in vain, she felt him invade her and thought she would throw up. Suddenly he moved his hand away from her mouth. In that second, she punched him hard in the face and as he reeled back, she lifted herself up and hit him as hard as she could in the groin. He screamed, rolled over and fell headfirst onto the floor with a thump.

"Ahhh fuck," he moaned, "What was that for?! Shit that hurts."

Amy shuffled down the bed, tumbled off the end and fell forward. In a second, she stood and looked to see where he was: still on the floor. Her heart was beating so fast it felt as if her chest might explode. Suddenly she realised she was only wearing one shoe. "Shit!" she said looking round. Amy glanced in Jimmy's direction as he sat up. He was staring at her as if about to leap up and grab her.

"Don't you dare touch me," she snarled. Then she saw it: her shoe was poking out from under his left leg. She held out her hand. "Give me the shoe."

He looked down, removed the shoe, and threw it violently toward her. Amy moved her head aside as it flew past and hit the wall. As she turned around to retrieve it, Jimmy jumped up and went to the door, leaning against it facing her in the room and blocking her exit. "You're not going anywhere, you silly bitch." Now with both shoes on she picked up a bottle of scent from the dressing table and held it aloft. She could feel it shaking in her hand. "Open the door!"

Slowly, he shook his head.

Amy threw the bottle with all her force toward him. It missed his head by a fraction, crashed against the bedroom door and smashed, the glass and scent exploding onto the side of his cowering head. "God!" he said as he fell forward. It was her chance and she pulled the door so hard it swung wide and hit the side of the wardrobe. "Look what you've done!" she heard him call. She almost fell down the stairs, her hands gripping the banister saved her as she stumbled into the hall. She sensed people turning around, wondering what on earth was going on. Outside she stopped, her breath uncontrollable, gasping for air. She could still feel him, as if his fingers were still there inside her. She wondered in that moment if the feeling of disgust would ever leave her. The next thing she knew she was running as fast as she had ever run in her entire life.

CATHERINE

CHAPTER 12

September 2018

It was Monday morning and Catherine went straight to see Professor Morehouse, tapping more heavily on his door than she meant to. "Come in." He jumped up from behind his desk, standing in his usual pose, hands in pockets, eyes sparkling, eager to hear what she had to say. "How's it going?" He began.

"Good. Very good," she replied.

He gestured for her to sit. She noted the chair was already occupied by a pile of books. Catherine carefully stacked them on the corner of his desk. Looking round she could see the whole room was a mess. There were papers strewn across the floor and on his bookshelf a stained mug, from which she guessed the smell of stale coffee was emanating. Sensing her disapproval he said, "Yes I know, it does need a tidy-up."

"It's fine," she replied as she sat down.

"You okay?" he asked. "You look… flustered."

"I am. Let me take you through this and you'll see why." They sat opposite each other at his small conference table. "The study of the atmosphere of exo-planet Proxima Centauri e. You remember the research project you helped me start a couple of years ago."

"Of course. What's up?"

Catherine could hardly speak and took a second to gather herself. "In the last few days, we have identified water, oxygen and carbon dioxide in the data."

"Brilliant," he exclaimed and raised his arms as if he'd scored a goal.

"That's not all though Stuart." She carefully laid out six printed graphs, as if presenting evidence in court. He picked them up, one by one, taking time to study each page. Suddenly he ran his fingers through his hair and looked straight at Catherine. "Bloody hell." He picked up the final sheet. "Confidence level?"

"High."

Professor Morehouse stroked his chin. "Good God Catherine."

"Scary, isn't it?"

"It sure is." He sat for a moment staring straight ahead deep in thought. Then he looked back at her. "Take me through the details." For two hours he quizzed her on everything, then sat back and smiled. "Looks good to me."

"Yes and we've run it by the geophysics department to see if there are any mechanisms for this that we haven't thought of. The answer looks like a 'no'." She hesitated then asked, "What next?"

"Firstly, you need to talk with Professor Norman in Chemistry. Secondly, we'll give your results to a couple of researchers within my group. Given it passes their scrutiny, then we need to inform the higher echelons at the uni. The implications for us all and the uni are so huge, it needs careful handling."

Catherine looked down as she shuffled together the sheets of paper.

"And this is potential Nobel prize material. You do understand this?" he continued.

Catherine nodded. "That scares me to be honest," she replied.

"Why?"

"It just does. I can't explain."

Stuart looked quizzically at her. "Listen, I'm not receiving a second Nobel prize Catherine. This is not mine, it's yours. You must be shown as the lead researcher and take whatever credit comes along."

"But you were my supervisor when the project began and the more senior, so…"

The professor held up his hand. "Stop. It's kind of you, but not right. All the work, and the novel approach came from you, not me. I cannot take the credit."

"Stuart." Catherine sighed, looked up at the ceiling and then back at Stuart, "I know."

"Send me the paper and I'll get things moving." He put his hands in his pockets. "I'll call Prof Norman and do the introduction." He smiled. "History will remember you, Catherine!"

"I…" but her voice trailed off.

****

John and Catherine sat in their garden with a bottle of chilled white wine. The girls were in bed, although they could hear them chatting through the open bedroom window.

It was mid-September, two weeks since she had met with Stuart. The nights were still warm, although a hint of moisture in the air signalled the end of summer.

"Are you sure you're okay?" John asked. "You've been so distracted."

Catherine looked down, observing the golden liquid as she swirled it around in her glass. She caught the fragrance of grapes and honey. She decided it was time to say something. "I'm sorry." Catherine gently squeezed his arm. "It's a work thing."

John stroked her hair. "I was worried."

She looked up at him. "There's no need to be." She took a deep breath. "Listen. I need to tell you something."

"Sounds ominous!"

"It's… the team have made a hugely significant discovery. Or it looks like we have. I'm consumed by the whole thing."

"Excellent! Why didn't you say before?"

"I should have, I know. But we agreed to keep it a secret. It's still early days. If we announced our results and the peer reviews found our paper to be flawed, then instead of it enhancing the uni's reputation, it could damage it."

"I get that, but you can tell *me* about it, surely?"

She rested her head back down. "I told my team they shouldn't reveal it to anybody, including family. So I felt I should do the same."

"You serious?"

"I am. I know it sounds crazy."

"It sure does."

"Please?" she whispered.

He smiled and kissed her. "Okay. It must be pretty amazing. But I won't push it further."

"Thanks," she replied. "You know I'll tell you as soon as I can."

"Of course. It is good though?"

Catherine looked down at her glass. "Sure." She nodded, "it is."

"Okay. No more discussion. More wine?" He held out the bottle.

"No thanks. I'm really whacked. I think I may go to bed."

****

"God, you made me jump!" She'd opened her office to find Professor Morehouse sitting in her chair. He immediately got up and walked towards her. "Thought you'd want to know right away." He stuck out his hand to shake hers. "Congratulations. My team found nothing wrong."

"Oh gosh. Really? Nothing?"

"Nothing material shall we say."

"Fantastic!" she replied.

"How's it been going with Prof Norman in Chemistry?" he asked as he took a seat.

"He's confirmed there's no known mechanisms for this occurring in the absence of life, as we thought."

He smiled, "That's amazing, Catherine."

She took a deep breath. "It is, I know, but Stuart, listen this is… too big for me to handle."

"Of course, it isn't!" he smiled, trying to reassure her. "I'll support you at every step. You know that."

She sighed, ignoring his comment, and looked away. He didn't understand. How could he? How could anybody? "I know you will," she replied.

He looked perplexed. "You don't seem very pleased."

"Oh it's okay. Sorry." She tried to pull herself together. "What next?"

"Right. You, me and the Vice Chancellor are meeting at ten this morning."

"I've not prepared anything."

"You don't need to. It's a chat to bring her into the loop. You'll be fine."

****

Catherine had met the VC at university fund raisers and departmental gatherings and had warmed to her from the start. But she had never been in her office. Looking around now she was surprised at the state of it: the desk stacked with papers, the floor so littered with piles of magazines Catherine had to step carefully to take her seat. The shelves were shambolic with old manuscripts, empty fizzy drink bottles, an out of date calendar, odd looking trophies and wonky picture frames with faded photos of what Catherine assumed where kids at swimming galas. She tried her best not to catch Stuart's eye and could feel him looking at her. The VC lowered her large frame into the seat at the head of the table. "Okay, right, you've called this meeting Stuart; you want to kick it off?"

"Actually, I'll hand straight over to Catherine if I may."

The VC turned to Catherine. "Before you begin, please bear in mind my knowledge of astronomy is limited." She smiled and sat back in her chair.

"Understood," replied Catherine, "And do stop me whenever you want." She glanced at Professor Morehouse, then continued. "Let me make a short statement upfront, so you know what we are dealing with." Catherine took a deep breath. "We have strong evidence for the existence of an advanced life-form on another planet."

Her announcement was greeted by silence as the VC glanced at Professor Morehouse as if looking for confirmation. Getting no reaction, she sat upright in her chair and stared back at Catherine. "Right. That's quite a claim, Professor. Enlighten me."

Catherine smiled. "I'll give you some context first, then fill in the details." She took a deep breath and continued. "Many stars in the night sky have their own planetary systems, similar to our own solar system. This has been known and researched for almost twenty-five years. We call these planets exo-planets and the one of interest orbits a star called Proxima Centauri, about 4 light years away."

"Okay I'm with you. So, tell me about this planet."

Catherine sat upright. "It's a rocky planet, so in that respect it's like earth, although it's almost twice the size. Such planets are called super earths." Catherine glanced at Stuart, then back at the VC. "The point is, Vice Chancellor, we have detected something unusual within the atmosphere of this planet. In a nutshell, we've detected Chlorofluorocarbons, or as we call them in everyday language, CFCs."

The VC frowned. "You mean what is emitted from aerosols, air conditioners and fridges?"

"Yes, precisely. Although we no longer allow them to be produced on earth as they are an industrial pollutant. And," Catherine paused, to ensure she had the VC's full attention. "There is no known mechanism for these gases to be produced naturally."

"So?" asked the VC.

"We are confident that the only way these gases can exist in a planet's atmosphere is by the activities of an industrialised society," replied Catherine.

There was a moment's silence as it sunk in. Then the VC slowly stood up and went to the window, looking out with her back to them. Eventually she turned around, blew her cheeks out and folded her arms. "By industrialised, you mean, sophisticated, like us?"

Catherine nodded. "You could say that, yes."

"Gosh. I don't know what to say," replied the VC. "It's shocking."

"It's difficult to form the words," added Stuart. "This is big. For humankind. And for the university."

"Absolutely," said the VC, sitting back down.

Catherine glanced at Stuart and then looked directly at the VC. "I need to add a major caveat, before we extrapolate too far."

The VC shuffled in her chair. "Go on."

"We will not make the claim that we've definitely found extra-terrestrials. It's not as if we've received a signal as such, so our evidence is indirect, rather than direct. We will present the evidence as it is and let the scientific community, and the world at large, draw its own conclusions."

The VC thought for a moment. "But as I understand it, unless some team somewhere comes up with a highly unusual mechanism for these gases to occur naturally, then everybody will conclude that we have indeed found an advanced life-form, right?"

"Indeed," replied Catherine, "But *we* won't make the bold claim. We will present evidence of what we have found. That's it."

"Yes, I get it," replied the VC. "But for our understanding in this room, the world is going to say that humankind is no longer alone, right?"

"Very likely," replied Stuart.

The VC put her hands behind her head. "Think how advanced they may be. There are so many implications and things we need to think through." She turned to Catherine, "there'll be huge attention on you in particular."

Catherine stiffened and looked down at her hands. She could feel they were clammy.

"And we'll need to prepare for the onslaught of worldwide media attention. It's going to make this university even more prestigious. And your department," she added, looking at Stuart."

"Indeed," he replied.

"And having a woman make the discovery is a perfect narrative," she added.

Stuart glanced at Catherine. "The Vice Chancellor is right, it will be you, not me."

Before Catherine could reply, the VC asked, "what's the timetable?"

"We'll write-up the paper and submit it to the Nature Journal," Catherine began. "We need two months for that. Then, under embargo, they'll send it to eminent researchers of their choice who will review it and no doubt come up with questions. Nature will send those questions to us and we'll need to answer to everybody's satisfaction before Nature will consider publishing. We may need to do some more work in order to satisfy them. That's about it."

The VC shifted in her chair. "So two months to write up and say two months to receive and answer the questions?"

"If all goes well let's assume it would be published in January," replied Catherine.

The VC clasped her hands together and thought. "Could other research teams be studying the same planet?"

"Could be," replied Catherine.

Stuart looked at the VC. "Although Catherine and her team have used a novel technique, which on balance, probably puts us ahead, even if other similar research is going on."

The VC hesitated, processing what she had heard. "It's critical we are first, so we have to move fast."

"We will," replied Catherine,

"This is Nobel prize material," added Stuart.

Catherine felt the knot in her stomach return. She knew the VC would back her being as the lead researcher. She'd want a woman to take the credit as a starter.

After they left Stuart walked by her side along the corridor. "Well done," he said. "That was pitched just right."

Catherine bit her lip again. "Good," was all she could muster.

"Let's get a coffee," he added. "We must discuss the timetable and who does what when."

"If you don't mind Stuart, there are some other things I need to take care of right now. I'll give you a call later," she said as she turned to go back to her office. All she could think about was where this was heading and the consequences on her and her life.

CATHERINE

CHAPTER 13

September 2018

Back in her office Catherine cancelled her meetings for the rest of the day and headed out to her car. It was nearly two o'clock by the time she reached Brancaster. She turned right before The Ship and headed down the lane to the car park by the sea. The sun shone and the air smelt fresh as she got out of the car and stretched. Families were queuing for sea food in front of a small hut. Catherine had no appetite so decided to walk the long way around, avoiding the hut and aromas. She removed her heels and walked barefoot across the dunes to Brancaster beach. The sea rippled over her feet and she broke into a run, the water splashing up her legs and wetting her dress. Then for a moment she felt free: she imagined it would all be okay. She wouldn't be exposed and her life would be normal; she would be safe.

After a while she stopped and put her hands on her hips and looked out to sea. Deep breaths calmed her and for a moment she felt hungry. A good sign she thought. Yes, I will be alright. Although deep down she knew she had little control over events and their consequences. How would it end? Her mind flipped between optimism and despair: life continuing as it had been against the bleak way it might turn out. After a while she made her way to the back of the beach and sat on a sand dune, drawing her legs up and resting her head on her knees. This beach always brought her conflicting emotions and she wondered why she had thought it was a good idea to come to Brancaster. They'd had a great family holiday here, and it was a beautiful place, but still, it left her with an uneasy feeling in the pit of her stomach. For a while she watched a woman with two young children and a puppy, playing at the water's edge. The girls were enticing the young dog into the shallow water, laughing, giggling, oblivious to the world around.

Eventually she lay back watching the clouds skid across the sky. The sun and breeze felt good on her face. If there really was alien life out there, what were they like? How advanced were they? Were they watching the earth right now, she wondered?

Her mind crept back to what she could see happening within months: the huge publicity surrounding the discovery, herself interviewed on TV, in newspapers, magazines; endless scrutiny of her life. She must have drifted off as she was suddenly jolted awake by the buzzing of her phone. She sat upright and saw her phone half buried in the sand.

She tried her best to sound calm. "Hi! John." But her voice was shrill.

"Hi there. Just wondered what time you'll be home. The girls have made biscuits and they're keen for you to try them."

"Oh, what time is it?" She glanced at her watch.

"Four thirty," he said. "It sounds windy. Where are you?"

"Outside in the car park. Just getting some air."

"Sounds like there are kids there."

"Yes. Somebody's brought their kids in today."

"You should do that sometime. Anyway, what time? Don't forget I have squash at seven thirty."

She had forgotten. "There's one thing I have to finish off, so I should be there in time. Although I'll miss the tea. Tell the girls I'll have the biscuits for breakfast."

"You okay?"

"Of course. See ya!" And with that she hung up, brushed the sand from her clothes and ran back to the car. "Damn it," she said as she screeched out of the car park. And this was just the beginning of the plates she'd have to spin, she thought.

****

"Did you win?" she asked later that evening as John returned from his game. She could see he looked happy.

"Despite being late, I did."

"Sorry about that," she replied. "Come and sit next to me, there's something I need to tell you."

"Like, why is there sand in your car, for example?"

She felt herself flush. "What?" An answer flashed into her head. "I wore those old trainers in the boot. Can't have used them since we were on holiday."

He didn't reply as he carried his kit bag into the utility room. She could hear him taking his sweaty clothes out and stuffing them into the washing machine. "What is it you want to tell me?" he called out.

"The work thing we talked about," she called back.

"Be there in a minute!" It sounded like his head was in the machine.

"Right," he said as he came into the room and flopped down next to her. "What's been happening?"

She took one of his hands in hers.

He leant over and kissed her hair. "Should I be worried?"

She could smell his deodorant. He must have sprayed himself after the game. She turned to him. "It's serious."

He frowned. "Serious-good, or serious-bad?"

Catherine ignored his question and went through what she had told the VC. John listened in silence, watching her eyes, her hand gestures, unnerving her with the intensity of his stare. "Well? What do you think? Say something!" she begged.

John sat back in the chair. "I'm married to one of the most brilliant scientists in the world. And I guess you will go down in history."

Catherine bit her lip.

"What is it?" he asked.

"You could be right about being famous and remembered. That part scares me." She took his hand. "You do realise what this means, don't you?"

"You'll be asked to go on 'I'm a celebrity, get me out of here'? Oh no, don't tell me, 'Love Island'?"

She couldn't help but smile, although it confirmed he had no idea what was about to hit them.

"Very funny. Listen, there will be intense scrutiny of us, you, me, the girls, our lifestyle. Can you imagine? You remember the phone hacking? They'll be going through our bins before you know it."

"That's a bit extreme, isn't it? We've got nothing to hide anyway."

"Everybody's got something to hide. Or at least things they don't want the world to know."

John thought for a moment. "Not really. Surely the alien story will be way more interesting than anything about us! You're overreacting." He hesitated, then added, "but if you say so, I agree, we'll be careful. How long before this stuff comes out anyway?"

"A few months. It will be orchestrated by the uni."

"Can we get advice?"

"Maybe. That's a good idea. I'll ask. In the meantime, we keep ourselves to ourselves." She knew the seed had been planted and now needed to change the subject. "Let's open a bottle to celebrate the good things about it all."

"And raise a glass to the little green men," he replied as he stood up. John walked to the kitchen and called out. "I meant to mention, you're already famous." He came back with The Times. "Here, in this supplement, an article on STEM and school initiatives to encourage pupils to study those subjects." He handed the page to Catherine and tapped on a picture of her and the Head. "Good, eh?"

She looked with horror at the photo from the school speech and glanced over the half-page article.

"Was it written by that journalist we met?"

"Martin Mitchell, yes. Did you ever get to speak with him?"

Her heart sunk. "No and I wish he hadn't written it without speaking with me first."

John sat down next to her. "It's okay, isn't it? You don't sound pleased."

"I'm not. Anyway, enough. Where's the wine?"

As John went to fetch the bottle, she closed her eyes. She knew she was already losing control. How was it going to end?

AMY

CHAPTER 14

As Amy ran from the party, she kept glancing behind her, petrified Jimmy might be following her, but there was no sign. When she felt she'd run far enough from the house, she slowed her pace, eventually stopping outside a row of dimly lit shops. She put her hands on her hips, looked up to the sky and gasped for air. Then it dawned on her, Tamsin's mum was collecting her. She glanced at her watch and realised her friends would probably be looking for her by now. They might even phone Mum if they couldn't find her. Her heart pounded as she wondered what she should do. There was no choice; she'd have to go back.

    Amy tentatively approached the house, her senses on full alert. There was no sign of Tamsin's mum so she crept along the front hedge and hid behind a tree, leaning against the rough bark. She couldn't control her shaking so sat down, her head against her knees as she let the tears flow. Amy gasped for air, at the same time trying to keep quiet in case she was heard. The night air was fresh and she breathed deeply trying to calm herself, but the vision of what had happened exploded in her head like a flash-back in a violent movie. How she hated him. Her chest tightened as she thought of him back in the party chatting, laughing, not giving her a single thought. She could kill him right now. "Damn him!" she cursed. Suddenly she heard a car enter the drive and saw Tamsin's mum at the wheel.

    Amy wiped her eyes on her sleeve and blew her nose. She stood up, brushed herself down and took a few deep breaths. She'd have to appear normal she thought as she walked over to the car. Amy tapped on the window. "Hi, I'm first out but I'm sure they'll be here in a minute," she said brightly.

As Rachel and Tamsin appeared they looked distraught. "Where have you been!?" asked Rachel, "we've been looking for you everywhere!"

Amy opened the car door. "Sorry, I was in the garden talking to some of the uni friends." She saw Tamsin and Rachel exchange glances. "Right by the hedge at the back," she added.

As they squashed into the back Tamsin asked, "didn't you have a coat?"

Oh damn, thought Amy. "I'll get it another time," she replied.

Mrs Hewitt turned round smiling. "We can wait, it's fine."

Amy froze. "No, we'd better go, it's getting late and my mum will be wondering."

"You're stuck in the middle," said Tamsin opening the car door. "No problem, I'll get it."

"Thanks," Amy replied.

Rachel leant across and touched Amy's arm. "Sure you're okay?" she whispered.

Amy turned away looking out of the window, then back at Rachel and swallowed hard. "Of course," she replied as brightly as she could.

"How was the party?" asked Mrs Hewitt looking in the mirror.

"Great!" replied Rachel. "Everyone was there."

"Not too much to drink I hope girls."

"We're okay, Mrs Hewitt," said Rachel slurring her words. Tamsin jumped in the open door and threw Amy's coat onto her lap. "There you go."

"Err, what's that smell?" asked Mrs Hewitt turning to her daughter. "Have you just put perfume on?"

"No, of course not," she replied. "It's from the bedroom where the coats were. The whole room stank of it. A perfume bottle had been smashed and there was glass on the carpet."

"I shan't ask any more," replied Mrs Hewitt as she reversed the car out of the drive.

"Thanks for the coat," whispered Amy as she put her head back and closed her eyes. It took all her will power not to burst out crying.

"You're shivering Amy, why don't you put your coat on?" said Rachel. But Amy couldn't answer: she was totally numb and checked out.

After they dropped her off, Amy stood outside her front door plucking up the courage to enter. What if Mum was still up? Would she blurt it all out? It was all she could do to bend down and retrieve the key from under the mat. Her hand was shaking as she slowly put the key into the lock. The house was in darkness. She gently closed the door and stood motionless, listening. To her relief the house was in silence. What she most wanted was a long shower or a bath, but it would wake her mother. At the top of the stairs, she heard her mother call from her bed. "Hi Amy! Are you okay?"

"Okay! She called back, hoping she hadn't shouted too loudly.

"Tell me about it in the morning. Goodnight!"

"Night," she whispered. She'd never be doing that. Amy opened her bedroom door, gently closed it and threw herself onto the bed. She felt a sickness in her stomach and a thumping in her head. She thought how she really hated him. How could he be so cruel, humiliate her? Debase her like that? If only I'd kicked him hard while he was on the floor, she thought. Amy violently moved one leg backwards and forward imagining herself kicking him in the head and then his stomach. I'm going round there tomorrow to tell his whole family what he did to me. How he assaulted me. After a while she rolled over onto her back and sobbed uncontrollably. At some point she must have drifted off as it was after three before she finally climbed into bed – shattered.

"Can I come in?" she heard her mother ask. Amy rolled over on to her side and saw it was after nine in the morning. At least she'd managed some sleep, she thought.

"I'll be out soon!" she called. After she was sure her mother was downstairs, she crept into the bathroom and showered until the water ran cold. She scrubbed herself hard wherever he'd touched her. Back in her room she lay on the bed, tears flowing, until suddenly Billy was there and leapt on her bed. Quickly he snuggled up to her and she held him close, and soon they both fell asleep.

"Come on you two," said her mother waking them up. "It's a lovely day and you should be out there."

Amy opened her eyes and the memories came flooding back.

"Oh Amy, you look dreadful. You were drinking, weren't you."

"I…"

"What did I say before you left?"

Billy sat up, his hair in all directions. "What are we doing today?"

Amy put her hand through her damp knotted hair. "Thanks for asking if I had a good time."

Her mother put her hands on her hips. "Did you?"

"Not really," she replied and slumped back down on the bed.

"Suit yourself," her mother replied. "Hangovers are horrible and you've only got yourself to blame. Maybe you'll listen to me next time," she added. "Come on Billy, get dressed: leave your sister in peace." As Mum shut the door, he snuggled up against Amy again.

"What time is Dad coming over?" she asked.

"Don't know. This evening sometime," replied Billy. "How long am I staying with Dad?" he asked.

"Most of the holidays, I guess. I'll miss my little brother," she said, tears welling up. "I'll come over, maybe this week to see you."

"Dad said he's taking me away."

"Really? Where?"

"Bristol."

"Bristol?" That's where his girlfriend lives, she thought. "Are you staying with his girlfriend?"

Billy sat up. "Yes. Dad said she has a big house and a son a bit older than me. He's really cool according to Dad, good at football. Dad said he was going to teach me cricket too."

Her heart sank. Nobody had told her Billy was going to Bristol. And why hadn't she been invited?

"Why aren't you coming too?" he asked.

She put her hands behind her head and looked up at the ceiling, thinking for a moment. "I guess Dad doesn't want me."

"Of course, he does!" replied Billy.

Amy took a deep breath and concentrated on holding back the tears. "No, Billy. He doesn't," she replied as she turned her face away. For a while they lay there with Billy chatting and her not listening. The thought of being stuck here with Mum was another nightmare.

JOHN
CHAPTER 15

October 2018

John opened the car door for the twins as he watched them run down the drive. They had matching pink shoes, grey duffle coats and small pink rucksacks which bounced on their backs as they skipped along. Both girls were brimming with enthusiasm, unlike himself: Catherine had hardly been home for the last month, ever since 'the discovery', as they called it.

"Bye! Thanks again!" He called as he waved to his mum. "See you tomorrow."

"We did space at school today!" called Chloe, waving a painting in front of him. "Look!"

He took both their paintings; each had a large yellow sun surrounded by a variety of what he assumed were planets. "It's the Solar System. Which planet is this?" he asked, pointing to a splodge of blue, white, and green paint."

"The Earth!" said Chloe.

John smiled. "We'll put them up in the kitchen with the others." He carefully rolled up the paintings and put them in the boot with the rest of their kit.

As they drove away his phone rang on the hands-free. "Hello?"

"Is that Mr John Holmes?"

He hesitated, wondering if this was a random sales call. "Yes. Who is this?"

"Detective Inspector Jane Flanders from the Cambridgeshire police."

"The police? What's it about?"

"It's nothing to worry about sir. I need to talk with you in confidence. Is this a convenient time?"

"Who is that, Daddy?" Called Ruth from the back. There was a moment's silence before anybody spoke.

"Can I hear someone?" asked the Inspector.

"School run," said John.

"Hello!" called Ruth from the back. John picked up his phone so the girls couldn't hear.

"Can we talk when it's more convenient?"

"Is everything alright? Has somebody been hurt?" asked John.

"No, not at all. We just need your help and you're not to be concerned."

"If you say so. Listen, I've got your number so I'll call you once I'm home. In about ten minutes. Is that okay?"

"That's fine Mr Holmes. One thing before you hang up. It's really important you don't mention this to anybody at this stage. I mean, it is absolutely confidential."

John gripped the steering wheel harder. "Okay," he replied, then killed the call.

"Who was that, Daddy?" asked Ruth.

"The police," replied Chloe.

"No it wasn't." replied John.

"Yes it was," replied Chloe. "I heard it."

"And me," added Ruth.

John looked in the rear-view mirror. "It was somebody from school just pretending. Don't you do pretend at school?"

"Why did she have a funny voice?" Asked Chloe.

John smiled to himself. "She didn't have a funny voice, Chloe, it's called an accent. I think she's from the northeast, probably Newcastle."

"I was an astronaut today," said Ruth.

"So was I," added Chloe. "We went to Mars."

"There you go then," said John. "You must have just been pretending as you're not on Mars, instead you're about to arrive home for your tea."

****

"D.I. Flanders," came the reply.

"It's me, John Holmes returning your call."

John had made the girls' tea and gone into the garden. He stood watching them through the patio window, chatting away, not a care in the world. He'd paced around the garden before calling, trying to imagine why the police wanted to talk to him. He'd not witnessed anything, not heard about a local robbery. There was no hint of anything wrong at school.

"Thank you for calling, Mr Holmes."

John interrupted. "Before we go any further, I should say you need to convince me this is not a hoax, otherwise I'm cutting the call."

"You are welcome to cut the call and phone the station in Cambridge if that would help?"

John hesitated. "Carry on for now," he answered.

"Let me say you are not under suspicion for having done anything wrong. This is really important for you to know. You are a POI, so your cooperation is entirely voluntary, although it would be appreciated.

"What's a POI?"

"Oh sorry, jargon for a 'person of interest'. Someone who can help us but is not under suspicion. Again, I want to emphasise you're not a suspect, we simply believe you can aid us in an enquiry."

"Okay carry on." He was walking around the garden with the phone pressed against his ear. With his other hand he picked up the girls' toys and placed them neatly against the house. First the scooters, then a football, and finally a muddy skateboard. He decided he must cut the grass one more time before the winter sets in.

"We would like to meet with you on an informal basis to ask a few questions. As I said, it is voluntary."

"About what?"

"I cannot say over the phone. We only need about thirty minutes and we can do it in a café or if you prefer you can come along to the Cambridge police station. Although we recommend a café. It's more conducive to the informality of the meeting. Most people prefer not to risk being seen walking into a police station, if you see what I mean."

"When are you thinking?" He watched as a robin hopped across the lawn and disappeared under a bush.

"This week? After school?"

John dropped the bike he was holding. "How did you know I'm a teacher?"

"We're the police Mr Holmes."

"I guess that's how you got my mobile number?" There was no reply, so he continued. "How many of you? Will you be in uniform?"

"No uniform and two of us. Nobody will know. It'll be like friends meeting for a coffee as far as anybody else is concerned."

He thought for a moment. "I can do tomorrow around two, in Blossom café, Church Street. It'll be quiet by then. I'll only have an hour as I need to get back for another lesson."

"Thank you, we'll be there." She hesitated before adding, "one more thing."

"Go on," he said, wondering what she was going to say next.

"You mustn't mention this call, or our meeting, to anybody. It's sensitive information. This includes your wife."

"You know I am married then?"

No reply.

"I'll find that difficult."

"It's important."

John thought for a moment. He felt uncomfortable keeping a secret from her. "If I have to." He hesitated then asked, "How will I recognise you?"

"We'll recognise *you* Mr Holmes."

****

Catherine gently pushed open the girls' bedroom door, trying not to wake them. It was almost eight and she'd just got home from another exhausting day. She and her team had received an avalanche of searching questions from Nature's independent researchers. They were making good progress, but it was challenging.

She adjusted Ruth's blanket, kissed her daughter's forehead and knelt down in front of Chloe on the lower bunk. Suddenly Chloe opened her eyes. "Mummy," she whispered. She stroked her hair and kissed her cheek. "Time to go to sleep my little darling."

"Have you seen our paintings?"

"No, where are they?"

"Daddy put them up in the kitchen." Chloe turned over on to her back. "He talked to a policewoman today."

"A Policewoman?"

"In the car, on the phone." Chloe stretched, yawned and closed her eyes.

"Sweet dreams," Catherine whispered. "Love you." She pulled the blanket up and crept out of their room.

John was sitting marking books. He looked up as she came into the lounge. "Good day?"

"Long," she said, kicking off her shoes. "Tea?"

"Not me," he replied without looking up.

Catherine returned a few minutes later with her drink. "Chloe said something odd just now."

John tensed. "Not the police thing by any chance?"

"Yes. What's that about?"

John's mouth felt dry as he said. "They were in the car when I got a call from a community police officer. They are giving a talk on policing and I'm coordinating the visit to the school."

Catherine picked up a magazine and fanned the pages. "Right." After a minute she tossed the magazine onto the chair. "I'm exhausted, I might go to bed."

John turned. "It's not even eight thirty."

She put her hand on his arm and gave it a squeeze then leant forward with her elbows on her knees, covering her face with her hands. He could see she had started to cry. He put his arm around her shoulder and pulled her close. "What is it? Tell me."

She shook her head. "Nothing."

He waited a moment before replying. "It's so not 'nothing' Catherine. Please."

She moved his arm away from her shoulder and flopped back in the chair, staring at the ceiling. "We've already talked about it: I don't want anybody to ruin our lives." She wiped her eyes and turned to face him.

"Not this again," he replied.

"Oh John, sometimes…"

"What?"

"Well, you have no idea." The anger in her voice unnerved him.

"No idea about what?"

"Life. You don't know how hard I've tried. You trundle along in your own little world sometimes."

"What do you mean, 'my own little world?' That's not fair!"

Catherine sighed. She hated herself for starting this argument. "Listen, I'm tired and I'm sorry. I didn't mean it." She pecked him on the cheek and squeezed his hand. "I'll feel better in the morning."

"You can't leave it like that."

"Forget it. I didn't mean it and I'm knackered." She stood up to go. "Don't feel you have to come up soon. Finish your marking."

"You haven't eaten anything."

"Not hungry," she said, as she left the room.

"I'll be up soon," he said to the back of the door. John gathered the books into a pile and put them on the floor. Opening his laptop, he typed 'Detective Inspector Jane Flanders' into Google. He couldn't find any names of police officers, apart from the top brass: they didn't seem to publish them. What on earth did she want with him? Maybe he'd tell Catherine if she was still awake when he went up. But then again, the last thing she needed was to worry about that too. Anyway, it may be trivial and she need never know or perhaps he could tell her tomorrow night, after it was all over.

JOHN

CHAPTER 16

October 2018

"Shit" he whispered to himself as he checked his watch. Within minutes he was driving out of the school gates, relieved he'd not met anybody on his way to the car. The last thing he needed was a chat with a pupil or staff member.

As he reached the edge of town, he came round a bend too fast and braked sharply with cars queuing in front of him. His phone shot off the passenger seat into the well. "Damn it." He leant over but couldn't reach it as his seat belt tightened. "What the hell." A glance at the clock showed he had ten minutes to park and walk to Blossom's. He stared at the cars in front. "Come on, come on." He hit the top of the steering wheel with his palms. "For god's sake, what's going on?" He wound down the window and stuck his head out, trying to get a better view. It made no difference. A car further ahead turned around and drove back past him. "What is it?" he shouted, but the driver didn't hear him.

"Bugger, I'm now officially late." As he drove past Blossom's his luck changed: There was a parking place no more than five metres ahead. He nipped in, despite a car coming the other way indicating it was about to take the spot. He ignored the hoot and finger, removed his seatbelt and ran back toward the café. "Oh, my phone," he murmured and almost bumped into a woman standing by the door.

"Mr Holmes?"

"Yes, sorry!"

"Inspector Flanders," she replied, smiling and sticking out a hand. "You can call me Jane."

John shook her hand and studied her face. She was striking; not what he had expected at all. Her eyes penetrated him and his first thought was he would struggle to ever lie to this woman. She was dressed in a black suit and white shirt. He judged she was in her early or mid forties.

"Shall we go in?" she said, opening the door.

"Sure," he replied, then added, "Is your colleague already here?"

She half turned, "let's sit here, it's private." She smiled again. "No, it's only me after all. Too much on."

It wasn't only her looks that unnerved him: it was the informality of it all. He wondered if he was being softened up for some tough questioning. But about what? The waitress offered a welcome distraction and he took the opportunity to study the DI as she turned to look at the waitress. Her hair was auburn, tied in a bun, her ears small and he could make out tiny gold earrings.

As the waitress walked away the D.I. rummaged in her handbag. "My I.D.," she said, opening a small black wallet. John glanced, hardly able to read it and nodded, sat back and folded his arms. "What's this about?" he began, suddenly feeling more confident. Without answering she took a notebook and pen out of her bag.

"I'll be taking notes," she said as she carefully placed the notebook in front of her. Then she clasped her hands together and looked him in the eye. "Listen, as I said when we first spoke, you are here on a voluntary basis, you are not a suspect in anyway and you are simply helping us with an enquiry. I can't tell you what it is about or who is involved or anything about our on-going investigation. And I can't answer any questions you may have."

John nodded. "Okay."

"We may need a follow-up or you may never hear from us again."

John began to feel uneasy and glanced around the café checking there was nobody he recognised. "Alright," he replied.

There was an awkward silence as their drinks arrived. The waitress seemed to take an age to place the cups in a particular position. "Is there anything else I can get you?"

"No," the DI replied firmly, then added, "thank you."

John went to lift the cup from the saucer but changed his mind as he felt his hand shaking.

The DI put her glasses on and picked up her notebook. "Right," she said, looking at him over her glasses. "When, and where did you first meet your wife?"

AMY

CHAPTER 17

It was the morning after the party and Amy was lying on the settee in a complete haze, pretending to read Just Seventeen Magazine. She let it drop to the floor, the pages skewed in an odd way. She sighed, half sat up and rubbed her eyes.

"It's like living with Eeyore," said Mum. "If you're going to be so miserable then why don't you go out for a walk, at least get some fresh air."

"Might as well, there's nothing else going on. God, I hate Sundays."

"Hangovers more like. Off you go," added her mother as she disappeared into the kitchen.

"Can I come?" asked Billy.

"No," replied Amy standing up.

"Can I go with Ammy?" he called towards the kitchen.

"If you want," came the reply.

Amy stretched her arms almost touching the ceiling and looked down at Billy. "I'm going by myself, but I'll be back before you go with Dad."

Billy looked pleadingly at her. "Are you going to the Witch's Tree?"

"Not sure," she said, and with that, she put on her boots and walked out. Before she had gone more than a few steps she heard Billy behind her. "You're going to the Witch's Tree, I know it!" he said. He was wheeling his bike beside him.

"You need to go back inside, Billy. I'm not going to the woods; I'm going for a walk into town and Mum won't like you going there."

"Are you sure?" he asked. "You've got your boots on," he said. "Looks like you're going to climb trees."

"Billy, just go back, I need to be alone!" He started to cry and she immediately regretted her tone. "Look, I'll be back soon," she said stroking his hair. "Off you go."

In the woods, Amy took the path leading to the river and her favourite tree. She'd sit by the bank and distract herself: Throw stones, count the ripples, maybe watch the ducks; feel the coolness of the river on her feet. A picture in her mind's eye of dappled sunlight sparkling on the water lifted her mood. Suddenly she heard a woman's cries coming from the direction of the river. Her first thought was the woman had lost a dog. Instinctively she walked toward the calls, making her way through a narrow path between the tall bright green ferns, pushing them aside, carefully avoiding the nettles. She knew the route well and exactly where the path emerged into the clearing. On the edge of the riverbank was the Witch's Tree, partly overhanging the water. As she approached the clearing, she heard more distinctly the word, 'please'.

Amy made no sound as she stood motionless on the edge of the clearing. The woman had her back to Amy and was standing at the base of the Witch's Tree, calling upwards, as if someone was in the tree. For an instant, Amy wondered if it was some sort of ritual, as she couldn't see anybody through the foliage or sitting on a lower branch. The hairs on the back of Amy's neck stood up as the woman slowly turned around to look in her direction, as if a sixth sense had told the woman

Amy was there. Immediately she recognised it was Jimmy's sister, Tina.

"Thank God it's you!" exclaimed Tina. "Come over here, I need your help!"

For a split second Amy contemplated running. But something in Tina's voice made her stay. "What is it?" she asked as she approached. Tina had a towel around her shoulders, shorts over a wet costume and her wet hair hung down her back.

"I brought Jimmy here to get him out of the house while others cleared up."

Amy gasped, as a tight knot formed in her stomach.

"He was still high and making a nuisance of himself. We've been swimming. I've just got out of the river and seen he's climbed this tree," she added, pointing up. Amy followed her gaze and at first couldn't spot him. She took two steps forward so as to be closer to the trunk and craned her neck. Initially, she only saw his legs as the foliage and branches obscured much of her view. Amy put her hands on her hips and looked at the ground, wondering if she was going to be sick. She took a deep breath and turned to Tina; her mouth wide open. "How the hell did he get up there?" She'd never been that high in any tree and wouldn't dare. "That must be getting on for twenty feet." Her first thought was she hoped he fell and hurt himself. She could see the distress written across Tina's face.

"I'm frightened," Tina replied. "He's been up there at least twenty minutes; motionless and he's not responding to me calling. It's as if he's in a trance and stuck there. I think he could fall at any moment."

Amy glanced back up the tree and thought he deserved his predicament. She looked back at Tina. "What are you going to do?"

"I don't know!"

"He'll probably come down soon enough," replied Amy. She knew that to be unlikely but the longer he spent up there the better.

Tina put her hands on her hips and glared at Amy. "Are you crazy?! He could fall at any moment. You do realise he could be killed, don't you?! He needs our help!"

Amy thought for a moment. "What do you want me to do about it?"

"Stay here while I go and get help. He's weird and not talking to me but maybe he'll talk to you, as a friend. You can keep him calm until I get back."

Before she could stop herself, she blurted out, "a friend!?"

Tina looked at her quizzically. "Yes, a friend." There was a moment's silence before Tina added. "Oh, you're not pissed with him because of the silly spat you two had last night, surely? This is life or death, Amy!"

Amy couldn't bear the idea of staying with him. "No, it's not that," she replied. Suddenly she had a feeling of power over him. "How about I go and get help and *you* stay here?" She could leave and take her time or not do anything. She imagined herself saying later, 'Oh I didn't realise it was important. He looked fine up there.' She was shaken from her thoughts by Tina.

"You're not listening!" Tina bent down and grabbed her shirt. "I'm going to get help," she added as she threw off the towel and struggled into the shirt sleeves. Tina turned to go.

"Wait!" called Amy, but Tina had gone, quickly disappearing into the ferns.

For a moment Amy stood there in silence, scarcely able to comprehend what was happening. She was in two minds as to what to do. Eventually she slowly walked around the tree, all the time looking up at him. Amy could see him standing there, rigid, staring straight ahead. She noted the branches she knew so well up to the broomstick. Then she stopped walking and studied the branches beyond that point, craning her neck, stepping backwards and to the side to get a better view. Suddenly, Amy leapt up, grabbed the first branch, swung her legs and hauled herself up. She stood on the first branch, deftly stepped onto the next, then quickly and with ease, pulled herself up onto the broomstick, just six feet off the ground. She stood there a moment contemplating what Tina would be doing and how long before she returned. The nearest house was at least five minutes away and she hadn't even set off in the right direction. Then, someone would need to be home and then they'd probably phone the fire brigade before coming back to the woods. She'd be gone at least fifteen to twenty minutes. Amy looked up through the leaves. "Jimmy!" she called. "I bet you're glad to see me!" She lifted herself onto the next branch. "I'm coming up," she called. Amy gingerly put her foot on a short length of broken-off branch and hugged the tree as she eased herself around the trunk. Her mouth was dry and her hands clammy. Amy could see him clearly now. The leaves at the end of the branch on which he stood were continuously shaking. She heard the noise before she'd worked out what was causing the rustling. Now she had to climb beyond the highest point she had been and it took a minute for her to work out how she could get to him. How had he managed it? The drugs masking his fear? She glanced down and swallowed hard as she saw how far away the ground appeared. Then she hesitated and looked across to the river, the sparkling water peacefully making its way downstream. Amy clung tightly to the tree, heart thumping, wondering if she had the guts to go any further.

On impulse she grabbed a small branch and hauled herself further up. Now she was directly below him and could see how he had managed to get to where he was. She could smell the weed emanating from his clothes. One last pull-up and there she was, standing on the same branch, him six feet away and her up against the trunk. She felt the power over him and it made her feel good.

He made no move or acknowledgement of her presence: remaining rigid, aside from his shaking legs. He stared straight ahead, wide-eyed, holding on to the branch in front of him. Her first thought was he looked quite secure, and it would be no issue for him to shuffle along toward the trunk. But then again, she recalled a dream, being high up, on a rickety structure, not daring to look down and too petrified to move.

"Jimmy, it's me."

He flashed a glance in her direction, quickly returning to staring ahead. It was as if looking to one side might cause him to fall. "I fucking know it's you."

She moved one foot about six inches along the branch and brought the next alongside. It shook even from this gentle manoeuvre.

"Shit!" he called.

Amy assessed the branch, wondering how far she could go. "Remember last night Jimmy?"

"What do you want?" he growled.

"Remember all those horrible things you've done to me over the years? And as for last night. You disgust me."

"Piss off."

She gently moved herself six inches further along the branch, feeling it shake underfoot.

"Don't do that!"

"Just say you're sorry Jimmy, that's all."

"You're crazy!" he replied. "Anyway. What *about* last night? You were weird if anything. The way you came on to me."

Hearing his words, she felt the pressure rising in her chest. Amy bent her knees, then straightened them, causing the branch to bounce.

"Shit!" he called. "What are you doing? Stop it!"

Amy took one step back towards the trunk and began to bounce up and down, making the far end of the branch flick its leaves. 'Swish,' they went as Jimmy visibly moved up and down with the movement of the branch.

"I'll fall off!"

But Amy couldn't stop herself as she increased the intensity of her movements. "Sorry is all you have to say," she said, staring at him. "Why can't you just say it?" She hissed. But he stared straight ahead, gripping the branch in front of him, hanging on for dear life. She was about to give up and leave him to sweat it out when the loud crack took her by surprise. She gasped as the branch snapped about a foot away from her feet. She had been looking at him the moment it happened.

"Ahhh!" he cried as his feet dangled below him. In that moment he turned and stared at her, his gaze searing through her. He swung his legs as if that would help but it made it worse. "No!" he called as his hands slowly slithered off the branch that held him in space. Amy screamed as she watched him fall. He made no sound as he fell through the air, hitting a branch and somersaulting as he plummeted. As he spun it was as if he looked straight at her again, eyes wide, piercing her. Amy not only heard but felt the thud as he hit the ground. She could hardly bare to look down and when she did, she saw he was motionless, half in the water half out, and legs splayed. Her white knuckled hands were locked on the branch in front of her and she wondered if she could release her grip. Finally, she stepped toward the trunk and grabbed the nearest branch to steady herself.

As she dropped the last few feet to the ground, she realised she had no recollection of climbing down. She could have easily fallen too, she thought. Amy dashed over to where he lay sprawled on the ground with his legs dangling over the riverbank. Her heart raced and the ringing in her ears was excruciating. There was no movement from him, and she could see his head was in a sickening position, making her retch on the ground close by. She crawled on all fours back toward his body and leaning over put her ear to his chest, trying her best to ignore the thumping of her own heart. There was no beat.

Amy held her hands to her face. "Oh my god, my god, my god," she cried, "What have I done?" She fell backwards onto the grass. Briefly she lay there, still, the only sounds she could hear were the birds twittering in the Witch's Tree overhead and the river at her feet, bubbling gently over the rocks. In a dreamlike moment it was as if nothing had happened. Suddenly she heard a voice, making her leap up as if she'd been caught. As she turned around, to her horror she saw Billy, crying and calling her name. "Billy!" she screamed. "What are you doing here?" He was standing at the edge of the clearing, no more than ten feet away, his hands gripping the handlebars as if the bike was holding him up. As their eyes met, she knew, just knew, he'd seen it all. Amy ran over to him, glancing around to see if there was any sight of Tina and help. Nothing.

"Oh Billy," she said kneeling in front of him. "There's been a terrible accident. Did you see it?" He nodded through his tears. "How long have you been here?" she asked, her mouth so dry, it was difficult to form the words.

"I saw that woman run off and you starting to climb."

"Come here," she said wrapping her arms around him and squeezing him tightly. Her heart sunk. "Does Mum know you're here?" She whispered.

She could feel him shake his head. "I couldn't find her and wanted to catch you up."

Amy released her cuddle and leant back, looking him straight in the eye. "Listen to me Billy," she said, now moving closer. "Listen very carefully. It was an accident. Do you understand?" He nodded as he wiped his eyes. Amy took a deep breath, again looking about her for Tina and whoever she would bring with her. She turned back to Billy and put her hands on his shoulders, her face inches from his. "The police will be here, and they'll want to question everybody. You could be in trouble if they see you here. Plus, Mum will be very cross too," she added as an afterthought. "And we don't want that, do we?" Billy shook his head and began to sob, rubbing his face as the tears flowed. Again, she looked around for Tina. Nothing.

She turned back to Billy and put her hands back on his shoulders, getting his full attention. "Look, go home. Mum will be wondering where you are. Say you went to look for me, got to the edge of the woods, gave up and came home. You never saw anything, okay?"

He nodded.

"Billy, look at me," she said lifting his chin with her finger. "You never saw anything, right?"

He nodded.

"You must never ever say anything to anybody, then you'll be safe. Do you understand?"

He nodded.

"Promise?"

A small whimpering voice answered. "I promise."

Somehow, she managed a smile, trying to reassure him. "Then everything will be fine and you've got nothing to worry about!" She kissed him on his forehead, gave him a tight hug, then said. "Now go, quickly!"

As he turned, his wheel became entangled in bracken. He leaned over the handlebars trying to free the wheel, pulling at the bike at the same time. Amy frantically looked around for Tina. "Let me do it," she said pulling hard on the bike. She glanced around again. "Wait," she said. Amy wiped away his tears with a tissue. "Everything will be okay," she whispered into his ear. "Just trust your big sister." She struggled up and stood back. "Go!" She pushed his bike to get him moving. "Go! Go!"

He had just disappeared into the ferns when she heard rustling and voices from the other side of the clearing. She turned and saw Tina with a man, both of them breathless. Neither had seen Jimmy lying on the ground. Tina called in her direction as they ran toward the tree. "What's happened?" Tina looked up the tree and for a second all three were silent. Confused, Tina walked around the tree looking up, trying to spot him.

Amy stood motionless unable to speak or move.

"Where is he?" asked the man. Slowly they both turned to look at Amy. She tightly closed her eyes and pointed toward the riverbank just below the tree. She felt dizzy and just before she collapsed, she heard Tina's piercing scream.

AMY

CHAPTER 18

July 1993

Jimmy's body was surrounded by kneeling paramedics. The police had rapidly cordoned off the whole area with blue tape and led a hysterical Tina away to an ambulance. Amy saw one of the paramedics turn around and look at a policeman and shake her head. Standing next to Amy was a paramedic and a policewoman. "You okay Miss?" asked the paramedic.

Amy shook her head. "I think I'm going to be sick again." Her teeth were chattering and she was freezing.

"Here." The policewoman put her hand on Amy's back and gave it a rub, then put a blanket around Amy's shoulders. "We're going to take you home now; can you walk to the car?"

At first, she didn't answer as she was staring in the direction of the body. She saw the policewoman and paramedic exchange glances.

"Amy?"

"What?" she said through chattering teeth.

"You said your mother was at home?"

She nodded, just before her stomach flipped and she bent double, vomiting over her shoes.

Amy sat in the back of the car, squeezed between two officers. The penetrating noise of their crackling radios unnerved her and made her head thump. On her left was the officer who had rubbed her back. Amy couldn't stop shaking. Being sandwiched between these two made it worse and the car was stuffy enough to make anyone feel sick. They're going to know, she thought. She went over and over in her mind what she would say, how she would explain what had happened. And Billy, would he keep quiet as she had told him to?

"Wait here will you," said the driver as he opened the car door. "I'll have a quick word, then we can go in."

Before the officer got to the front door, she saw Mum open it and look over the officer's shoulder toward the car. The officer had his back to her and blocked her view of Mum as the two of them spoke for what felt like an age. Suddenly her mother came running to the car and threw open the door.

Amy was engulfed by her Mum's tight hug, squeezing the air from her lungs. "Amy, Amy, my poor darling. It's unbearable. Come here," she added, squeezing her even more tightly.

Amy buried her head into her mother's shoulder and sobbed. "I saw it happen," she managed through her tears.

Her mother rocked Amy slightly from side to side, still hanging on to her as if their lives depended upon it. "I know. Poor Jimmy. And the family, my God." Mum pulled away, hands on Amy's shoulders. "We'd better go inside."

"Can we come in?" asked the police officer. "We just need to ask a few questions while her memory is fresh."

Her mother looked at Amy. "Are you okay with that?" she asked. Amy nodded and they walked toward the house.

"This tea's very sweet," said Mum, handing Amy a mug, "it's good for shock." Then she turned to an officer, "will you excuse me, I need to check on my son." Shortly she returned. "I've popped him next door until his father gets here." She looked at Amy. "Dad's coming over as fast as he can."

One of the police officers got out her notebook and pen. "As you know Amy, tragically this was a fatal accident and therefore it will be subject to an investigation and a coroner's report. As the only witness we need your help to establish precisely what happened. Is that okay?"

"Yes," she answered and swallowed hard. Her hand shook as she sipped the tea. Amy's mind whirled and her heart raced as she wondered if she'd remember what to say. She had the same feeling she'd experienced once in an exam when she panicked, thinking she'd forgotten everything.

The police officer shifted in the chair. "In a few days' time we will need you to come to the station and write a statement and sign it, in the presence of your mother, or father obviously. You're sixteen, correct?"

She nodded.

The officer smiled. "You are not in trouble. We simply need your help with this exceedingly difficult situation and we'll be as quick as possible and then leave you alone."

"If it could be quick," added her mother. "She's clearly in shock."

"Of course." The police officer hesitated, before adding, "if you could talk through your movements this morning, how you came to be there and what you saw?"

"I went for a walk in the woods…I needed fresh air. It was about an hour or two ago." She turned to her mother, "about three ish?"

Her mother nodded and looked at the policewoman. "Yes, just after."

"I came to that clearing and saw Tina. She was frantic, distressed."

"You know her then?"

"Not really. I've met her, including last night, but I don't know her as such. It's Jimmy I know from school. I've known him since we were young. We are in lots of the same classes. She's his older sister."

"Okay. When you say, 'last night' what was this?"

"A party at Jimmy's house. I went with friends."

"Right, so did you arrange to meet today in the woods?"

"No." She took a sip of her tea, her hand shaking so much she thought she'd spill it. "It was a coincidence."

"Okay. And what happened after you saw her in distress?"

"She told me Jimmy was up the tree and when I looked, I was shocked at how high he'd managed to climb."

"Amy likes climbing trees, always has," interrupted her mother.

Amy continued. "Tina wanted me to help. She asked me to wait while she went to get someone." Amy hesitated, wondering if she should mention it, but did anyway. "She said

Jimmy had taken a tab and she was worried 'he thought he could fly.'"

"LSD?"

"I don't know. She said 'tab', that's all… and I could smell weed."

The officers looked at each other.

"Right. So, tell us what happened next."

"Tina said she had to go and I must stay with him. There was no discussion and she immediately ran off to get help."

"What did *you* do then?"

Amy felt she was getting into her stride, but knew she had to be careful as the lying was about to begin. "I called up to him a couple of times but he took no notice so I decided to climb up some of the way so I could see him and he could hear me. I thought that may help. I got up as far as I could, a few branches below him. When I spoke to him, he was unresponsive, staring straight ahead, zombie-like. I said, 'I can help you get down'. 'I can guide you'. Things like that. 'Don't worry, I'm here'. But it made no difference. He just stared ahead, gripping the branch in front of him." Amy started to cry and covered her face with her hands. "It was horrible." Her mother put her arm around her.

"Take your time," said the officer. As her tears subsided, the officer asked, "how long were you up there?"

Amy thought for a moment. "I can't say. It feels like a bad dream now."

"Five minutes, ten?"

"She said she doesn't know," interrupted her mother.

They ignored her and continued. "Can you tell us what happened next. Take as much time as you need. We know it's difficult."

Amy snuffled and nodded. "He started to make a funny noise, like crying, whimpering and then started jumping up and down on the branch. I called out to him to stop but he continued. It was crazy. Then the branch broke and down he crashed." She put her head in her hands and sobbed.

"Can we finish?" asked her mother.

"We'll only be a minute," replied the officer. "We're nearly done."

Amy blew her nose. "I clambered down the tree and ran over to see where he was lying. It was horrible. Horrible. It made me sick. Then after what seemed like ages, Tina returned with some man and well, at first, she didn't know he had fallen…. then I pointed to Jimmy…..she screamed. The next thing I knew the paramedics arrived then you."

The officers looked at each other, then at her mother and back to Amy.

"Is there anything else you would like to tell us?"

"I might remember other stuff but I think that's it," she replied. Her mother was holding her hand and gave it a squeeze. In that moment it struck her, she couldn't remember the last time she'd held her mother's hand.

The officers stood up. "You've been very helpful; we appreciate it at this difficult time. I'm afraid though there is one more task before we go. Could you please put your clothes and shoes in this," she said, handing her a large clear plastic bag.

We need them for routine forensic analysis. You'll get them back in due course."

Her mother stood up. "You seem to be treating my daughter like a suspect."

"No, not at all," replied the officer, smiling. "It's simply routine."

Amy began to shake and ran to the kitchen to be sick, but only retched, her stomach was empty. Suddenly her dad crashed through the back door, dragging Billy behind him. "Oh Amy!" he called, then hugged her so tightly she thought she would suffocate. "You don't need to tell me; I'll get it from Mum." During the embrace she looked over his shoulder at Billy. In the moment, Amy put a finger to her lips, holding Billy's frightened gaze. Her father let go and turned to Billy. "Amy has witnessed an accident and is upset, so give her a big hug." Instead, Billy burst into tears and ran out of the room.

"I need to put my clothes in here," she said, holding up the bag. "Then be by myself for a while, if that's alright. I'll have a chat with Billy too," Amy added.

"Amy are you sure you're okay?" asked Dad.

She turned around. "I don't know. I need to lie down for a while and see."

After she had given the clothes to the officers and they had finally left, she went back upstairs while her parents talked in the kitchen. She tapped on Billy's door. He was lying on his bed, his hands covering his face, crying. She slowly sat down beside him and stroked his hair. "It's horrible I know Billy, but it was an accident. A terrible accident." He rolled over and looked up at her.

"Here," she said handing him a tissue. "Blow your nose."

He arranged his pillows and sat up. "I'm really frightened, not saying anything, pretending I wasn't there. Do you think they'll find out?"

"Never! Don't worry."

Billy rested his head on her arm. "I feel a bit better now," he mumbled.

"Good. It's our little secret, forever." She stroked his hair again. "Nobody will ever know, I promise," she added, smiling. "Remember what I said." He nodded and slithered back down and rolled on his side facing her. Amy took hold of his hand. "Just trust your big sister and everything will be fine."

"Thank you, Ammy," he replied as she gave his hand a gentle squeeze.

Back in her room Amy sat on the edge of her bed. Suddenly she couldn't swallow and struggled to move her limbs. Feeling nauseous, she fell forward flat on her face. "Oh God," she cried as she rolled over. Amy gasped, her chest rising and falling, out of control, unable to suck in enough oxygen however hard she tried. Amy propped herself up on her elbows. Gradually she let herself lie back as the room spun around her, waves of nausea swirling around her head. The next thing she knew, Dad was leaning over her shouting. "Come quickly!"

Later, with Amy tucked up in bed, her mother explained, "it was a panic attack, brought on by it all."

Amy turned away and pulled the covers up to her neck. "Will it happen again?"

"Maybe," her mother answered. "Perhaps we will get you help."

That was never going to happen thought Amy. Changing the subject she said, "how's Billy?"

"That's kind of you," Mum replied. "He'll be fine but I'm surprised how upset he's been. It's as if he was there not you. Although I popped in his room just now and he was fast asleep."

"Good," she replied, cuddling her hot water bottle. She began to feel sleepy herself.

JOHN

CHAPTER 19

November 2018

"Where did I first meet my wife? That's an odd question. Why do you want to know?" asked John. "What has Catherine got to do with anything? It was yonks ago."

The DI put down her notebook. "Mr Holmes, this will take forever if you are going to ask questions that I can't answer. Can we keep it that I ask the questions and you answer them?"

John shifted in his chair, sat upright and brushed imaginary crumbs from the table. "Understand. It's just that...."

"Please?"

John nodded and bit his lip.

"So?" she prompted.

"We met at university. I'd gone up to study English at Balliol College Oxford and she was in the same year studying physics. We met at a freshers' drinks thing. It was October 1995 and we've been together ever since."

"She didn't do another degree or go to another university prior to Oxford?"

"No. She came straight from school, like me. We're the same age."

"And which school did she attend?"

"Actually, I'm not sure, we've never discussed it." As he said it, he thought it sounded weak, but it was the truth. The DI took off her glasses and carefully placed them on the table. She looked up at him. "That's odd, isn't it?"

"Well." John thought for a moment, then folded his arms. He pictured Catherine lying next to him in the single bed in his tiny room in Balliol, one leg over his, her head resting on his shoulder. He could smell her hair, recall the softness of her skin. He vividly recalled the moment he asked about her childhood and feeling her body stiffen. Her abrupt response, 'I find it very hard to talk about. Too hard to be honest,' had taken him by surprise. It had seemed so easy to talk until that moment and a silence hung in the air. Eventually she told him about her being orphaned and her tough upbringing after her parents' deaths. He recalled the feeling of her tears on his arm as she'd explained she had no relatives. She had turned to him and said, 'I have put that part of my life behind me. It's the only way I can survive.' He'd gently kissed her. 'I understand.' He decided to never raise the subject again.

"It's not so odd," he replied. The DI picked up her notebook and began to write. "She moved schools a lot," he added. "Her parents died in a car crash when she was about nine and she was fostered after that and moved around."

"Really? No relatives at all?" she pushed.

"No." John kept his arms folded. Why was she asking this nonsense?

"Where did she grow up?"

"In Hertford."

"Hertford. I see. Has she ever mentioned Harlow in Essex?"

"I don't think so, no. Why?"

The DI ignored him. "And when it came to the wedding, nobody came from her side, is that right?"

John thought back to the discussions they'd had and the difficulties caused by her only wanting a small wedding. His parents had been so disappointed. If she'd had her way then they'd have been married in secret. "We had a small wedding. A few of my relatives and, from her side, only uni friends. I knew them all anyway. Joint friends really." John looked down at his now cold coffee. "I'm not sure this is going anywhere. Can we finish?" he added, looking up.

"It appears there is a whole chunk of your wife's life you know very little about, Mr Holmes."

"I've told you, it's not relevant. She was orphaned and that's that. It's not a subject we've ever talked about. It's very painful for her and I'll not exacerbate it."

"What was her name when you met her?" asked the DI.

"Her surname was Motson."

"Catherine Motson?"

"Yes."

"Okay. And has she ever mentioned somebody by the name of 'Jimmy Evans'?"

"No. Who's he?"

"Or 'Amy Ridley'?"

"No."

"Sure?"

"Completely."

The DI continued scribbling in her notebook.

John felt a tightness in his chest. "Who are these people?" As he asked, he began to feel angry. "I find all this bizarre, if you don't mind me saying. These weird questions with no explanations."

The DI shut her notebook. "I think we're done for now. I've got all the information I need at this stage." She smiled at him. "I appreciate your time and I'm sorry if it's been somewhat confusing."

"O… kay," he replied. "It's been more disturbing than confusing," he added, pushing his coffee cup aside.

"I know it's not easy. Listen, I need to get going," she said, as she stood up. "In the meantime, don't mention our talk to anybody and especially not your wife."

Left sitting alone at the table, he wondered what on earth that was all about. He toyed with his spoon, twiddling it around between his thumb and forefinger. 'Jimmy Evans', 'Amy Ridley'. Reaching down he removed his laptop from his bag. Firstly, he typed into Google, 'Harlow' but saw nothing of interest. Then he typed 'Amy Ridley' only to be presented with a long list of women on Facebook, Linked-in and Instagram. He searched through a dozen or so and felt he was going down rabbit holes. He did the same for 'Jimmy Evans' but couldn't get past a dead actor who dominated the listings. John glanced at his watch. It was time to go, so he slammed his laptop shut, and headed off.

"Damn," he said, peeling the parking ticket off his windscreen. He threw it on the seat and reached down for his phone lying in the footwell. "Damn," he repeated. There were six missed calls from Catherine. He needed time to calm down so drove back to the school, replaying each of the DI's questions in his head. He was about to dial Catherine when she rang. He took a deep breath.

CATHERINE

CHAPTER 20

"What's up?" John said as he answered Catherine's call. "You, okay?" he asked.

"More than okay," she replied. Catherine was standing in her office looking out over a white frosted field.

"What time did you leave this morning?" he asked, hoping she wasn't going to ask where he was.

"Five thirty. Glad I didn't wake you."

"I don't mind when you do. We've hardly seen you these past few weeks. Look, I've got to go, my next lesson is in a minute."

"Don't you want to know why I'm excited?" asked Catherine.

"Sorry, yes, go on."

"It's done. The paper's been submitted. Now we just wait for more questions and with luck it'll be published early in the new year."

"Sounds good."

Catherine felt deflated by his coolness. "You don't sound excited."

"No. I mean yes. Of course. Wow, yes. It means we'll have Christmas together. The girls have missed you."

She watched a rabbit hop across the grass. It wasn't the first time he'd said how much they had missed her recently. She had missed them too. "I know it's been difficult. But now it can all change." She thought for a moment, then added, "for a short while at least."

"I know, it'll go crazy once it's out." She could hear the despondency in his voice.

"Anyway," she said, trying to lift the mood. "I've booked us into that new Italian at seven thirty tonight to celebrate. Can your parents take the girls?"

"Lovely idea, I'll sort it. Shall I see you there?" replied John.

"No, I'm coming home early so I thought we could, you know, celebrate before we go out."

"I love you!"

"Love you too!"

"Must go!"

For a while Catherine stared out of the window. Over the last few weeks her mind had been so immersed in the science she'd thought little of what was to come. She flopped into her chair and closed her eyes. Adrenaline had masked her exhaustion and the adrenaline was now fading fast. She must have nodded off as the next thing she knew was her desk phone ringing. She fumbled for the receiver. "Hello."

"Professor Holmes, this is the VC's secretary. She needs to see you this afternoon at three thirty, can you be there?"

"Of course. I have a tutorial at four, but yes. What's it about?"

"I think she wants you to meet somebody. Apart from that I've really no idea."

Catherine gently knocked on the VC's door. A moment's silence then an authoritative voice from within. "Come." Catherine tentatively opened the door. "Ah, Catherine good afternoon." The VC was sitting at her conference table. Catherine wasn't sure what made her feel uneasy, but she felt her ears were burning. Positioned opposite was a petite young woman. Catherine judged she was in her late twenties.

The VC turned to the woman. "This is the lady we spoke of, Professor Holmes."

The woman stood up and outstretched her hand. "It's an honour to meet you," she said. "I'm Sophie Howells from PRE."

"From?" Catherine shook her hand and looked at the VC for an explanation.

"Sophie is from the PR company we are using for the announcement and all media follow-ups. She will also act as your agent."

Catherine pulled out a chair and sat down. "Agent?"

"Agent, yes," replied the VC. "Best if Sophie explains."

Sophie's over-confident delivery and sentences which sounded like questions, irritated Catherine from the outset.

"This is clearly the most amazing story and if we all get it right, well, I cannot begin to tell you. It's so exciting isn't it!?" She smiled at Catherine, adding, "I will ensure you have the right type of exposure and maximise the opportunities for you and the university? It'll be brilliant for you."

"It really will be!" added the VC.

Catherine stiffened as she turned to Sophie. "When you say 'exposure', what do you mean, exactly?"

"There will be global interest in this story and in you?"

Catherine nodded. God how am I going to work with this woman, she wondered.

"So that means demands from newspapers, TV stations, publishers wanting your story and of course an on-line frenzy?" enthused Sophie.

Catherine froze. "It all sounds ghastly." She thought for a moment. "What do you mean by 'my story'?"

"So, every media outlet will like, want a story? Some will want the science angle, others the human side: maybe charting your journey from childhood to where you are now? That's without the speculation of what these aliens may be like."

Catherine turned to the VC, trying to gauge if she was thinking the same way. She quickly got her answer.

"And Sophie will find you a literary agent as there will be high demand for a book."

"More likely a multiple book deal?" added Sophie. "We'll have like, a bidding war."

"You will be known worldwide for this Catherine. You need to be prepared," added the VC. Catherine dug her nails into the back of her hand. Glancing down she could see the red marks and quickly covered one hand with the other.

"It's not only a fame thing," added Sophie. She turned to the VC. "It's a case of maximising the reputation and income for the uni." The VC nodded at a silent Catherine before Sophie continued. "I will ensure we maximise your income too? We at the agency see you becoming a celebrity and multi-millionaire very quickly. There are like, so many endorsement opportunities?" There followed an awkward silence as both waited for a response from Catherine.

"I'll have to think about it," she replied. "It's not something I want or will be seeking."

The VC folded her arms. "The train has already left the station, Catherine. It's now a matter of us handling it right."

"I agree we need to handle it correctly," she replied. Catherine then turned to Sophie. "But if your company is so good at controlling the media then why can't it choose to keep me low profile? Put the uni in the spotlight?"

Sophie smiled at Catherine and replied as she might to a child. "I don't think you quite understand. But don't worry, we will sort everything."

Catherine turned to the VC. "I don't feel entirely comfortable with this, Vice Chancellor. Do we have to do it this way?"

The VC sighed and smiled. "I'm afraid so, Catherine. The population of the earth is about to learn we are most likely not alone. If that's not a story we need to manage and exploit, I don't know what is."

Catherine stared at the VC. She could feel her heart racing and her anger rising. She wasn't going to solve it now, so looked at her watch. "I do apologise, I have a tutorial." She stood up. "I'm already late and they'll be waiting in my office. Will you excuse me?"

"Yes, yes you must go," replied the VC. "We'll talk later and Sophie will follow up with you directly. We need everything in place for when the news hits the airwaves."

"Nice to meet you," added Sophie. But Catherine was already at the door. "You too," she replied, without turning round.

CATHERINE

CHAPTER 21

November 2018

As Catherine stepped outside, the chilled night air made her gasp. It was dark and a gentle rain fell, the droplets caught by the glow from the orange lights illuminating the ancient walls.

Catherine loved this route through the college and murky weather could never detract from the majesty of it all. She would often take a stroll and remind herself of how lucky she was to be doing the job she loved in the most beautiful and privileged of surroundings. But not today. Her head pounded and her mouth was dry. At that moment she hated everything about where she was. She rarely left the uni at this time of day and the roads around Cambridge were jammed with parents collecting their children from school. She closed her eyes as she waited in a long queue at the lights, the rain now lashing the windscreen. She was still wearing her wet coat and the inside of the car smelt musty.

Catherine's mind raced. She felt trapped by what she had done. All she had ever wanted was to find the right partner, nurture her children and never have them experience what she had as a child. And now this discovery was going to wreck everything. She seemed to have little control over the events that would lead to her past catching up with her. Everything would change, wouldn't it?

As the car pulled away, Catherine called her mother-in-law. "Hi, it's me."

"Hello Catherine. Everything alright?"

"Yes, you know, busy, busy." There was a moment's silence before she continued. "There's been a change of plan as we're not going out tonight after all and I wondered if I could come and collect the girls?"

"Oh. They're about to have their tea."

"That's fine, I'll be there in twenty minutes."

"They were looking forward to staying over."

Catherine took a deep breath. "I know. I'm sorry. Could we make it another night this week instead?"

"I suppose so. Grandpa will be disappointed."

"I have to go. The traffic's manic. See you soon."

****

Catherine and the girls were sitting at the kitchen table each with a large sheet of paper and paint splashed everywhere as John entered the room. She saw the confusion on his face, so she smiled and said, "Slight change of plan."

"Hello Daddy!" exclaimed Chloe.

"We are painting pictures for you," added Ruth as she ran a brush thick with purple paint across the sheet.

"They look wonderful," he replied as he opened the fridge door. "No restaurant tonight, I assume," he added as he took a beer from the shelf.

"Sorry, I'm exhausted," she replied. "Take-away instead?

John kissed her hair. "Lovely idea," he replied as he sat down. "I'm shattered too. Tough day, one way and another."

"Me too."

"Chat later?"

Catherine smiled at him. "Sure."

"That looks rubbish Mummy," said Chloe pointing at Catherine's painting. Paint dripped off her brush onto the table.

"Mummy always does rubbish paintings," added Ruth.

"I'm trying my best!"

"What is it?" asked Chloe.

"Looks like an alien," said John leaning over.

The girls giggled as Catherine splodged green paint over the paper. "Yup, they're little green men from a planet far away. What do you think?" she said turning to John.

"As the girls said, I think it's a bit rubbish. What do you say, girls?"

"Rubbish!" they replied in unison.

Catherine smiled. "Well, I like it."

****

After dinner they took their second bottle of wine to the sitting room. Catherine lay down on the settee, her head resting in his lap. She loved lying like this, looking up at him as they talked. She had fallen in love with him on the first day they met.

"What are you thinking about?" he asked.

"Only how much I love you," she said.

He smiled and stroked her forehead. "I love you too," he replied, as she closed her eyes. "Tell me about your day."

Catherine opened her eyes. The peace she had felt disappeared in an instant. "I hardly want to talk about it. I met with the VC and some dreadful woman who is going to 'manage me.'"

"Manage you? Nobody could do that!"

"Very funny. I mean, when it all comes out, there'll be countless demands. Books, TV, radio appearances. God knows. She's going to manage all that. Be my agent."

John gently stroked her hair. "I can't imagine what it's going to be like."

"I'm not sure I can cope, John. I don't want any of it. Can we just disappear?"

"There's nowhere to hide. And imagine if we did, the story would be even bigger."

Catherine smiled. "Daily Mail headline: 'Discoverer of aliens is abducted.'"

"There you go," he replied. For a while they stayed silent, each with their own thoughts. The first bottle of wine had relaxed them, the second making them melancholy.

"What about your day," she asked. "Did it make you want to run and hide?"

John sighed. "Not really. It was just the usual stuff." There was a moment's silence before he asked. "I know so little about your early life."

Catherine tensed. "There's not much to know."

"It's on my mind for some reason," replied John.

"Really?" She sat up and topped-up her glass. "Why?" She held the bottle out for him.

John frowned. "No more wine for me."

Catherine sipped from her glass. "We've been over this before." She watched him playing with his wine, swilling it around the glass. "Why the interest all of a sudden?"

"No reason." He hesitated, then added, "It's just that I know so little."

"There's not much to know, that's why. I was orphaned, moved around from family to family."

He hesitated as if contemplating whether to ask something…. "I don't even know where you grew up. Apart from it was Hertford. Where were all the foster homes?"

Catherine felt her anger rising. "I've never visited the house *you* grew up in. Couldn't even tell you the address."

"Fair enough. It's just that…"

"What? Tell me."

"I don't know – it's that I don't have an image in my mind of you growing up. You've seen photos of me as a young boy and teenager and I've never seen a single one of you. Sometimes I wonder what you were like, that's all."

"As a young teenager I had lanky blond hair, spots and braces then later blossomed into the beautiful woman you met at Oxford. Swan-like!" She smiled at him as she dug him in the ribs. "Enough?" Her attempt at lightening the mood hadn't worked as John looked down at his hands without replying. She felt a knot in the pit of her stomach. "I don't think I've got a photo," she added.

"Didn't you keep *any* mementoes? You must have had one or more nice foster parents?"

Catherine yawned. "Please, not now. I'm really tired. Can we change the subject?" She gently stroked his hair.

But John continued. "Once you're a celebrity the press will want to know. Plus, your foster parents will all come forward claiming they made you what you are now."

"I don't think I'll be *that* famous" she replied, smiling. But her casual remark hid how she felt. How was she going to cope with it all? "I'm going to have a long soak then go to bed," she suddenly announced, swivelling her legs to move away.

John sighed. "Really? Okay, we'll talk about it another time."

"Maybe," she replied as she headed for the door.

JOHN
CHAPTER 22

November 2018

John stood in the kitchen and listened as Catherine went upstairs. Once he could hear the bath running, he opened his laptop and started typing. He began searching again for the names the DI had mentioned. It took him nearly an hour before he hit on it: A newspaper headline from late July 1993.

TRAGIC ACCIDENT – LOCAL BOY FALLS TO HIS DEATH

As he scanned down the article he nearly skipped past the page as the accident had been in Harlow not Hertford. But then the DI had mentioned Harlow too, hadn't she? This train of thought was brought to an abrupt halt. There was a picture of the boy standing next to a girl labelled: 'Jimmy Evans with his older sister Tina' - taken a few months before his tragic death. He stared at the photo, enlarged it on the screen. He guessed the boy was mid-teens and the girl late teens. He enlarged it further and centred the screen on the girl. Suddenly the hairs on the back of his neck stood up. "Oh my god!" he exclaimed. "What the?!" As he leapt up, his chair fell over behind him. "Shit," he said picking it up. John paced the room, running his hands through his hair. Eventually he leant over the table and stared again at the image. He knew that face: It had to be the younger face of the DI, surely? But how could that be? "What is going on?" he whispered. The detective's name was Jane, wasn't it? He stood back from the screen, leaning against the sink, then leant forward and tapped to zoom-in on her face. He sat down again and stared at her. It was her: he was sure. It was the DI alright. "Christ!"

He read on further and discovered the boy had fallen to his death from high up in a tree. His sister had been there and witnessed the tragedy along with another girl, Amy Ridley. *That's the other girl the DI mentioned. That's right, she'd said, have you heard the name, 'Amy Ridley?'* The article reported how Amy had clambered up the tree to try and save him prior to his fall.

John sat back in his chair, folded his arms and stared at the screen. His eyes were tired and his head ached, so he slammed his laptop shut. What was going on? How can DI *Jane* Flanders have been *Tina* Evans? And who was Amy Ridley? Why was she so important? Sounds like she was a hero. He thought about asking Catherine but decided against it, she had enough on right now. Anyway, it might lead to her finding out about his meeting with the DI. He thought for a moment - he'd start by phoning the DI to ask her about the picture of her and this Jimmy Evans. That needed clearing up for a start. He pushed his chair back and went upstairs to bed. Catherine appeared to be fast asleep.

****

John pulled his collar up in an attempt to keep out the biting wind and thrust his hands deep into his coat pockets. It was lunchtime and he'd left the school and gone for a walk. He found a bench by a small pond and sat for a while wondering what he would say. The gusts of wind made the water ripple and the reeds flutter. He didn't have long so he got out his phone and searched for received calls and redialled the number he had for the DI. But all he got was one long continuous tone

- no such number. "Damn it." He Googled the local police station and after a confusing call discovered there was no 'DI Flanders' stationed in Cambridge or at any other station as far as they knew.

As his last lesson filed out he opened his laptop and studied the Harlow Chronicle article again and made a note of the reporter, Peter Leech. He phoned the Chronicle. Just retired. He searched and within minutes found the reporter on multiple sites. Mr Leech had written a novel and had an author's profile. "Gotcha," said John as he wrote down his number. He checked his watch and dialled it straight away.

****

It took John less than an hour to drive from Cambridge to Harlow. He'd phoned-in sick to give himself the whole day. He only needed to be back to collect the girls at four-ish. John quickly found the small coffee shop in Harlow Old Town. The main street was drab and quiet, and he wasn't surprised to be the only customer as he entered the café.

"Sorry sir, our machine's broken again, we're only serving instant."

"Really?" John ordered tea and took it to a corner table and within minutes in walked a man with old fawn trousers, a tired looking jacket and uncombed greying hair.

"Peter?" John called, hoping it was him.

Cigarette smoke wafted from the man's clothes as he slumped in the chair opposite John. "Peter," he said holding out a hand.

"Thanks for coming," said John, as Peter took a seat. After getting him an instant coffee and politely enquiring about his novel, which turned out to be self-published, Mr Leech asked, "What do you want to know?"

John took a deep breath and folded his arms. "It's a long story which I won't go into, but I've recently met this lady here," he said, pointing to the photo of the young Tina. "I'm trying to find out more about her and," he looked up at his companion, "the other girl mentioned in your article, Amy Ridley."

Mr Leech tried to stir-in the undissolved coffee granules floating on the surface of his drink. "Okay," he began, "Are you wanting to date this woman or something? Is this why you've got me here?"

John was horrified. "No, no not at all. Listen, I'll tell it to you straight. I was approached by a detective, a Jane Flanders, in my hometown of Cambridge." John could see he had the reporter's attention. "She interviewed me in a café, not as a suspect I hasten to add, but seeing if I could help her in some investigation."

"I'm still none the wiser, but let's start with; what sort of investigation?"

"Actually, I'm now pretty sure there is no investigation, which I'll explain in a minute. Anyway, she asked about my wife Catherine and she also dropped the names of these three people in your article," he said, tapping the newspaper cutting.

Mr Leech leant back. "I remember this story - it really gripped the town. Keep going," he added.

"The thing is, when I went to contact the DI, I found her number no longer existed - so I contacted the police station, and nobody had ever heard of a DI Jane Flanders."

Mr Leech sipped his coffee. "That's disgusting." He hesitated then added, "the coffee I mean."

"I chose tea," replied John. He paused, wondering if Mr Leech was losing interest. "The thing you should know, Mr Leech, is that this so-called detective is her," he said, stabbing the image of Tina. "I'm sure of it."

"Now you've got my attention," said Mr Leech as he turned and beckoned over the waitress. "I'll have a tea please and you can take this away," he said as he handed her his mug. John waited for the waitress to leave. "So how can I help?" asked Mr Leech.

John put his hands on the table. "Maybe start by telling me what you recall of the incident."

"Fair enough. As I said, it was a tragedy. I reported on it and followed up further as the story went on for a while. This Jimmy kid and his sister were in the woods. I can't recall why they were there, but I think he may have taken LSD, so perhaps they went there just to take the drugs, I'm not sure. Anyway, Jimmy was about sixteen and his sister Tina a few years older. For whatever reason he climbed up this tree, probably because he was off his head, and then got stuck up on some crazy high branch."

The waitress plonked a tea mug in front of Mr Leech. He looked down to observe creamy milk floating on the surface. "Thanks love," he said to her back. "Where were we?"

"High and high-up," replied John.

"Quite so. Then this Amy girl, who it turns out knew Jimmy at school, rocks up, Tina runs off to get help and while she's gone Amy climbs up the tree to help him." Mr Leech moved his tea mug aside and entwined the fingers of both hands as if about to deliver something significant. "And that's when it got interesting."

"How so?"

"The police were involved, obviously, given there was a death. The conclusion was, Amy Ridley was a hero, who, as I wrote, bravely went up the tree to try and save her friend. I interviewed Amy over the phone and she was quite cooperative. She refused to give me a photo and said she'd only agree to the interview if we didn't print one. I said that was fine although I confess I would have printed a photo had I been able to find one. Let me think…..oh, I did talk to some of her friends too and she was an ace student apparently."

"So that was that?" asked John.

"Not quite."

"Go on."

"Well, I think it was about a month after the accident when I got a call from the mother."

"Tina's and Jimmy's?"

"Yes, Mrs Evans, Silvia as I recall."

John sat upright in his chair.

"She called me at the newspaper office and asked if we could meet. Said she would bring her daughter. I thought, well, the original story had made the front page and if she had more, it might have legs."

John nodded, desperate to hear what he was going to say next.

"Look, I need a cigarette, do you mind if I pop out for a minute?" asked Mr Leech.

John's heart sunk. "Yes, sure. Fine." Five minutes later Mr Leech was back, more smoke wafting around his person. "Sorry about that, can't kick the habit. Where was I?"

"Mrs Evans and her daughter, Tina."

"Ah yes. They came to the newspaper offices. I remember Mrs Evans was dressed smartly in what looked like expensive clothes and as I recall, wafts of perfume. Couldn't get rid of the smell for days. Nice enough though. She was still upset from the loss, obviously."

"What about the daughter?"

"Tina, bloody scary was my first thought. She was pretty, no doubt about that. Like her mother. Training to be an actor if I recall correctly. But the interesting thing is, they were livid about me making this Ridley girl a hero as they claimed that she had lied and had caused Jimmy's death."

"Really? How? Why? Did the police believe them?"

"I know they interviewed Amy, maybe more than once, but nothing came of it."

"Blimey."

"Mrs Evans said the only reason the police didn't take it further was because her daughter Tina, had, 'had a little smoke' and therefore her evidence wouldn't stand-up in court. Actually, come to think of it, maybe a month or so after their visit to me, Tina was arrested for supplying class A drugs to her brother. It could have led to manslaughter, but in the end, they couldn't prove anything so all charges were dropped. The police never established who supplied the drugs."

"But the fall was an accident, right?"

"Well, there's the thing," continued Mr Leech, now in his stride. "In my office, Tina took over the conversation from her mother. It was like she was spitting nails, full of hate for this Amy girl. She said Jimmy and Amy had arguments all the time and the night prior to Jimmy's death, Amy and Jimmy had had a big argument at a party at the Evans's house, which she says she and others witnessed. Amy hit Jimmy according to her. She also said Amy fancied Jimmy and wouldn't leave him alone: 'stalker' she said. It had gone on for years, or so she said. Tina suggested Amy had followed them to the woods that day, rather than happening upon them. Tina ranted all this at me."

"Blimey," he repeated.

"Then she said, and I can picture her telling me, 'Amy deliberately killed my brother. Murdered him.' I looked at her mother who sat passively, letting her daughter make this accusation. I remember it, like it was yesterday."

"That's one hell of an accusation."

"It is. They wanted me to investigate and then write a story revealing what Amy had done - according to them anyway."

"Did you?"

"No! Of course not. I wasn't some sort of investigative journalist, and it was the local paper, reporting on fetes, local football, and holes in the road. No-way would the editor be interested in something like that."

John sighed. "I guess not."

"But I did have a conversation with a police friend of mine, off the record. The fact is, they were a bit suspicious of Amy's story and suspected she had at least been on the same branch that morning, which she claimed not to have been. They found forensics proving she had recently been on that branch, so she may well have been up there that day and could have done something, even by accident. But Amy claimed she'd climbed up there the day before. She often climbed trees apparently. Her mother confirmed she had gone to the woods the day before and there was another witness who said he'd seen her going into the woods. So, the police couldn't build a case."

"Wow. And was there a suggestion of a relationship between Jimmy and Amy?"

Mr Leech sat back and folded his arms, as if contemplating whether to speak further. After a pause he continued. "At the time, my daughter was a cook at the school. The rumour was that Amy and Jimmy did hang out a lot, but that was all. My daughter was at the party though, and she corroborated Tina's claim of the argument at the party."

"A big leap to say it was motive for murder."

"Exactly. But I have to tell you, through my daughter, I heard more."

John leant forward, "Go on."

"Following the tragedy, the Evans family waged a war of words on Amy. When I say 'family' I mean the mother and daughter. Tina in particular. The father wasn't around as far as I recall."

"What do you mean, 'waged war?'"

"Tina wheedled her way into Amy's circle of friends. I heard she used her acting skills, but you don't know what to believe, do you? She sidled her way into Amy's circle and then isolated and poisoned the relationships. It seems she was an expert at it." Mr Leech hesitated. "I remember now, it's coming back to me - there was a memorial service for Jimmy and most of his school friends were invited. Even my daughter went. But they excluded Amy, that's right. It was a celebration of Jimmy's life and the kids ended up drinking too much. That's when Tina started poisoning Amy's relationships with her friends. Sort of isolating her. According to my daughter anyway."

John sipped his now cold tea. "It's all horrible. Either this Amy accidently caused his death or at a stretch deliberately, or she was doing all she could to save him and was a hero. Either way it's dreadful for both sides." John sat back and thought for a moment. "This is all fascinating, but why on earth would Tina contact me now? Plus, lie about her name, pretend to be a policewoman and ask me about my wife and if I knew about, what turns out to be her, Tina, and her brother? She must have known I'd track this picture down," he added, pointing to the cutting. "And then also mention the name of Amy Ridley. It makes no sense."

"I can guess," replied Mr Leech. "From seeing how she behaved back then; I suspect Tina is playing with your head. She doesn't care if you find out she is Tina Evans. She wants you to find out in your own way about this tragedy and Amy Ridley."

"Why? And why didn't she just tell me about it?"

"She led you here, didn't she?"

"Maybe. Seems all a bit convoluted."

"Well, as I said, she's playing with your mind, and I suspect she's really getting at your wife. Or," he said, raising a finger, "Trying to drive a wedge between you and your wife, isolating her, like she did Amy."

The mention of Catherine made him shudder at the duplicity of what he was doing. Here he was secretly meeting this reporter, knowing the lies he would later tell Catherine about his day. Perhaps he should tell her everything? He thought for a moment. No, he decided, he couldn't possibly do that.

"A wedge between us? Why?" asked John.

"That's what you need to find out."

John sighed. "I need to find Tina and also Amy Ridley."

"Not sure there's any point trying to find Tina, she'll only mess with you further or refuse to talk. Amy is the key here, don't you think?"

"Key to what?"

"No idea, but there's obviously something going on, or gone on, that's connected with your wife – which you're in the dark about. Maybe your wife knew Tina or Amy or all three of them?

"Impossible."

"Well, it's an itch you've gotta scratch. Why not simply ask your wife?"

"Ha! Definitely not. She's going through a lot right now plus she hates talking about her past. Her parents died in a road accident, and she was fostered." John thought for a moment. "I've already searched on social media for Amy Ridley and the only thing of relevance I came up with was your newspaper article. No trace of her now and she's probably married, so her Ridley surname means nothing."

Mr Leech looked down at his drink as if not listening, then suddenly said, "Hold on, now I come to think of it. Following my interview with Amy and her refusal of a photo, I approached her mother to attempt to get one. She was no help, but then I found out Amy had a younger brother, who soon after moved away with the dad to Bristol. What was the son's name? It's in there somewhere," he continued, drumming his fingers on the sticky tabletop. "Ah! That's it – Billy, that's it, William, Billy Ridley."

AMY

CHAPTER 23

July 1993

"I don't want to see anybody!" Amy sat at her desk; bedroom curtains closed with her back to her mother.

"But your friends are downstairs, they want to see you."

"Tell them I'm fine."

Her mother stepped into the room and lowered her voice. "It's not just about you being fine, it's your friends wanting to support you."

Amy turned around. "Please, I don't need support. I need peace. Tell them whatever you want!"

Five minutes later her mother was back. "It's been two weeks now and you know tomorrow we're going to the police station. Have you written your statement?"

"Of course," she replied without turning around.

"May I see it?"

Amy opened her drawer and held the paper over her shoulder. She tapped her desk with her pen. "I've been more precise on the timings. When I left home, things like that."

Her mother scanned it and placed it back on Amy's desk. "I'll leave you in peace," she said touching her shoulder. As she left, she hesitated, "One thing, I had a call from Dad.

Seems like Billy is being very difficult at this new woman's house. Dad says he hardly recognises him and wonders if he's still suffering from the shock of the accident."

Amy swivelled round. "Has he said anything?"

"Not as far as I know. It's Dad assuming that's the reason, although I think it's more to do with Billy being away from home. What does he expect?"

"Tell Dad I'll have a chat with Billy," said Amy, "and let him know I'm alright. Perhaps that'll help?"

Her mother smiled. "That's kind, I'll let him know, maybe you can speak with Billy this evening?"

"Okay," she replied. As soon as her mother had gone, Amy stood in front of her mirror, staring at herself in silence, digging her nail into her arm. She imagined the blood from an open wound and how the badness inside her had to come out: She deserved the pain and the scars, she told herself. Then she sat on her bed with the blade and cut herself where she had made the bright red mark.

****

Amy met with Catherine in the park. She'd only been out once in nearly two weeks and this was the first time she'd spoken with Catherine since that fateful weekend.

"Let's lie down," said Catherine, "Watch the clouds drift across the sky." They lay there in silence until Catherine asked, "Do you want to tell me?"

Amy began to cry and wiped the tears away with her sleeve. She had to wait for her gasping to subside before she could speak. She explained all about the party and what Jimmy had done and then the tragedy the following day. She watched

Catherine intensely, wondering if she was being judged negatively. But in her heart she knew Catherine understood.

"It wouldn't happen to you," said Amy. She turned to look at Catherine. "You're in control of your life, but me," she looked away, "things happen to me and I react."

"What happened to you is shocking and not your fault. Don't be hard on yourself," replied Catherine. "He was evil. It could have happened to anybody. Maybe he assaulted other girls too?"

Amy shook her head. "I don't know," she replied, her voice trailing off.

"And as for the accident," continued Catherine, "few people would have had the guts to climb up there, I certainly couldn't have, and fewer would have been willing to help after what he did to you. You're an angel. Really!" Amy remained silent, not knowing what to say.

They both sat up. "You did what you could," said Catherine, "I'm proud of you."

"You're my only true friend. Nobody but you can help me through this."

"I'm here for you," replied Catherine, "whenever you need me, you know I'll be there."

Amy smiled. "Thank you. I'd better be going. Everybody's watching me like a hawk, worrying that I might harm myself. There will be a search party out in a minute. See you soon?"

"Anytime," replied Catherine, "I'm around."

As she walked up the hill she stopped, turned and looked down toward the park, with the climbing frame where she had first met Catherine. Suddenly Amy bent over double, her hands on her knees, her chest rapidly rising and falling. Physical pain from the guilt, she thought. Gradually she straightened her back to stand upright, hands on hips, now staring up at the sky. The white puffy clouds and glimpses of blue had been replaced by a uniform greyness. "And I couldn't even tell my dearest friend the truth," she whispered.

"The headmaster's called," said Mum as Amy opened the back door.

She tensed. "It's the holidays, what does he want with me?"

"They want to recognise you with a bravery award when you return to school in September."

Amy's heart raced. Oh God, she thought, no way. She imagined herself walking onto the stage in assembly, unable to look the headmaster in the eye. "I don't want anything!" she replied. "Anyway," she added, "one minute he's going to suspend me then he's holding me up as an example."

Her mother looked quizzically at her. "Don't be childish, Amy."

"The Evans's haven't even had the funeral yet."

Her mother shrugged her shoulders. "Guess they want you to know how proud they are. How you were willing to risk yourself for someone else."

Amy knew her voice sounded panicky as she replied, "I'm going to my room."

****

"In here," said the officer opening the door for Amy and her mother. Amy's mouth was dry and when they offered her a glass of water, she wanted to accept but with her hands shaking she declined. A smell hung in the air and at first Amy couldn't place it. Suddenly she realised it was the smell of the police officer she had been squeezed up against in the police car. It made her feel nauseous.

The room had one bulb hanging from a cord that was too long. In the corner was a table with a clock that had stopped and to its side, a plastic plant. The grey lino floor had black scuff marks dotted about. She stared at them imagining someone being dragged in or out screaming, objecting to being questioned. Amy was jolted from her thoughts by the officer.

"This shouldn't take long. Have you brought your statement?"

"Yes," she replied as she and her mother sat down opposite the two officers.

"Sorry it's so stuffy in here, as you see it's windowless and what with this weather…"

Amy wished they could just get on with it and get out of there. 'It'll all be over soon' she told herself.

"We need you to sign the statement and your mother to witness it," she began. The officer smiled as Amy pulled the envelope out of her bag and slid it across the table. The officer picked it up and read it through as they sat there in silence. Then she looked up. "So, no changes from your verbal statement on the day?"

Amy swallowed hard and felt the sweat under her arms. "No."

Instead of returning the document to Amy for signing, the officer carefully placed it down in front of her and smoothed her hand across it as if attempting to remove any creases.

"All okay?" asked her mother. "Amy is keen to put this behind her."

The officer smiled. "We just need to clear up a couple of things if we may?"

"Shouldn't take long," added the other officer. "We know this is all very difficult for you."

Amy stared straight ahead and could sense her mother looking at her. The officer smiled again, then began. "Tell us about your relationship with Jimmy."

Amy moved her position and sat on her hands. "What do you mean? I didn't have a 'relationship' if that's what you mean?" She hated the way she'd answered that, too aggressive she thought.

"How long have you known him. How did you two get on, did you see him out of school, that sort of thing."

"Why do you ask?" interjected her mother. "She simply wants to sign her statement and go. How is this relevant?"

"If you don't mind Mrs Ridley, we would like Amy to do the answering for herself."

"Does she need a lawyer?"

The officers looked at each other then back at Mrs Ridley. "She can do, and we can rearrange this for another day. It's all very straightforward."

Amy looked at her mother. The idea of coming back appalled her. "No, let's do it now," she said. Her head instantly filled with thoughts of his bullying, the unkind notes, the name calling, the teasing and worst of all, his assault. She felt her throat closing and had to pause before answering. Then she wondered, what had they heard? Eventually she began: "I've known Jimmy since infant school. After that we lost touch as we were in different classes, then at the current school different Houses and had different friends. Although in the last couple of years, we've had more contact and common friends as we have been doing the same GCSE subjects."

"Carry on."

"Err, we may have met outside school, can't remember. I mean I can't say we never did, although not often or planned… apart from the other Saturday when me and my friends went to a party at his house."

"The night prior to his death."

Amy noted the officer hadn't used the word 'accident'. "Yes," she replied.

"And did anything happen between you and Jimmy at the party?"

Again, she felt her mother staring at her. "I hardly saw him the whole night. Not until the end when he went on at me about something."

"What was that?"

"I can't remember. Trivial. He was high on drugs and very drunk, so he didn't make sense."

"The reason we are asking is that there are witnesses to say it was a serious row."

Amy shifted in her seat. "No!" The word came out louder than she'd wanted. She stopped and took a deep breath. Her legs began to shake under the table. "It was nothing and I came home as normal with my friends; it didn't bother me. I knew he wasn't in a fit state."

"Why is this relevant?" asked her mother.

"We just need to clear a few things up." The officer turned the page of her notebook. "Would you say you two had a toxic relationship – sort of bullying each other? Provoking each other?"

"No."

"So, you're saying you weren't angry that night?"

"I wasn't angry! Ask any of my friends. Or Tamsin's mother who gave us a lift back."

"It has been reported that you hit him in the face during the argument, is that true?"

She felt herself blush. "No, that's ridiculous. Who said that?"

"It doesn't matter who said it. We just want to know, yes or no."

"No."

"But it is true that you've hit him before, correct?"

Amy clasped her hands together and could feel the stickiness of her sweaty palms. She looked from one officer to the next as she thought of how she might best answer.

"Well?" prompted the officer.

"It was more like a playful slap, after he said something. No big deal and we made up pretty quickly."

The officer smiled. "Sorry to have to ask these questions." She looked at Mrs Ridley. "We're nearly done, then Amy can sign and you two can be off."

Amy clasped her hands on the table, encouraged by what the officer had said.

"Just to clarify, in your statement you said you stopped at 'one or two branches below where Jimmy stood,' correct?"

"Yes"

"Now the forensic team have identified fibres that precisely match those of the jumper you were wearing, on the tree trunk at various points, including at the height of the branch where Jimmy stood, indicating you had been on the same branch. Would you like to amend your account in the light of this evidence?"

Her heart raced and the words came out even before she had thought what she would say. "I've climbed that tree countless times. Everybody will tell you I've been climbing trees in that wood since I was a kid."

The officer didn't immediately answer, as if contemplating what she had said or perhaps letting her answer hang in the air. She tapped her pen on the table. "It is very unlikely those fibres would last more than a few days on the trunk as any rain or weathering would remove them, so they had been deposited very recently."

Amy froze, unable to speak. Suddenly the interminable silence was broken by her mother. "Amy went to the woods on the Friday morning." Her mother turned to her. "That's right, isn't it?"

Amy gulped for air. "Yes! I was there on that branch on the Friday morning."

"Really?" quizzed the officer. "And are there any witnesses?" she added.

Amy turned to her mother, who answered the officer. "Well I recall her saying that morning she was going to her reading tree…. you see she goes there to read, that's the same tree, and she came back late morning to meet friends."

"And I saw a neighbour at the edge of the woods on my way back," added Amy. "And my friends made a joke about me going to the tree to read. You can ask them. And Mr Jones the neighbour who saw me leaving the woods."

"Okay," replied the officer. "That's helpful. And you were wearing the same jumper as you were on the Sunday morning?"

"Yes," she answered.

"It's her favourite," added her mother. "In fact, I recall she was wearing it."

"Okay we'll want to speak with your friends and the neighbour Mr Jones, to corroborate your account."

"I think that's enough," said her mother. "She's not answering anything now until we have a lawyer present."

The officers looked at each other, then turned to Amy. "Excuse us a moment, will you?"

Alone in the room Amy's mother stood up and looked down at her daughter. "Why are they asking you this?" Amy put her elbows on the table and her head in her hands. "I've no idea," she said half-shaking her head. After what seemed like an age the door opened and in-walked one of the officers. "It's fine, you can sign the statement and go. You've been most helpful, and we know it's been difficult for you. Sorry we had to ask those questions, but I think we're done."

Amy felt her shoulders drop as she puffed out her cheeks. She had to take a few deep breaths before she was able to sign her name. As they walked out, she tensed, thinking they might ask her one more question, trying to catch her out, but to her relief they seemed uninterested in her now.

"Glad that's over!" she said as they left the station. But her mother didn't answer, instead she marched on ahead. Amy walked one pace behind her to the car, half expecting her to swivel round and ask, 'what's been going on?' Or perhaps 'well done darling I'm glad it's all over.' But nothing, just an awkward silence. The doors slammed and still nothing, so she stared out of the window as her mother drove away. Amy thought about the guilt she had felt, especially after the chat with Catherine, but she couldn't conjure it up. If it was there under the surface it was trumped by the relief of getting through that interview. She was free from the police at least.

"Not sure you'll get away with that," said Amy as they sped through a red light. She looked at her mother whose gaze remained clamped on the road ahead. For no reason Amy opened the glove compartment, looked inside, then flicked it shut. She couldn't bear it any longer. "What a waste of time that was."

"Amy," said her mother without taking her eyes off the road.

"What?"

"For whatever reason I recall exactly what you were wearing when you went to the woods on Friday morning and it wasn't that jumper." Her mother pulled up sharply outside the house, switched off the ignition and turned to her. It was still in-gear and the car lurched and beeped at them as she spoke. "Tell me!" Her mother gripped the steering wheel. "How come they found a match?"

"Mum!" she screamed. "I wasn't wearing the jumper when I left the house or when I returned as it was hot, but I took it with me and was wearing it in the woods as it was cooler in there." She thrust open the car door and got out. Leaning in she shouted, "You're no help!" And slammed the door shut in her mother's face. Immediately she felt guilty. Her mother had helped, she told the police she recalled her wearing the jumper.

Back in her room she lay on her bed and cast her mind back to the interview. The police had seemed satisfied in the end. But she'd lied; she'd not taken the jumper that Friday morning. And Billy, she still hadn't spoken to him. She got up and rearranged the things on her desk. She needed to speak with Billy and soon.

AMY

CHAPTER 24

August 1993

"You need to tell me the truth Amy." She knew it would be coming at some point, but she still hadn't thought how she'd answer her mother. There'd been a horrible tension in the house for a week since the police interview and she'd avoided her mother at every opportunity. They were sitting in the garden having lunch and she slowly put down her knife and fork. "What about?"

"You know very well what about. This thing with Jimmy and you. It doesn't add up and we both know it. The sooner you come clean, the sooner I can help you."

Amy sat back and sighed; her appetite gone. "We've never really got on, that's all there is to it." She folded her arms and looked straight at her mother. "We've had arguments but then he's had arguments with others in the class. He's very competitive... *was* very competitive. I didn't like him."

"So that was all?"

"Yes Mum, don't keep going on about it!"

"It's just those police questions. And you hitting him. Then the next minute you're risking your own safety trying to save his life."

"Just because someone pisses you off it doesn't mean you'll never help them."

Her mother thought for a moment, biting her lip. "I guess so."

Amy tried to eat but instead pushed her food around her plate. Yesterday she'd received an evil letter from Tina. *I don't believe it was an accident. I know how you chased my brother, despite his rejections and how you used to hang around outside our house. I even saw you once myself. I know you two argued and I know you drove him crazy.* And other horrible accusations. And the scariest bit: . *We've spoken to the police and we will not let it drop until the truth is out. Be warned.* Amy shivered at the thought of the police interviewing her again.

Her mother interrupted her thoughts. Well?"

"I need to go out," said Amy, standing up.

"But you've not finished."

"I'm not hungry."

"I don't know why I bother to prepare these meals sometimes. Where are you going?"

"It was a frozen pizza Mum - with a salad from a packet."

"Don't be so ungrateful. Where are you going?"

"For a walk."

"Be back before dark," she replied, picking up the newspaper.

"It's August. I'll be back long before that."

She climbed a tree in a different part of the woods, leant against the trunk and pulled out Tina's letter. Suddenly she felt dizzy and clambered down as fast she could. She'd only just touched the ground when she bent over, her hands on her knees and threw up her dinner, being sick from the bottom of her boots. When she got home, she tore the letter into tiny pieces and stuffed them under the other rubbish at the bottom of her bin.

"There's a phone call for you!" her mother called from downstairs.

Amy opened her door. "Who is it?"

"Someone from the Paper."

Amy stood in the kitchen. "Hello?

"Amy. My name is Peter Leech and I'm a journalist on the Harlow Chronicle, have you got a moment?"

Was this Tina's doing? she wondered. "What's it about?" She looked at her mum who was standing watching and waved her away.

"I'm writing an article on the tragic death of local boy Jimmy Evans. I understand you were heroic in your attempts to save him. We want to include a section on how you tried to save him and something about you too." He hesitated and she wondered if he was waiting for a response. Not getting one he continued. "Could you answer a few questions now? Have you got a photo we could use?"

Amy slowly pulled out a stool and sat down. It dawned on her; this was a chance to get her story out there.

"Hello?" he said.

"Sorry, I'm still here. I was thinking."

"Take your time. If you want to ask your parents first then go right ahead."

Amy looked through the window at her mother stretched out on a lounger smoking. "Can we do it now?"

"I'd be delighted."

"What do you want to know?"

"As a starter, how well did you know Jimmy and were you close friends?"

"Since we were very young. And yes, we were good friends. We had our moments of course but yes, we kinda got on pretty well."

It was forty-five minutes before she hung-up, confident that he would write about her heroic attempts to save the life of a good friend. She liked the man despite his persistence in trying to get a photo.

****

The whole of the school entrance hall was buzzing with excited parents and students. It was the day of the GCSE results and Amy had tried her best to hang back but to no avail - so many of her peers had approached to offer sympathy for witnessing such a tragedy or to offer admiration for her efforts. Now she was pleased she'd done that newspaper interview as her heroics were being recognised. True to his word, the journalist hadn't included a picture of her - only one of Jimmy and Tina.

She stood away from the crowd and carefully opened her envelope, slowly running her finger along the seam. She pulled it out and held it upside down and then flipped it over. Ten A grades. She smiled to herself and thought how she would meet up with Catherine as soon as she could; she was bound to have stormed it too. And maybe the Tina thing will go away and that will make everything good. She was getting over the Jimmy tragedy and with these results…. she sighed, glanced down, and re-read the grades, taking time on each line. As she looked up, she scanned the crowd for Tamsin and Rachel who she'd so far avoided, knowing their results would be poor. And then she spotted them on the edge of the playground. She stared, hardly able to believe her eyes. Standing talking to them was Tina. She squinted in the sunlight, at first believing her vision was deceiving her. What on earth was Tina doing? She didn't even attend the school. She stood rigid and watched as they appeared to be engaged in deep conversation. After what seemed like an age Tina walked off without seeing her. Should she go over?

"Hi, you two!" she began.

"Hi there," replied Tamsin. "Bet you got all A's!"

Amy smiled. "How did you know?" she said holding out her results.

"Educated guess," replied Tamsin without taking the sheet of paper.

"And you haven't got that black cloud hanging over you," said Rachel.

Amy was taken aback. "What do you mean?"

"You know, sometimes you're a bit moody."

What a horrible thing to say, thought Amy. "Oh, sorry," she replied. "And yes, I got the best results I could have hoped for."

Suddenly Rachel said, "These results have confirmed it. I'm not going into the sixth form – there's no point. So I'm going full time at the salon."

"And I'm going to try and get a job as a waitress," added Tamsin, "I've done enough hours at weekends."

Amy's heart sank, she'd really miss them and suspected they would all soon drift apart.

"Let's have a group hug," added Rachel as she held out her arms. They stood there a while with their heads touching, cut off from the outside world, promising to stay close. Suddenly Amy said, "Wasn't that Tina, Jimmy's sister earlier?" She spotted a fleeting glance between the two before Rachel answered, "Yeah. So sad isn't it."

"They're having a memorial service to celebrate his life and invited us, well, pretty much everybody," added Tamsin. They separated from their hug and stood facing each other. "Why can't you come?" asked Rachel.

"What do you mean?"

"Tina said you couldn't come," added Rachel.

Amy thought quickly. "Oh, right, not sure. It's all a bit much for me," she added.

"Tina said something about not being able to have a funeral yet due to…what did she call it?" asked Rachel turning to Tamsin.

"Coroner's report," answered Tamsin.

Amy had already been asked by the coroner for the same statement she'd given to the police. "Not surprised," replied Amy, "apparently, it always happens when there's a fatal accident."

There was a moment's silence before Tamsin said. "Amy. Tina says you're under investigation by the police. What's that about?"

Tamsin's words sent a shiver through her. "What?!" She looked from one to the other. "No!"

"That's what she said," added Rachel. "That you may be arrested for causing his death."

"We didn't believe her," Tamsin quickly added.

She felt she'd been punched in the stomach and the elation of the exam results vanished in a second. She looked from one to the other. Oh God, they believed her. She thought for a moment. "He was off his head and thought he could fly. It's really sad… and… I've got no idea why Tina would make such horrible stuff up about me." She felt the tears flow as it all came back. The two girls put their arms around her.

"Oh Amy, we didn't mean to," said Rachel, squeezing her tightly.

"He was off his head the night before, he probably never came down," said Amy through her tears.

"He was crazy," added Tamsin. "But it was an accident, right?"

Amy felt the adrenalin hit her stomach. "Of course, it was an accident!"

"No, I mean… I didn't…"

Amy pulled out of the huddle. "Please don't! It's hard enough without your friends deserting you!"

"We're sorry, we didn't mean to upset you!" added Rachel. "Come on, forget about them, let's go to Nando's, we can celebrate your exam results and our new lives."

Amy wiped her eyes and was about to say 'great' when she spotted Tina at the school gates watching them. "I'd better get back," she said. "I promised my mum I'd let her know my results as soon as possible."

The girls stared at her. "Really?" said Rachel.

But she ignored the response and as she walked away Tamsin called, "Where are you going?"

Amy turned. "I'm going out the back way, I need a longer walk." She had her back to them as she waved and then called out, "I'll be there later!" Quickly she broke into a run, afraid Tina might come after her.

AMY

CHAPTER 25

It was her 17th birthday, 4th September 1993 and the first day in the sixth form. She'd only seen her mother for a few minutes in the morning.

When she got home from school, her mother was still at work and probably going out to meet friends. Dad called as she sat alone in the house, so at least he was excited for her. She'd managed to talk with Billy who had been uncommunicative, but he hadn't said anything to Dad: that much she had established. How long it could go on for she didn't know. She began to scratch the side of her thigh, pushing her nails in harder with each stroke. She looked down to see she had drawn blood. I deserve it, she thought, as she dabbed the wounds dry.

Catherine had got the same results as her. The plan was they'd do the same A levels, pure maths, applied maths, physics and chemistry. Then try and go to the same university, Cambridge, or Oxford perhaps. Catherine wanted to study Cosmology or perhaps Physics and Astronomy. It made Amy think she might want to do the same subjects.

On the mat were four envelopes all addressed to her, three birthday cards and one hand delivered envelope. It contained a scruffy handwritten note.

Come on Amy, we both know what really caused his death – you! You'll NOT get away with it and we're talking to the police and the coroner so expect a knock on the door very soon. You'll go down for a long time.

She opened the front door to see if anybody was there. Glancing up and down the street there was no sign of Tina and she had no idea what she would have done if she'd spotted her. She slammed the door too hard and went into the kitchen.

"Happy birthday!" said her mother as she walked in. Amy had screwed up the note and put it in her pocket. "What's wrong with you?" asked her mother, "seen a ghost?" She did her best to smile as her mother handed her an envelope. "Didn't know what to get you so there's a voucher. Get some clothes you like. Perhaps not jeans," she added with her back to her. "Something pretty?"

Amy only just caught her mother's last words as she'd already walked out on her way to her bedroom. She needed to dispose of the note at the bottom of her bin. How long is this persecution going on for? She'd be frightened by every knock at the door.

****

It was October when the headmaster gave a talk about Jimmy's life during morning assembly. He told the whole school that the funeral was to be the following week, which would 'give some sense of closure' for the family.

Amy sat rigid as he told the school about Jimmy: how special he had been. The kindest of boys, academically talented and funny! He told a story of how Jimmy had ad-libbed in a school play and brought the house down. "Not funny," whispered Amy. How he had been a credit to the school, his family, and the whole community. Amy felt her toes curl and her back ached as she sat rigid in the chair. He talked about how he had worked in a charity shop on Sunday mornings. Really? Thought Amy. Throughout the talk she fixed her gaze halfway up the curtain on the left hand side of the stage, never taking her eyes off the target. How could the Head say such things, had he no idea? The Head's words faded as her mind drifted back to the party, up in the bedroom. Suddenly her leg kicked the chair in front of her hard, as she relived the moment she had pushed Jimmy off. The girl in front turned round. "Sorry," whispered Amy. The Head's words were sickening and she felt the urge to shout out: 'Jimmy Evans raped me!'

After assembly, she shut herself in the toilets and missed the first class.

****

The inquest into his death was to be held at the end of the month and Amy was required to give her account of what happened. Her mother had arranged a solicitor who had advised her to tell it straight, simple facts in chronological order. Not worth the money for that advice she'd thought. She had practised her speech in front of Catherine a hundred times. What really scared her was that the inquest was open to the public, journalists and of course the entire Evans family.

"Have you got a moment?" said the Head catching her up. She sat in his office, sullen faced.

"Very impressive results," he began. But she knew this wasn't the reason why he'd called her in. His office was cluttered with books and papers, and she wondered how anybody could work in such a mess. There was a smell of stale coffee emanating from a cup that hadn't seen a fresh drink in what she guessed were weeks.

"Thanks."

"Listen," he said adjusting his position, "I know we talked earlier about a bravery award, you know, given what you did on that afternoon." He drummed his fingers on the desk as if playing a tune. "In hindsight it's not the best time right now, not with things as they are. I'm sure you understand," he added.

"Oh yes," she replied, "no problem." She hesitated then plucked up the courage to ask. "What things?"

"Well, it's not all tidied up yet," he replied, readjusting his position. The drumming continued.

She so wanted to say, 'the police investigation you mean?' But dare not.

"We'll still do it of course," he said, leaning forward as if trying to reassure her.

"I don't need it."

"You deserve it."

"I don't want it. It's embarrassing."

"But you took a risk to your own life in attempting to save somebody else's and that deserves recognition."

"I'd much rather not Mr Stirling, if that is okay?"

He sat back and put his hands together as if in prayer, drawing them to his lips. "Let's talk about it another time," he said before suddenly changing tack. "Have you been interviewed by the police about the drugs at the party?" he asked.

His question made her jump. "No!" she replied too loudly. "I had nothing to do with any of that."

He smiled as if trying to reassure her. "I'm sure you didn't Amy, you're not that sort of girl, I know. But I'm aware they are interviewing many of the partygoers. I suspect when they find out who supplied the drugs to Jimmy then they'll be able to go after them. It looks like the drugs contributed to the tragedy," he added, shaking his head.

After an awkward silence she said, "Can I go now Mr Stirling; I'm going to be late for my class."

He glanced at his watch. "Oh goodness me, yes of course. We'll speak another time," he said as he stood up. "Well done again on your GCSEs," he added as she left his office. She blew her cheeks out in relief.

CATHERINE

CHAPTER 26

November 2018

Alone in her office, Catherine sat in silence, staring straight ahead, dreamlike. A noise from down the corridor brought her back to reality and as she looked down, she saw she had been scratching the back of her hand, leaving bright red marks. "Damn it," she whispered. Suddenly her desk phone rang. Her pulse raced as she picked up the receiver and slammed it back down. Within seconds it rang again and this time she answered, "Yes?" she said tentatively.

"Ah Catherine, at last!"

"What can I do for you, Sophie?" she replied. Catherine studied the back of her hand. She'd have to buy hand cream on the way home. It looked terrible.

"It's what I can do for you, Professor. We have so much to talk about?"

Still distracted, Catherine replied, "Go on."

"I understand the uni plans to announce early January - so we need to get a lot of things sorted?"

Catherine felt her heckles rising. "Is that a question?" she asked irritably.

"Sorry, is what a question?"

"Doesn't matter."

"Oh, okay. Anyway, when can we meet? The first priority will be planning your media appearances. Have you done this before?"

"Done what?"

"Been on the radio, TV. That sort of thing?"

Catherine leant back in her chair and looked up at the ceiling. Before she had a chance to answer Sophie continued. "We'll give you training anyway? Let's get together in the next day or so. How about tomorrow, ten at our office in Cambridge?"

Catherine sighed again. She'd have to rearrange things but there seemed little choice. "Ten it is."

****

Catherine followed Sophie through the buzzing office. It was such a contrast to the uni environment: cool furniture, no piles of books, and everybody fashionably dressed.

"In here," said Sophie opening a glass door to a conference room. The table which dominated the room was oval, oak and shiny and had a complex looking speaker phone and controls for a huge TV on the far wall. Catherine wondered how much all this 'advice' was costing the uni.

"For conference calls," commented Sophie, seeing her glancing at the screen.

"Yes, I know what they're for." She put her bag on the floor and sat opposite Sophie. "Is anybody else joining?" she asked, noting the table could probably accommodate fifteen, twenty people.

"Nope, just us. In fact given the security required, only one senior manager knows what we are discussing, in addition to me."

"Good," replied Catherine as a young man brought in a tray of coffee and biscuits.

"Okay let's get down to business," began Sophie. "Firstly, what's the latest on timings?"

Do I *have* to do this, wondered Catherine? No choice she thought as she adjusted her position and sat upright. "We're ploughing through the questions we've received. Assuming our answers are satisfactory we would expect publication early to mid-January."

"Is there a deadline to make the January issue?"

"It's weekly."

"Oh great, that's easy then."

"And on-line too."

"Of course."

Catherine took a sip of coffee. Way better than the uni stuff, she thought.

"Okay, here is the proposal?" said Sophie, sliding a sheet of paper across the table. I'll go through it, so that's just for reference?"

Catherine glanced down and then turned the sheet over. Two pages of everything she didn't want to do. She could feel her stomach cramp.

"I'll run through a rough timetable and we can discuss it from there. But we will take care of everything, all the planning, everything. All you'll need to do is turn up and explain to the world what you've discovered. It's so exciting."

Feeling her hand shaking, Catherine carefully placed her coffee cup on the table.

"Are you okay Professor?" asked Sophie.

Catherine took a deep breath. "I'm fine thanks."

Sophie continued. "The uni will draft the press release and we will hone it. It will be translated into over one hundred languages and sent to all the global news agencies the same day as the Nature Journal is published. Let's call that day 1."

"The world will go crazy," said Catherine.

"We will make sure of it," replied Sophie, making Catherine's heart sink.

"You will need to clear your diary for a month at least."

Catherine sighed. "Really?"

"Absolutely. Day two and for the following week at least, you'll be going from one radio and TV station to the next. We will keep it all in the UK but expect to be interviewed dawn to dusk. The morning of day two I'm sure you'll be on breakfast TV and radio and then by the afternoon when the USA wakes up it'll be repeated. We will handle all the requests, schedule your diary and get you to each place on time. There'll be the Asian networks in the morning of day three. There will be requests for interviews on daytime TV and radio; it'll be endless but we'll choose carefully. Also the requests for articles, so I suggest you prepare three versions so you are ready – dead simple, medium and more sciency.

"Sciency?"

"Yes, for the more thoughtful mags. The actual science magazines will extract from your paper I guess, so you'll only have to maybe have a short interview?"

"Where's the toilet?"

"Down the hall on the left."

Catherine clasped the sink with both hands and leant over as she thought she might be sick. She looked at herself in the mirror. How did it come to this? She'd been so happy, her life so in control. And now the most amazing thing she could ever have dreamt of was happening, yet, she couldn't want it less.

"Okay," started Sophie as Catherine sat down. "Week two we'll arrange interviews for you and the VC with the wider media, to promote the uni. Then assume week three you'll be in the USA, 'on tour'. By week four I will have set up meetings with agents and publishers for your book.

"Book?"

"Yes, the demand will be huge and I'm sure we'll have a bidding war. If we don't secure a million pound advance then we'll not be doing our job right. Then over the coming weeks we'll give you media training."

Catherine looked at her watch.

"And we may have to arrange security for your family, just to be on the safe side. You can't be too careful, an escort for the kids to and fro from school, that sort of thing."

Catherine stared at her. "Why?"

"Most celebs need the peace of mind. There are nutters out there and who knows how they may react to what is being claimed."

Catherine clenched her toes, doing her best not to react.

"And we'll manage your social media sites to send out the right messages at the right time. Have I missed anything?" Added Sophie.

"Doesn't sound like it," replied Catherine, making an effort to smile. She hesitated before adding, "Listen, I appreciate it. I don't know what I'd do without your support. It's a world I'm completely unfamiliar with."

"My pleasure," replied Sophie.

Catherine hesitated as she looked at her watch again. "Apologies though, but I must be going." Within minutes she was driving too fast back towards her office.

Catherine spent the afternoon in a daze, sitting at her desk, working on the responses to Nature, but making little progress. Her mind couldn't move on from what faced her. She kept re-reading Sophie's media agenda, eventually screwing it up and throwing it in the bin. By four thirty she was heading to the departmental drinks, determined to be there first to get a much needed pick-me-up.

"You're late!" exclaimed Catherine as she put an arm around Neil's shoulders.

Neil looked at her quizzically. "I'm hardly late, it's only five thirty!"

"You've been missing the fun!" replied Catherine holding out her glass. "You'd better get this re-filled for me."

"Oh, right," replied Neil, taking her glass. "Red or white?"

"Whatever," she called after him.

Just then Lucy appeared at her side. "Ah Lucy," she said a little too loudly, "it's your round!"

"Arrive early, did we Prof?"

"I possibly did!" said Catherine as she walked off to look for Neil and her glass.

"Oy!" she called looking over Stuart's shoulder. "Neil, make it quick; a gal could die of thirst over here!"

"Everything alright?" asked Stuart.

"Couldn't be better. Had a meeting with the PR woman today and we're all set to be global super stars. Now where's that drink?" she said looking round. God she felt dizzy. Another wine should help. For the next half hour, she went from group to group, talking loudly, leaning too close, swaying.

"I'm fine!" she said as Neil helped her into the taxi.

"Put your leg in first," he said trying to steer her in the right direction. "Thank God for that," he whispered as she slumped into the cab.

"Take me home, Jeeves!" She called to the driver.

He leant out of the window and spoke to Neil. "If she's sick in my cab that'll be one hundred quid plus the fare."

"She'll be fine," he replied.

"She'd better be."

The garden path was swirling round, round, round and round as she tried to walk in a straight line. She put her foot in the flower bed and felt the mud squelch. "Oh, whoops! Now, where are my keys?" she said as she leant against the door. She rummaged in her bag again. "Ah! You little fuckers, gotcha," she said and promptly dropped them on the floor. As she bent down to retrieve them John opened the door, whereupon she fell in.

"What the?" he couldn't finish the sentence as Chloe appeared by his side.

"Mummy!"

John helped her up. "Your Mum's fine, she just tripped, go back into the kitchen, I'll be with you in a minute."

Catherine put her arm around John for support. "I'm shit-faced," she whispered.

"Well, who'd have known! You'd better go upstairs. I'll bring you water and pain killers."

"Which way is it?"

"What?"

"Only joking," she said as she kicked off her shoes and grabbed the banister. "I need to go to bed. Ahhh, I think I'm gonna be…"

****

The next morning John left her lying in bed as he readied the girls for school. By five he was back home having collected them from his parents. Catherine's car was in the drive.

"You're home early," he said as they walked in. "What time did you make it into work?"

Catherine was stretched out on the settee reading a magazine. "I didn't go in, too knackered after yesterday."

John tossed his keys into a tray, "I'm not surprised," he said as he turned to leave. After making the girls their tea he came back to join Catherine, who hadn't budged. "Shove over," he said moving her legs.

"If I must."

"What was that all about?"

"What was *what*, all about?"

"You know, last night. Getting lathered. It's not like you."

"Nothing really, just had a bit too much fun. It can happen. No harm done."

For a minute neither said anything. "What's wrong with you?"

Without looking up from her magazine, she replied, "Nothing."

"Yes there is."

She looked up. "John, for god's sake, please, give it a rest, can't you see I'm tired?"

"But what's up with you?"

Catherine dropped the magazine on the floor and stood up. "I'm going upstairs to be with the girls, they won't hassle me." As she got to the door she turned, "Oh and you may want to explain how we have a speeding fine from the M11 the other week. I was at the uni and you were, well, I thought at school. The letter's on the kitchen table."

JOHN

CHAPTER 27

November 2018

John sat in the corner of the staffroom with his laptop on his knees. He was anxious about lying to Catherine over the speeding fine.

"I lent the car to another teacher so she could get to an interview after her car broke down," he'd said.

"Make sure she pays the fine," Catherine had replied as she grabbed her keys and bag before making for the door. He was worried that when she had more time to think, she might not believe his story.

He continued to tap away searching for William, Billy, Bill Ridley. He just couldn't let it go; it was an itch he felt he had to scratch. First he searched Twitter, then LinkedIn, Instagram and finally Facebook. He assumed Billy would be in his late thirties or maybe early forties and hoped still in or around Bristol. There was only one with that name and he clicked on him, scanning across the images, his heart racing. It seemed odd to be looking at this stranger and he wondered for a moment why he was doing it at all. Then he spotted it; born in Harlow and it appeared he lived there now too. God it really could be him. He checked on his birthday; born August 1984. John looked out of the window and watched as a crow mobbed a red kite. His mind drifted as the crow ducked and dived, eventually forcing the kite to accelerate over the treetops and out of sight.

Returning to his screen he clicked on Billy's Facebook friends. His mouth went dry when he spotted her: he wouldn't forget that face in a hurry, so-called D.I. Flanders, or as he could now see her real name, Tina Evans. John slammed his laptop shut, put it aside and stood up.

"You okay, John?" asked a colleague.

It caught him by surprise; he'd been in his own world. He put his arms above his head as if stretching. "Yeah, just needed a few seconds break," he replied. "You know what it's like," he added smiling.

An awkward silence followed, then John sat down and with shaking hands opened his laptop and now clicked on Tina's Facebook page. She was no police officer that was for sure. An infant schoolteacher and into amateur dramatics and she lived in Harlow. It all fitted. He would think what to do about it later. For now, he clicked back to Billy and crawled over his images and page. Works for a mental health charity, FirstStep in Harlow. He pondered what to do, did he really want to pursue the whole thing? But there was a connection wasn't there: between Catherine and Tina, Amy and Jimmy. Surely? Was he really going to track-down Tina, talk to Billy, do what Tina wanted him to do? Perhaps that reporter was right, this is Tina screwing with his mind. Perhaps he should report her to the police for pretending to be an officer. But what was the point and how could he go through with it without Catherine spotting something. He'd nearly been caught out by the girls talking about the phone call from Tina in the car and then there was the speeding fine. John smiled to himself, thinking about what a poor private detective he would make, unable to hide anything. Hopeless. He shut his laptop, having first noted down the charity's phone number: it was lesson time.

CATHERINE

CHAPTER 28

Catherine sat at the kitchen table working. She heard the front door open and Chloe and Ruth chatting to John as they scrambled down the hall.

"Hi Mum!" They both gave her a big hug.

"Hello girls." She pulled them both close.

"You're hurting me," cried Ruth. Catherine released her grip. "I'm making tea today, what will it be? It can be a treat."

"Dad's promised us sausages, we went to the shop," replied Chloe as she took off her coat, leaving it on the floor where she stood.

John appeared in the kitchen doorway. "Hi."

She noticed he hardly made eye contact. "Hi," she replied, looking at her mobile.

John dumped the shopping on the worktop. "Tea's already sorted, but you can cook it if you want." He had bought a newspaper and was looking at the headline as he spoke. Catherine's chair scraped as she stood up and opened the cupboard for the frying pan. John opened the fridge, took out a can of beer and left the room.

Later, after the girls were in bed they sat in the kitchen and ate. "How was your day?" asked John.

"Okay. Yours?"

"Okay."

"Why didn't you go in today?"

"I don't always need to."

"Why is that?"

"Oh, for goodness' sake John, haven't you heard of the internet?"

He slammed down his fork. "Alright, alright!" He sat back and folded his arms as Catherine continued to eat. "You know what I mean."

"I don't really, no. If I want to work at home, I work at home."

"What's up with you?"

"You," replied Catherine. "There's something going on that you're not telling me."

"No there isn't."

"I don't believe the story of the car by the way. Plus you're always on your laptop and shut it when I come in the room."

John bit his lip. "You can speak to her if you want. She'll confirm she borrowed the car."

Catherine couldn't eat, her mouth was dry and her stomach cramped. "It's more than that. You're doing something and hiding stuff."

"I'm not 'up to' anything. What about you? Getting totally blathered the other night. That's not you, is it? What prompted that?"

"What do you mean, 'what prompted that?' You know damn well what prompted it – our lives are going to be transformed in a few weeks and I don't want it!"

"What don't you want? You'll be feted, we'll have all the money we've ever wanted and you'll get any job and funding you want. Oh… and that's apart from a Nobel prize in five, or ten-years' time. I just don't get it."

Catherine pushed back her chair and stood up. "No, you really don't, do you!" She put her hands on her hips as she looked down at him. "All I've wanted is to do my research and raise a family in peace. In private, just us." She briefly looked away, thinking. "I don't want my difficult teenage years dragged up and paraded. I don't want the outside world intruding, spoiling what we have built together. And that's what's going to change."

"Why will it spoil what we have?"

"It just will. It's intrusive. I value our own world." Catherine hesitated, then added. "Right now, I need your support, not your hostility." She could feel the tears coming as she left the room and went upstairs. She threw herself on the bed and sobbed. Her heart ached as she thought of John. Did she deserve him? Catherine pulled the duvet over her and curled up into a ball. She despaired of her past; agonized over the lies she had told. It was bound to all come out with this fame and if she lost him, or her girls, that would be it, she couldn't go on. Perhaps she should tell him? Of course she wouldn't, she thought. Instead, she would do whatever it took to keep her past in the past.

Soon Catherine heard the bedroom door open. Quietly John came in and lay next to her. He put his arm around her and pulled her close and kissed her hair. "Sorry," he whispered, "I didn't mean to upset you." He squeezed her closer, "I love you," he said kissing her cheek. His lips touched her tears and as he moved back, he gently wiped them away.

"I'm sorry too," she replied. "It's all so stressful."

"I want to help."

Catherine thought for a while then turned over and lay on her back, her hands behind her head. "You can't really. It's moving fast and there's no stopping it." She turned back to him, their faces inches apart. "You must promise me something though."

John smiled, "Of course, anything."

"Whatever happens, you must still love me." She started to cry as the words came out.

"Hey, hey, stop it - I'll always love you. What are you talking about?"

"Just promise me. Say it to me."

"I promise I'll always love you."

"Whatever happens?"

"Whatever happens."

CATHERINE

CHAPTER 29

December 2018

It was late evening, 23rd December and she'd spent the morning with Sophie and the VC then the remainder of the day working in her office. She rested her elbows on her desk and rubbed her temples. At that moment her phone pinged; a text from John: *planning to be home this xmas?* The anger welled up and she instinctively texted back. *I'm trying my best here. Give me a break.* She threw the phone back on the desk and leant back in her chair. Perhaps she should get home? Damn it, of course she should. Suddenly she was jolted from her thoughts by her mobile ringing. "Now what?" She said as she looked at the screen. A London number she didn't recognise. She hesitated, wondering whether to answer.

"Professor Holmes," she said.

"Glad I caught you Professor; my name is Alison Wright and I'm the CEO of the company that owns the Nature Journal."

Catherine's heart raced. "Good evening." Her mouth was dry and she reached for her water.

"I have some news and wanted to tell you personally prior to sending you the email. But first, may I ask, are you sitting down?"

JOHN

CHAPTER 30

Earlier that day, John had taken the girls to his parents to get a break and some peace at home. He'd hardly seen Catherine over the past few weeks and it annoyed him. After the 'will you always love me' conversation, he'd decided not to contact Billy or make any further investigations. He was frightened of where it may lead. But then two weeks ago, he had waited one evening for Catherine to return from work, the girls desperate to decorate the tree. They had always done it together, but by seven and no sign of her he'd given in to the twins and the three of them had decorated it without her. They'd had a blazing row when she got home. Catherine had completely forgotten. That night he'd decided at some point he would contact Billy after all.

Back home at ten he made coffee, sat at the kitchen table and opened his laptop. He viewed the profile of Billy and Tina once again, pondering what to do. He just couldn't leave it alone. If Catherine had been more reasonable, he may not have bothered, he thought. But he needed to know what he didn't understand. He went into the hall and dug out the piece of paper from his coat pocket with the charity FirstStep number and sat back at the kitchen table, playing with the small square of paper; turning it around between his fingers, thinking.

"FirstStep, how may I help?"

"May I speak with William Ridley please."

"Who is it calling?"

"My name is John Holmes."

"Hold on please." He heard the muffled lady's voice call across an office. "Billy are you in?" He couldn't hear the reply, then she said, "Hold on I'll transfer you."

"Hello, how can I help?"

Anxiously he replied, "My name's John Holmes and I'm sorry to bother you. I was wondering, am I right in thinking you've a sister called Amy?" But he didn't get the chance to continue.

"Wo, wo hold on there, tell me who you are again."

"Of course." John felt he'd rushed in too fast and had better take it step by step. "It's a bit of a long story, have you got a few minutes?"

"Listen, I've not heard from her in over twenty years and I never want to. So firstly why are you asking about her?"

"It going to sound odd, but completely out of the blue I was contacted by a woman who turns out to be Tina Evans, who I think you know. I have no idea why she approached me. I live in Cambridge with my wife and kids and have no connection with Harlow or this woman Tina or your sister. I subsequently found out about the accident involving Jimmy Evans, Tina's brother, and I think I need to know more about Amy."

"Not sure I followed all that, but why?"

"Again, it's going to sound odd but Tina seemed to suggest there was some connection between my wife and her, or Amy, or something like that. It's all rather odd and to be honest I feel a bit daft asking you about it."

John could only hear him breathing at the other end while he waited for a response.

"How did you find me?"

"I talked to a reporter who covered the accident in the local paper, and he remembered Amy had a brother and that led me to you."

"Listen, John, isn't it? This is somewhere I really don't want to revisit. It's taken me years to get myself back together again."

"I'm sorry, I didn't mean to…"

"No, it's not your fault. I would also avoid Tina Evans, she's not so nice."

"I did hear that."

There was a moment's silence. "What's your wife's name?"

"Catherine. Holmes."

"Never heard of her. How old is she?"

"Forty two"

"Birthday?"

"Fourth of September."

A brief silence then, "Year?"

"As I said she's forty two, so nineteen seventy six."

The phone went silent. After what seemed like an age John said, "Hello?"

"I'm still here. I'm thinking. What does she do for a living?"

"Astro physics professor at Cambridge."

There was another silence before he heard a woman's voice in the background whispering, "are you alright?" He could just make out a muffled voice, "Not sure." Billy must have had his hand over the receiver. He heard the woman's voice again. "Sit down, Billy. Shall I take over?"

"You there?" asked John.

"Wait a minute," replied Billy.

John thought he detected a tremor in Billy's voice. "Listen, I don't mean to…"

"Does she have a birthmark on her neck?" interrupted Billy, his voice suddenly loud.

The hairs on the back of John's neck stood up on end. "Yes… she does."

The phone went dead.

CATHERINE
CHAPTER 31

Catherine laughed, nervously. "Yes, I am sitting down."

Alison Wright from Nature Journal continued. "Good. I'm delighted to inform you that all the peer reviewers were satisfied with your answers, so the great news is that the publication date will be Monday, 7th January 2019 with the digital version published at six o'clock GMT that morning."

"Alison, that's wonderful," replied Catherine. "I'll let the team and the Vice Chancellor know immediately."

There was a brief silence before Alison continued. "Given the significance of the news, I assume you are prepared?"

Catherine sighed. "I think so. The uni has a PR company so we will be as ready as we can be."

"I guess you understand what will be unleashed. There will be nobody more in demand than you. You're going down in the history books and you'll be one of the most recognisable people on the planet… this planet I mean."

Catherine managed a brief smile to herself. "I know, Alison. It's not without its downside."

Soon they finished the conversation and Catherine flicked off her desk light and stepped out into the cold night, the sky lit only by the orange glow of streetlights in the distance. As her eyes adjusted to the darkness she looked up at the stars and wondered if beings were looking at earth?

Perhaps contemplating what was living on this small blue dot of a planet orbiting an average star four light years away. What were they like? Did they kill and fight and love and worry and laugh and believe in deities? She shivered as she walked to the car.

With the engine running and the warmth coming through, she texted Lucy, Neil, Stuart and the VC. *It's happening. Heard from Nature Journal. We've done it. 7th January. Coordinate by phone tomorrow -I'm done!* Then she texted John. *Sorry! On my way now. It's all go for the 7th! I'll buy champers on the way home. luvs ya! C xx*

"I'm sorry," she said as she bounced into the sitting room holding the champagne. John was slouched on the settee watching TV. He quickly sat upright and she had the impression he'd been asleep.

"It's okay, you're here now." He stood up and gave her a hug. "Well done. You're amazing and sorry I was grouchy earlier. This news trumps everything."

Catherine went to the kitchen for the glasses and John followed. "How was your day?" she asked as she poured the sparkling liquid. It fizzed to the top and over the side. "Whoops, out of practise!"

"You'll be getting lots more practise over the coming weeks," he said as he picked up his glass.

"*We* will you mean."

"My day?" began John. "Not as exciting as yours! The girls were at my parents, they got back around five."

"What have you been doing? Apart from getting some peace and quiet."

"Just that," he lied. "That's what I needed really."

"Cheers," she said clinking her glass against his. She kicked off her shoes and let them fly across the kitchen. "We're going to enjoy this Christmas, make the most of it before the crazy stuff starts." She took another gulp and topped up her glass, spilling more on the table.

"I'm so looking forward to Christmas," he said. "I assume you're not working tomorrow."

"I'm not. I'm done. But I'm out in the morning."

"Where?"

"Shopping."

"Really? You're nutty, it'll be crazy. We've got everything."

"Wait and see. I'm getting something for myself. Now, pass me that bottle."

****

Catherine was heading home by ten thirty in the morning. She parked around the corner from the house and looked in the mirror, feeling her hair as she did so. In the years since she first met John, she'd let her appearance slip. It had suddenly dawned on her she needed to sort her appearance. Surely that would help.

"Oh my god!" exclaimed John as she walked into the kitchen. "What the?!"

"Mummy!" cried Chloe. Ruth ran into the room to see what the fuss was about and stopped still, staring at her mother, not saying a word.

Catherine swivelled round in a twirl. "Well, what do you think?"

"It's quite the transformation!" John moved closer as if peering at something he didn't understand. "It's… well," he smiled. "Like I remember you when we first met! The blond pixie cut!"

"Gorgeous, you mean," replied Catherine.

"Yes. I love it!" he said, as he touched her hair. "Although, it'll take a bit of getting used to. I… wasn't expecting it. You didn't say."

Catherine smiled. "I haven't finished yet," she said pulling a case out of her handbag. "How about these," she added, putting on a pair of glasses. "I've got three pairs, each in different coloured frames."

"You're full of surprises. Very hot!" He was quiet for a moment then added, "I didn't know you needed them."

"Oh well, you do now - distance seeing, so I'll wear these most of the time although I may need a pair for reading before long." Catherine removed them and popped them back in the case. She'd kept quiet about the fact they weren't lenses at all, but simply glass.

"It really does take me back," added John.

"Takes me back too," she replied. "Now let Christmas begin!"

AMY

CHAPTER 32

November 1993

She couldn't decide if she should look smart or casual for the inquest. In the end she grabbed her jeans, threw them on the bed and picked out a T shirt and jumper from a drawer. That'll do, she thought.

As she was about to enter the kitchen, she heard Dad come through the back door. "Hi," he said to Mum. Amy hesitated, her hand on the handle, listening.

"How's Amy?" he asked.

"Generally, or about giving evidence?"

"Both," replied Dad.

"Withdrawn as usual. Hardly goes out, except when she's meeting that friend of hers, Catherine. Otherwise, she's studying up in her room. No boyfriend yet. Sometimes I hear her talking to herself when I go past her room. But that's Amy, in her own world."

"Poor girl. What about giving evidence?"

"God knows. She's competent, but how she actually feels…"

"You think there's more to it… something she's not saying, don't you."

"I don't want to talk about it," replied Mum.

Amy gently let go of the handle and steadied her breathing, keeping as silent as she could.

"I'm more worried about Billy, if you must know," added Mum, "I'm at the end of my tether with him."

"What now?"

She heard chairs scrape as they sat down. "You know he's been a nightmare since the Jimmy accident. It's as if he was there, not Amy."

"Don't forget I had him over the summer: he wasn't easy when we were in Bristol with Janice."

"Ha! Now he's uncommunicative, moody, uncooperative and then yesterday we got this." The room went silent, and Amy guessed Dad was reading.

"Suspended?" he said. "For what?"

"It says, if you keep reading! Not doing his homework, rude to teachers and now he's been in a fight. They want a meeting before deciding."

"When?"

"Soon. Next week. I don't know!" Her voice faded … "I've got to call." There was another silence, before Mum said, "Perhaps he should live with you for a while." Amy remained motionless. There was a long pause and she wondered if they had heard her. She did her best to breathe as slowly as she could.

"About that…," said Dad.

"About what?"

"Look, I wasn't going to tell you today, of all days, what with the inquest, but in the new year, Janice and I will be moving in together." Before he could continue Mum interrupted, "but she's in Bristol!"

"Yes. I'm going to live with her. I start a new job in January at a private school just outside."

"What?! You didn't tell me!"

"I was about to. I only just heard I got the job this week."

"I didn't know you were applying!"

"Well guess what, we have separate lives!"

"Fuck you!"

"Come on, let's not argue," said Dad. "There's another thing, while we are being open."

"What?"

"I've made enquiries and Billy can attend the private school for a reduced fee. And Janice is fine having him live with us…. despite his behaviour when he stayed over the summer."

"You're going to take him away!?"

"Come on, we know it would do him good to be at an excellent school… just look at this letter…"

Amy heard a door slam as her mother went out into the garden.

"And he's not exactly flourishing living here, is he!" Dad yelled.

Amy gently turned around and tiptoed upstairs. Billy was a pain these days and nothing had been the same since Jimmy. But she had to keep an eye on him: stop him from speaking what was on his mind. How could she do that if she never saw him? And she loved him. "Please no, no, no. Don't leave me here Dad, please no. And don't take Billy, please," she whispered.

****

"I want to thank everybody for attending this morning," began the coroner. The courtroom was packed and stuffy, the atmosphere punctuated by wafts of freezing air as people came and went.

Amy had barely been able to stop herself shaking since she stood down from giving evidence. The coroner had been gentle and had smiled at her, encouraging her and at one point asking her to speak louder. Just as she thought she had the shaking under control another spasm seared through her body. The whole Evans family had glared at her while she had given her account of what happened on that fateful afternoon. Now Tina was staring at her, rather than the coroner. Amy tried as hard as she could, not to look in her direction, but she could feel her stare as if it were a laser beam - as straight as a die – burning her body from across the room. It gave her the creeps.

The coroner continued. *"To be clear, we do not assign blame in a coroner's court, and it is not my role to determine any issues of civil or criminal liability. The first and over-riding duty is to inquire how the deceased, in this case, James Declan Evans of Globe House, Harlow, came by his death."* She looked around the room as if checking all were listening. *"The autopsy shows the medical cause of death was by trauma to the head and neck consistent with,"* at this point she turned to briefly look at Amy and then back to her notes, *"with the fall from a tree in Burnt Oak Woods, from a hight of approximately twenty-three feet. The forensic examination shows impact occurred on at least three branches prior to the impact on the ground."*

Amy took a few deep breaths, attempting to calm herself and hoping upon hoping she wasn't going to throw-up there and then in the court room.

"This occurred at approximately two thirty on the afternoon of Sunday 25th July 1993. Forensic analysis confirmed the branch on which Mr James Evans stood, snapped, causing the fall."

Mrs Evans, who had sat motionless between her two children throughout the hearing, burst into tears, putting her hands to her face. The coroner hesitated and looked in the direction of a court official, who then went over to Mrs Evans and leant forward and whispered to her. Amy saw Mrs Evans shake her head. The coroner hesitated, while Mrs Evans blew her nose and wiped her eyes. Amy felt sick to her core. How had it all come to this? It wasn't only Jimmy's life that was finished, it was hers too. How could she go on after what had happened?

"I accept the forensic evidence, which is corroborated by the eyewitness, whose evidence I also accept. The witness stated Mr Evans began to jump up and down and walk further out on the branch." Again, she looked around the court before continuing. *"There is no evidence that this was an act of suicide, about which the law requires me to be satisfied beyond reasonable doubt. The toxicology report shows that Mr Evans had significant levels of the class A hallucinatory drug, lysergic acid diethylamide, commonly known as LSD. Given the indicated levels within his system, one can reasonably conclude he would not be able to make clear judgements as to his safety."* She hesitated. *"On these grounds, I am unable to record accidental death."*

There was a loud gasp from the direction of the Evans family. Was it Tina? Mrs Evans? Amy couldn't tell and dare not look over. Dad put his arm around her shoulder and pulled her close. It was the first sign of affection: her mother had sat rigid throughout.

"There is no evidence the deceased took the drugs involuntarily." She looked up again as if wanting the point to sink in. *"And therefore, the circumstances leading up to the death were not wholly a result of misfortune. The manner of death, the way by which the death was caused, is therefore by misadventure. This will be the recorded verdict. It is for the police and criminal justice system to establish how Mr Evans came into possession of these illegal drugs."*

Amy walked between her mother and father as they hurriedly left the court. She'd anticipated there would be journalists so pulled her baseball cap down to better hide her face. A group of journalists snapped away, but none approached and seemed more interested in waiting for the Evans' family who were yet to appear. Amy and her mother waited further down the road on the other side while Dad got the car.

"It's behind you now," said Mum, stroking Amy's arm.

Amy looked at her mother, incredulous. She has no idea, she thought. "Maybe."

"Why wouldn't it be?"

She couldn't possibly say how Tina had got in with her friends, including Rachel and Tamsin who hadn't returned calls or suggested meeting up since the day of the exam results. She knew why. They had been poisoned against her by Tina. Most of the sixth form had gone to the memorial service where Tina had spread rumours about her. She was evil. She felt isolated at school; everyone was cool toward her; agreeing they must 'go out sometime', but never actually doing it. Countless times she knew she'd missed nights out. The pain of hearing them talk at school about the fun they'd had over the weekend. It was unbearable. And as for a boyfriend - no chance. She had a neon sign above her head: 'could be dangerous', or maybe 'damaged goods'.

"I guess it is," replied Amy, just to kill the discussion. "Over, I mean."

"Look at that!" said Mum, pointing back toward the courtroom entrance. "What are the police doing?" Amy could see a police car parked right outside and three police officers standing at the bottom of the steps as the Evans family came down. "Let's go and see," said Mum.

"No!" But her mother was already striding back towards the court. Amy stayed put and despite craning her neck and standing on tiptoe couldn't see what was happening given the noisy throng of people surrounding the Evans's. A few minutes later the police car moved off with the whole Evans' family inside. As the car passed by, Tina, who was slumped in the back, suddenly turned and glared out of the window at Amy. It raised the hairs on the back of her neck. Her mother came marching back, arriving just as her father pulled up in the car. "Wow – Tina's been arrested, charged with supplying class A drugs and for the manslaughter of Jimmy!"

"Good!" said Amy as she opened the car door, "no less than she deserves." But that wasn't entirely how she felt. Sitting in the back of the car, the guilt began to creep into her head. What if Tina took the entire blame for Jimmy's death? Could she live with herself?

When she got home, she lay on the bed. On the one hand her mother was partly right, maybe she could move on, especially if Tina was out of the way. On the other hand, how would she feel if Tina was convicted? Riddled with even more guilt? And, she thought, how would the Evans family react? Wouldn't they come after her even more strongly? Momentarily she glanced up from her textbook with her pen in her mouth, tapping her teeth. I must ask Catherine what she thinks. At least her friends and all those around her would soon know she wasn't to blame for what happened; it had been Tina.

****

"Have you seen this?" asked Mum tossing the local newspaper across the table toward her, "seems like Tina has gotten off." Amy's heart skipped a beat. Tina had initially been released on bail the day after her arrest and hadn't wasted any time in sending malicious notes to her every few days. She read the brief article. "They've dropped all charges."

"Yes, and I heard from someone at work that the charges were never going to stick, and the police had to drop everything and release her."

Amy felt a tightness in her chest. "How come?"

"According to this lady who knows the family, Tina had been really worried by Jimmy's drug taking – to the extent she'd taken him to a clinic to seek help. Without the parents knowing, or so the story goes. The visit is in the clinic's records so she would hardly do that and at the same time supply him with drugs. Plus, the police haven't found anyone who claims to have seen her supply him. Or supply anybody for that matter. On that basis the police had to drop the charges."

"Have they arrested anyone else?"

"Apparently not. You were at the party and it's like nobody saw anything or noticed anybody taking or dealing drugs. You included. You all closed ranks."

"I saw dope but not hard drugs. I had no idea. But I'm sure if Tina had seen someone supplying Jimmy that night or the following day, she would have ratted on them by now, wouldn't she?"

"Who knows? It may have been the older brother, then what?"

Or, more likely his friend, thought Amy. And now, she knew her persecution would get worse.

Billy came into the room and Mum attempted to wipe the ketchup away from around his mouth. "What a mess." She looked up at Amy, "I'll be late home from work today. Can you get Billy's tea?"

"Whatever," Amy called as she closed the door behind her. It would give her the opportunity to speak with him.

Back home after school, Amy made Billy's tea. "Here you go little man," she said as she poured the beans onto the toast, spooning more from the pan to cover his plate. Amy sat down at the table, and they began to eat in silence.

"Did you know that Jimmy's sister is no longer being investigated by the police?" began Amy.

"Didn't know she was. What for?"

"Being involved in his death of course. Supplying drugs that made him climb that tree."

"Oh."

"You know what that means now of course?"

"No. What?"

"The police will want to know if anybody knows more. And if they find out somebody did know more and hasn't come forward already, after all this time, then they'll be in a lot of trouble for not saying something earlier."

"Please don't tell them Ammy, please!"

Amy leant across the table and touched his arm. "Billy, we have our secret, and nobody will ever know - I promise."

CATHERINE

CHAPTER 33

28th December 2018

"Sophie's coming to the house, so at least I'll be here," Catherine protested.

"I thought you weren't working between Christmas and New Year?"

"Really? With what's about to happen? John, she'll only be here for an hour."

"Alright, I guess so."

"You'll hate her, by the way. But between the two of you, you'll be running my life!"

"I'll keep out the way: take the girls to Mum's."

Five minutes before Sophie arrived, John and the two girls had tumbled out of the door each laden with all those bits and pieces to take to the grandparents, then John returning twice for things he'd forgotten. "For goodness' sake," she heard him mumble as he closed the front door behind him.

It was the first time Catherine had seen Sophie dressed informally and she looked even younger in jeans and a baggy jumper.

"We need to finalise arrangements prior to the 7th?" she began.

"Go on," replied Catherine tentatively.

"Firstly, what social media accounts do you have?"

"Only LinkedIn, no Facebook, Twitter or Instagram."

"That makes things easier," began Sophie. "No unwanted posts to delete. We will create a Twitter account and manage it on your behalf."

"Whoa, before you continue, I'm not having any social media accounts, managed by me or you. Just not happening."

"But…"

"Sophie, sorry no. You're not going to convince me, so let's move on."

Sophie shifted in her chair. "Understood."

"I don't mean to be awkward, sorry," added Catherine.

"No, it's fine." But Catherine could see her blushing, probably with anger. Sophie turned over a sheet of paper and crossed through some wording. As Catherine glanced at the paper, she could see what looked like a long list.

"Now I see you don't have a Wikipedia page, so we'll create that for you. I've got all your educational details and positions from the uni, but I need help with the section, 'early life.'"

"Sophie, I need to tell you one thing and that is, my private life will be staying private, and I'll be looking to you, as my PR agent, to help me with that. So, the entire focus will be about the discovery, not me. Please, nothing about my early life, or about my current life come to think of it."

Sophie frowned.

"I'm sorry, it's important to me," added Catherine.

"Yes, I can see that. You know it is going to be difficult though?"

Catherine sighed. "Yes. We'll have to do our best."

"Okay, we'll try." She took a sip of coffee. "What about phones, how many?"

"One."

"Right. We'll issue you with a new one and you'll have to only let trusted people know your new number. Destroy the old sim card."

"Really? What do I do about the WhatsApp groups I'm in? Like those for school arrangements and so on?"

"Good point. You simply decide who gets your new number. You'll need to get this sorted prior to the seventh. I've got your new phone in the car so you can start now."

"I'm not going to enjoy this one bit."

Sophie smiled. "It's not easy being a celeb! But hey, we'll look after you?"

Catherine didn't know what to say and felt her heart racing.

"Are you okay, professor?"

"Yes, fine. Can you see your own way out?"

Sophie stood up. "If you're sure?"

Catherine nodded, hardly able to swallow, let alone speak, and she quickly realised she couldn't move. She managed a brief smile as Sophie left and as she heard the front door close, she felt nauseous, fell forward, kneeling on all fours. Catherine gasped as she rested herself up on her elbows. The next thing she knew, John was standing over her and shouting at the children to go and play upstairs!"

She vaguely remembered the paramedics arriving and more clearly the ambulance. She certainly remembered lying on a trolley in A&E, feeling the cold sweat under her clothes. John had taken the children back to his parents' before driving to the hospital. Now they sat with the doctor.

"Mrs Holmes, I'm pleased to say there's absolutely nothing physically wrong with you."

John put his hand across and held hers tightly.

Catherine shifted in her chair. "Was it a panic attack?"

The doctor looked directly at her over her glasses. "Precisely. Sounds like it was a big one. Have you had them before?"

"May… be. I'm not sure."

"So you think you have."

"Not for a long time."

"Okay. What do you think may have triggered it this time?"

"Pressure of work, most likely."

"I can vouch for that," added John.

The doctor tapped the desk with her pencil. "Are there things you can do about it?"

Catherine looked at John and then back at the doctor and laughed. "I'm not so sure! The pressure is more likely to *increase*."

"What's your profession?"

"I'm an astrophysicist, a professor here in Cambridge. Normally you'd not think that to be a high-pressure job, but circumstances have arisen which changed things." She thought for a moment. "It's not my boss, or the volume of work. It's… things."

"Okay. Listen, I'm not able to solve this here for you, it's not my area, but you will need to seek help from the right professional if you want to control it. And you'll need to take a hard look at what you do and the precise underlying cause."

Catherine bit her lip and nodded.

"Because one issue is that the fear of it happening again can cause it to happen."

Catherine nodded again and John gave her hand another squeeze. They sat in silence on the way home, neither able to suggest a solution. In the end John said, "I'll just need to take better care of you."

She smiled and touched his arm. "You do already. I'll be fine. I feel better for getting that out of my system. It's as if it had been building up and now it's done, I feel more in control."

"Will it last, is the question. Especially with what's about to hit you."

Catherine thought for a moment. "Let's see," she replied. "Let's see."

CATHERINE

CHAPTER 34

7th January 2019

Catherine sat up in bed, "What the hell?"

John turned over, "What's that noise?"

"No idea," said Catherine as she slipped out of bed. "Feels like I've only just got to sleep."

She glanced at the clock – 4:30am. Gingerly she opened the curtains and stared out into the night. "Oh bloody hell," she exclaimed as she turned to John who was struggling to put on his dressing gown in the pitch dark. "It's begun, look," she said, pointing through a gap in the curtains. John leant over her shoulder.

"Christ."

Two large white vans with satellite dishes had parked in the road outside their house. A group of men and women were leaning against one of the vans smoking and chatting.

"What does it say on the van?" asked John.

"One says CNN and the other BBC."

"No need for your glasses," quipped John. "I'll make some tea. Keep the curtains closed," he added as he left the room.

Catherine sat on the bed and switched on her phone.

"You okay?" asked John as he returned with the tea, "you look dazed."

Catherine threw her phone across the duvet. "Take a look at that."

He studied the screen. "Christ, eighty seven messages? What, since we went to bed?"

"Yup," replied Catherine, covering her legs with the duvet.

"And is that your new phone?"

"'fraid so." Catherine fell silent then suddenly leapt up. "Right world, I'm as ready as I can be for whatever the day may bring," she announced as she clicked on Sophie's number.

John stretched and yawned. "As soon as the girls wake, I'll tell them their mother is famous." Then he came up behind Catherine and put his arms around her waist. "Shall I serve you your tea, madam, or will your butler be doing that?"

She dug him in the ribs then turned and they kissed. "Hope you didn't leave a crack in the curtain or we'll already have been papped!!"

"Stop it!" exclaimed Catherine. "They can't be that interested." She turned on the radio but heard nothing while she dressed. She picked out a new suit she had purchased for this day then sat at her dressing table listening to classical music until it was interrupted by the five o'clock news. She slowly put down her lipstick as she heard with horror her name. It had really begun. Was this the beginning of the end for the life she had built? Her legs began to shake and she could feel the dizziness creep into her head. "I must keep calm," she whispered as she took deep breaths. God, what happens if I panic during a TV interview? She paced the room, feeling trapped in the world that was being created for her: one she never wanted. One from which she saw no escape. She sat on the edge of the bed with her head in her hands trying to control her body.

****

It was just after seven when Catherine stepped out of her front door, with the family hidden away in the kitchen and the girls wondering what on earth was going on. The neighbours were either looking through their curtains or standing on their steps trying to catch a glimpse. There was no way she was going to make it to the taxi Sophie had sent, without saying something to the reporters and camera crews as they gathered around, blocking her path.

>   *"Have you made contact with them?"*
>
>   *"Are they dangerous?"*
>
>   *"Do they know we are here?"*
>
>   *"What do they look like?"*

Momentarily she wondered if she should just push through the scrum as if she were a harassed celebrity. But the type of questions forced her to stop. "Thank you and good morning! The key point is that we have found CFCs in this planet's atmosphere and these cannot occur naturally: I mean, they are only man-made, not produced in nature. We have no explanation as to how they could be in this planet's atmosphere other than they have been produced by an industrialised society."

"Have you sent them a message?"

"Have they already visited earth?"

"How long have you known?"

"Is the government aware?"

Catherine kept her composure. "Thank you all, I don't have any more to add at this point but I'm heading to the university now and we'll be making further statements shortly."

Sophie held open the taxi door as she almost dived in the car, throwing her overnight bag on the seat. "Phew!"

"Well done!" exclaimed Sophie. "All that media training is paying off?"

"They're crazy, but it'll die down as soon as they realise we know pretty much nothing."

Sophie turned to her, raising an eyebrow. "Yeah, right."

Catherine closed her eyes, relieved that no one had asked anything about her. But why would they at this stage? "For the time-being it's going to be full-on little green men," she said.

Sophie ignored her comment. "You have five television interviews this morning, all in the room we've prepared at the uni. One will include Neil and Lucy, one with the VC to promote the uni and three just you. At one o'clock there's a lunch at the uni with the department and you'll give a quick speech as we discussed, then at two, a car will take you to London for a round of more studio interviews and prep for the six o'clock news. That'll be a two minute live piece to add to their overall report."

"I've seen the schedule, you don't need to remind me," replied Catherine. Sophie took no notice and continued. "Tonight, you and the VC have a dinner in London with some members of the cabinet, not sure if the PM will be there."

"Yeah, that was a bit of a surprise. What do they want?"

"They need to know more behind the story so as to appear competent when questioned by the press." Sophie continued. "Then tomorrow it's radio stations, interviews, and phone-ins. We'll get you home tomorrow night before your travels start."

Catherine stared at the people hurrying to their destinations, bent against the biting wind. She wondered if they had heard the news that we may not be alone in the universe? Or maybe they hadn't checked and their worlds were yet to change. There would now always be a day before and a day after. Professor Norman had been quite adamant, the CFC gases they had detected could only be produced by intelligent life.

****

Catherine and the VC sat in silence in the back of a blacked-out Range Rover as it whisked them from The Dorchester Hotel to the Houses of Parliament. Neither could quite believe what was happening. As the car slowed by a side entrance, Catherine jumped as two lenses clunked against the glass and cameras flashed. She held up her arm to shield their view. Thank God she had done something about her appearance before all this kicked off, she thought. But the risk of being recognised was still there. Catherine turned to the VC. "How did they even know it was us?" she asked.

"No idea," replied the VC, "and it's not a case of 'us', it's more a case of you."

"I guess so," replied Catherine. She briefly thought of home and how John would be clearing up at this moment after the girls' tea and soon running their bath. She wished she could be there, back in a simpler life.

"You okay?" asked the VC looking at Catherine.

She turned and smiled. "Sort of. I feel as if we've been catapulted into a different world. It's unreal." She looked out of the window. How did it change so fast? "Please God," she whispered.

Security took no time and soon they were ushered into a private room with half the cabinet and the PM. After drinks, chit chat and the first course arriving, the PM got straight down to it.

"Tell me, Professor. What's your view? Because I've read a synopsis of your paper and you're very cautious, understandably. But let's hear it straight."

"It's more likely than not we have found we are not alone. It's toned down in the paper, you are right, for good scientific reasons, but if I were a betting woman, which I'm not, then I'd say yes, something's out there."

There was chatter around the table until the PM held up her hand and it fell quiet.

"How advanced?"

"We have no idea and we are a long way from knowing." Catherine hesitated to enjoy the moment of holding court with the most powerful people in the land. "But these CFCs can remain in an atmosphere for up to a few hundred thousand years. Here on earth, we've had them for what, less than one hundred years. So that could be an indicator. On balance they have probably been around much longer than humans on earth, thousands or maybe tens of thousands of years longer. So yes, they are probably more advanced although we have no idea about the environment in which they live, so it's a tough one to answer."

The PM put her hands behind her head and leant back. "Fascinating."

Lined up on a row of chairs, shoved against the wall, were what Catherine assumed to be half a dozen private secretaries or civil servants. They hadn't been introduced and hadn't been invited to eat. Suddenly one of them piped up. Catherine turned to look at her. She was not unlike Sophie: young, smart and confident.

"A good time to be burying the Brexit issues," she said. Some around the table stared blankly, others smiled and one went, "Hmph."

The Health Secretary added, "This announcement has completely buried our good news on the ten-year NHS plan."

Catherine couldn't resist it, "I'll let them know."

"Who?" he asked.

The PM interrupted, "Get a grip man, the Prof's joking, she means the aliens."

"Oh, right, very droll."

The PM continued. "Back to the main subject. If they are in any way more advanced then why haven't we heard from them already?"

"Good question and we can only speculate." Catherine took a sip of wine, her food untouched. "For a start they may have tried and we haven't noticed. Or perhaps they investigated our planet a while ago and only detected plants or primitive life forms and lost interest. Or they may not know we are here; the universe is a big place. Or they may have no interest in looking beyond their home. Perhaps they are so advanced that communicating with other life forms is not interesting to them." Catherine glanced around the room, so she wasn't just talking to the PM. "A super advanced life-form may have a completely different environment. I don't' know, maybe some sort of matrix perhaps, where every being is partly life as we know it, partly computerised and they exist in a beautiful virtual world. In those circumstances there is no need to go off looking for trouble or finding new things."

"Sounds like a film," said the PM, "continue."

"One thing to consider is that they may not exist now and we are just detecting a fossil, an echo of a former civilisation. There is a theory that states the reason we've never been contacted, is that technologically advanced civilisations have the power to, and ultimately do, destroy themselves. So, by the time they can travel interstellar distances, they've taken themselves back to the cave."

There was a moment while this sank in. "I can see that happening to humankind, can't you?" commented a minister. "So do you think we should make contact?" he added. Catherine recognised him as the Minister for Universities, Science, Research and Innovation – the VC had introduced him to her at an event in Cambridge a few months ago.

"That is something we, or humankind, are going to have to think long and hard about," Catherine replied.

"And who makes that decision?" he asked.

"I really don't know," replied Catherine.

"I think we'll need the science community involved," added the PM. "If all of humanity could be affected by humans making contact, then shouldn't it be an all-humankind decision?"

"Maybe," added Catherine. "There's an astronomer at the SETI Institute, that is, the search for extra-terrestrial intelligence, who argued for laws or treaties or some global agreement on what should be done in the event we detect life. He says without such an agreed way forward it is reckless."

"The aliens really might not be friendly," added the VC.

The PM seemed to ignore her comment and continued, "I cannot imagine how a global approach could be agreed." She thought for a moment, then added, "Maybe through the United Nations?" She hesitated then said, "And didn't the late Stephen Hawking say something about aliens?"

"He did," replied Catherine. "He thought it very unwise to reach out."

"We could find any rogue state or group sending whatever messages they wanted, couldn't we?" asked a minister.

"Absolutely, it's not difficult," replied Catherine. "We also have to remember we've been sending messages into deep space for decades. In 2008 NASA sent the Beatles song, 'Across the Universe' toward the North Star. That star is 430 light years away so the message hasn't arrived yet but it will in time. Not only that, prior to our TV and radios turning digital, our TV and radio programmes leaked out into space. So, aliens will be watching Big Brother, Are You Being Served? and Friends!"

The ministers laughed, one commenting, "that'll keep them away!"

Catherine wondered if she'd been talking too much, fuelled by the willingness of the audience to listen, plus her third glass of wine. The PM sat back, not appearing amused by the jollity.

"Catherine," she began, "could we send a spacecraft?"

Catherine looked across at her. "We could, but it would take a very long time to arrive. Although the planet is orbiting the nearest star to our own, the sun, Proxima Centauri e is nevertheless 4 light years away. This is not far in interstellar terms but it's huge in human space-travel terms. Even sending a signal, which travels at the speed of light, would take four years to reach them. Assuming they send a reply, that would take another four years to reach *us*, so even signals would make for a painfully slow conversation. But sending a spacecraft is considerably slower than that. Human technology is such that interstellar travel is simply not practical. Spacecraft are okay for reaching the moon or our planets within our solar system but going further afield – not really. Maybe within one hundred years we could have developed technology enabling travel at say, ten percent the speed of light. So in that case it would take a craft around forty years to get to the planet. Not so bad, I guess. But for now, it's not an option."

It was late by the time they left and made their way back to the hotel. As they walked in they spotted Sophie standing in the reception looking pensive. "How did it go?" she asked. "I couldn't wait until tomorrow to find out."

"We'll tell you but let's go to the bar," suggested the VC.

"It went well," began Catherine, "they were completely engaged, seemed to understand and were basically wrestling with what to do and how to control the narrative."

"Vice Chancellor?" asked Sophie.

"Actually, not so good from my side."

"Really?" asked Catherine.

"Yes really." The VC took a slug of her beer. "They were a bit frosty with me during the meeting. Then at the end, an aid took me aside and said the PM was disappointed the government hadn't been informed in advance, so they could prepare a response. The message was 'don't let that happen again.'"

"We missed that one," replied Sophie, "I should have thought of that, it's my fault."

"Not at all, it's mine," replied the VC. She downed her beer, slammed the glass on the table and waved to the waiter. "I should have thought it through. Now, let's have another drink and change the subject."

Catherine turned to Sophie. "So, what got you into PR?"

Sophie looked straight at Catherine. "Fell into it really. I did anthropology at Oxford, went travelling for a year not knowing what I wanted to do, then when I got back a friend said give this PR job a go while you look for what you really want to do."

"I had no idea you'd been to Oxford," replied Catherine. "Me too."

"I know," replied Sophie. "I then worked my way up from there."

"And now you manage clients like Catherine!" added the VC.

"A little more than that as I am the co-founder of this company. People tend to assume I'm younger than I am, I'm thirty-three." Clear message from Sophie, thought Catherine. She had underestimated this woman, that was for sure.

"And I have a five-year-old daughter, so I have a busy life."

There was a moments silence before the VC raised her second beer and said, "Cheers! Here's to us and our friends from afar!"

"Don't you start!" replied Catherine as she raised the last of her wine.

"Right, I've told you about me," began Sophie, "now you each need to tell me something about you we don't know."

As the waiter put the drinks down the VC said, "I'll start then. Did you know I used to be a competitive swimmer?" Catherine looked at the VC's large frame squeezed into the chair and wondered how that could be.

"Go on!" replied Sophie.

The VC turned to Catherine, "Hard to believe I know," then looked back at Sophie, "but I swam freestyle for

England as a teenager." She took a swig of beer before adding, "but it became clear I wouldn't quite make it and with the punishing regime of five a.m. training sessions I eventually gave it up. My parents were relieved," she added wistfully. "After that it was just county stuff and then it all faded into a memory."

"That's hugely impressive?" enthused Sophie. She turned to Catherine, "and tell us something about you we don't know."

The VC signalled for another round of drinks and the reluctant bartender sauntered over. "Same again please," said the VC, "and can you bring two bowls of nuts and some crisps."

Catherine adjusted her position to sit more upright, feeling she had gradually slouched down into the armchair. "I haven't anything that compares with being an international sportswoman!" She thought for a moment then said, "You know everything about me Sophie."

"Hardly," Sophie replied.

"Tell you what," began Catherine, "being in PR and marketing you must have some stories to tell. Come on, enlighten us ladies who hail from the insular world of academia."

Sophie hesitated as the barman replaced the empty glasses with new drinks and placed three bowls in front of the VC. "Will these be okay madam?"

As he walked away, Sophie began. "Okay, here's something you'd never guess of me?" She sipped her wine. "This goes back a bit." Catherine wondered what she was about to say.

"I had quite close links with the criminal world."

"Now, that's an opening statement!" enthused the VC.

"Love it!" added Catherine. "Tell us more!"

"After I came back from my travels, I joined a small marketing company in London, so I was about twenty-three at the time? I hadn't been in London long when I was out with a friend in some trendy bar when I met this guy. His name was, or should I say, is, Jack and basically, I fell in love with him there and then." She took another sip of wine as her two colleagues sat riveted. "He had the gift of the gab, was thirty, cool, very well dressed and good looking. I quickly found out he came from the east-end of London?" She smiled. "He couldn't have been more different from me, this naïve girl who grew up in a Cotswold village and went to Oxford. But there was something so refreshing and, I was going to say, 'honest' about him but that's the wrong word, 'direct' is a better descriptor. Anyway, we dated and ended up living together and had my daughter, although we're no longer together. But still friends," she added.

"And the criminal world?" prompted the VC.

"As I said, I was naïve. Oh, my goodness when I think about it! It wasn't until I was in the pub one day with Jack and a few of his friends that I twigged that many of them were really dodgy? The funny thing is that I was chatting with this guy, a close friend of Jack's at the time, and I asked him what he did for a living. He laughed so much I thought he would fall over? 'Didn't Jack tell you'? he said. 'I'm a fence'. As bold as brass! I thought he was joking at first, until he went on to explain the finer details of how he moved goods around in the most ingenious ways so as not to get caught."

"Oh my God!" said the VC. "Did you challenge your boyfriend on it?"

"Of course, and he found it enormously amusing that I hadn't already sussed it? He said he didn't 'do crime himself' as he put it, although he did manage a dog racing venue in Essex so God knows what went on there. That evening he introduced me to a safe cracker, a burglar, a scary drug lord, some guy who ran a bouncer business which sounded more like thugs for hire dot com, oh all sorts. I can't remember now."

"So the relationship didn't end that night?" asked Catherine.

"Not at all. We stayed together for another five years or so, I just avoided them. Mostly. But I must tell you, they would do anything to help me and Jack. I was what they called 'family.'"

"Bloody hell Sophie, you're' full of surprises," said Catherine. "And what about your parents, how did they take to Jack?"

"Can you imagine? 'Not well' is the short answer. In the end they made me choose between them and him, which was sad. But they have no idea I still see him once a week, and they obviously have no inkling he sometimes looks after our daughter. They'd go crazy."

"Goodness me," said the VC as she lifted the remains of her beer and grabbed a handful of nuts. Swimming as a teenager seems tame now!" She turned to Catherine. "We never got anything out of you."

"Maybe another night," she replied standing up. "Whoops," she said as she grabbed the side of the chair. "Been a long day and we've got an early start haven't we, Sophie?"

"Full-on chat shows, you'll nail it."

Ten minutes later Catherine was lying on her bed face down feeling drunk and talking on her mobile to John about her day. The camera vans had finally left and he'd taken the girls to his parent's. "I didn't mind you waking me, even if you are drunk as a lord."

She woke up at three, still lying on the duvet in her clothes and her mouth dry as old leather. Despite the grogginess, she felt empowered, excited, ready for more of the adventure. It was going to be okay, after all, she thought. She was on the ride of her life, and nothing was going to stop her or destroy her precious family.

AMY

CHAPTER 35

January 1st, 1994

"I hate myself, Catherine," she began. "Look at me. Mum not back from a New Year's Eve party with her boyfriend, me still in bed, having spent the evening in front of the telly. I didn't even make it to midnight. I'm seventeen for God's sake: I mean, who *wasn't* at a party last night?!" Catherine sat down on the edge of the bed and held Amy's hand. "And with Billy now living in Bristol, I'm here all alone." She sat up and took a sip of water. "I hate what I've become. I hate me. I hate what happened to me; I hate how I never said anything; I hate what I did; I hate how I behave every day: my friends are gone, no surprise; I'm poisonous; miserable to be with. All I do is study. Amy looked down at the fresh scars on her arm. I deserved what happened to me and I deserve what comes. I'm worthless." She began to cry. "And you'd never have got into the mess I did with Jimmy. Damn it! That whole Jimmy thing would never have happened to you in the first place! Why can't I be like you?!!"

"Maybe it's time to put some things behind you, look ahead," suggested Catherine. "You're judging yourself too harshly."

"Why do you say that?"

"You're always beating yourself up."

"Of course I am: I'm simply not a nice person Catherine. Not like *you*, anyway. You're as I'd like to be, honestly." Amy thought for a moment. "I don't just mean your circumstances; I mean what you're *like*. How you live your life. Everything! There's no pretending otherwise. The fact is, I wish I was you."

"Oh Amy! It's kind of you to say but, come on, don't be like this; you've got so much going for you! Think about it. This time next year you'll know which uni and that will be amazing. Eighteen months from now you'll have a new life."

"But I won't, will I? I'll be living somewhere else, that's true, but Tina will know where I am and the whole thing will haunt me forever. She's never going to stop taunting me and my head will always be filled with guilt. So, nothing'll change that much." She swung her legs out of the side of the bed and sat next to Catherine. "I see the whole nightmare stretching out in front of me - forever. Can't you *see*?!" Amy screamed at the top of her voice. Briefly she felt relief as she flopped back down on the bed. She put her hands behind her head and stared up at the ceiling. "What can I do?" Amy's mind skipped from one idea to the next, not alighting on anything that could alleviate her anxiety. Suddenly she sat up. "What is it about you?" she asked, "that makes me admire you so much?" Amy turned to Catherine and smiled. "I love your confidence; how problems seem to wash over you." She looked Catherine up and down. "You dress smarter than I do, that must make you feel better. You look after yourself. You're nice to people. You're kind. Thoughtful." Amy looked down at her hands, clasped in her lap. "As I said," she whispered, "I wish I was you."

They were silent for a while before Catherine said, "You've had an idea, haven't you?"

Amy nodded. "Maybe," she replied as she fell back onto the bed.

"Tell me," Asked Catherine, lying down next to her. "I want to hear." Amy thought for a while, wondering whether she should say: the ideas were ill-formed. But maybe… just maybe.

"You mustn't tell anybody, you promise?"

"Of course! You know you can tell me anything!" replied Catherine.

Amy turned to her, their faces inches apart. "You've been my closest friend throughout. I don't know what I would have done without you." She felt tears running down the side of her cheek and wiped them away with her sleeve.

"When did you think of it?" asked Catherine.

"Just now."

"Well go on then, tell me."

Amy took a deep breath and averted her gaze, not able to look Catherine in the eye. "I'm afraid to tell you."

"I know already," said Catherine, "and it involves us saying 'goodbye,' doesn't it."

She turned back to look at Catherine. She loved that face and wondered if she was doing the right thing, she'd miss her so much.

"How do you know?" asked Amy.

"Don't be silly."

"And you think it's right?"

"It has to be," said Catherine. "And you've been my best friend."

"You've been mine too," replied Amy. "I'll never have another friend like you, Catherine. I'll always remember this…. Us."

They were silent for a moment until Catherine said, "It's the right thing. You must. You can do it, you're strong enough."

Amy moved her head onto Catherine's shoulder and soon they both fell asleep. When she awoke, Catherine had gone and Amy knew it was for the last time, but somehow felt at peace. Things were moving forward at last. Maybe she could feel better about herself after all? She lay there a while thinking of the good times they'd had together and what it would be like now with her gone. Suddenly a thought occurred to her. She jumped out of bed and went to her desk and opened the drawer. Under a few sheets of paper was her blade. It took her a while to find the old sharpener amongst her pens. Carefully she screwed the blade back into the sharpener and was about to put it back into the drawer, when instead she opened her bedroom window and threw the sharpener as hard as she could into the street below.

Amy slept that night better than she had for a long time. But there was much to be done and as a start she'd need to go to the library when it re-opened in the new year. Time for a shower she thought, as she swung her legs off the bed. Then she'd need to go out for a long walk and get some fresh air. Amy yanked the curtains aside, almost ripping them off the rail. A heavy frost covered the lawn and sparkled from the early morning sunlight. She threw open the window and filled her lungs with the freezing morning air. "It's time," she said turning, "to change things, then end it. That's the way forward, isn't it," she said, half expecting Catherine to answer.

AMY

CHAPTER 36

One year later

Her heart missed a beat at the sound of the postman pushing the letters through the door. The same rush of adrenalin had hit her every morning for the past week. She was alone in the house, her mother staying with her latest boyfriend as Amy called him. 'Please don't refer to Robert like that Amy, he's a nice chap and it's been over a year.'

She ran to the front door to find a single letter on the mat. She bent down and picked up the solitary envelope and flipped it over. Her heart raced as she saw it was addressed to her. Amy had planned the whole letter-opening process and it didn't involve standing by the front door ripping the envelope apart. Instead, she returned to the kitchen, sat down and slowly sipped her coffee while turning the envelope around in her hand.

Amy pulled open a drawer and selected the sharpest knife. She positioned the tip of the blade into a small gap to one side and with a careful sawing motion slit the envelope from left to right. Amy closed her eyes, breathed deeply, and pulled the letter from inside, feeling the fold across the centre. It was only one sheet, did that mean a rejection? Still with her eyes tightly shut she ran her fingers over the surface, wondering if she could detect the quantity of text. Maybe she had the wrong side so turned it over but still felt nothing. This is ridiculous she thought and opened her eyes. As she rapidly scanned the page, her eyes alighted on the words, 'we are very pleased' and 'unconditional offer.' She had her place at Balliol College Oxford to study physics, beginning the following October. She put her head in her hands and sobbed. Was it relief she felt or elation? She wasn't sure as she wiped away her tears. She knew it was a different feeling, something that helped lift the weight she been carrying every day for as long as she could recall. Amy reread the letter over and over before carefully folding and sliding it back into its envelope. She'd have to think where to hide it. Suddenly the phone rang.

"Hello?"

"Morning. Are you okay? Sounds like you've got a cold."

"Hi Mum. No, I'm fine."

"Heard anything yet?"

Amy hesitated. "Yes."

There was a brief silence. "Go on then, tell me!"

Amy took a deep breath. This was the moment of no return: the first of many lies she would have to tell. She dug her nails into her arm. "I've heard from Balliol - I didn't get in."

"Oh, darling, I'm so sorry to hear that."

"It's fine Mum. I don't care. I've got an unconditional offer from Manchester and I'm going to accept."

"Well done. Exciting! You happy?"

"Yup. I can't wait."

"Congratulations darling. We'll need to celebrate. I can't wait to tell Robert; he'll be pleased for you too."

"Right," she replied. "Speak soon. I've gotta call my friends." Amy opened her wardrobe and slid the envelope under the clothes on the top shelf, carefully patting them down. Lying on her bed she cast her mind to her next task. She was so close, and when it was done, she would visit the Witch's Tree for one last time, to say goodbye to Amy Ridley forever.

CATHERINE

CHAPTER 37

9th January 2019

She was awake by six. Her head thumped and the dryness in her mouth hadn't gone away. She thought back to yesterday; they'd started drinking in the House of Commons and finished in the hotel bar after midnight. "Ouch," she whispered.

Catherine switched on the radio to be greeted with more discussions about her discovery. She flopped back on the pillow to listen for a while.

"Now we are returning to the story which has dominated the news over the past thirty six hours, and just in case you've been hiding in a cave then let me tell you that a team at Cambridge University has discovered strong evidence for an advanced lifeform on another planet. It's hard to imagine, I know: Aliens for real! Clearly the implications for humankind are enormous, but what of the implications for religion?

What about for me? thought Catherine.

To help us, we have with us this morning Claire Howell our Religion Editor

Catherine adjusted her pillows, sat upright and took a long swig of water. The interviewer continued. *"Given how tiny and insignificant we are in this vast universe, and with the knowledge we are now not alone, perhaps we should start with the question of uniqueness? Religions claim that humans are the pinnacle of God's creation, so how can that be squared with the fact that we are not alone?"*

It struck Catherine that humankind wasn't insignificant at all. Who said they were?

"Good morning. It is true that some may argue humans have a unique and special relationship with God which could not be shared with other intelligent life forms. But I think you'll find most religions view God as being kind and generous and the idea of creating many lifeforms fits within this idea. This need not devalue the love God has for humans at all and there's no reason why God would not love many beings throughout the universe. They are creatures of God after all."

Catherine thought back to a conversation she'd had with Sophie. She'd told her why she didn't believe in God. Sophie had listened respectfully then had made it clear she should never say that in public. "You'll be deluged with the religious nutters if you say you're a non-believer. Preferably be vague or worst case, lie by saying you do."

"And what of the Bible, Claire, why is there no mention of life further afield?"

"There are many things that are not mentioned in the Bible and it doesn't make them incompatible with the existence of a deity or the love of God for all life. There's no mention of the other planets or of the double helix, but that's fine, the Bible was for obvious reasons 'local' and written during a certain period in our history. But look at other parts of the Bible and in general terms it does talk about the wider creation, for example God being the creator of all things. There is no suggestion that God is less powerful or less relevant beyond the Roman world of that time."

"So do you think there's the danger that this discovery will make believers doubt or feel insignificant in the grander scheme of things and question if they really do believe?"

I hope so, thought Catherine.

"Again," she began, "I don't think God's love for us is in any way diminished by spreading it further, so no. Many religions believe that God named the stars, so why not embrace the inhabitants?"

"What about the Creationists - surely they will struggle with the existence of other intelligent life forms?"

"Creationists! For God's sake!" shouted Catherine.

"Any religion that takes their scripture literally will have to square the circle, that's true. But this isn't new to them. If you adhere to the notion that God created the world in seven days, and you reject Darwinism then you've already diverged from much of modern scientific thinking. In this case - if there's no clear evidence in the Bible – then in the creationist's world it is indeed rejected."

"We haven't got much more time, but I must ask you about Christian salvation -how is this possible for creatures who have not experienced incarnation?"

"That's an interesting question. There is an argument that God's incarnation on earth covers all beings throughout the universe. Jesus visited earth to cleanse all beings wherever they may be. Or you could argue that maybe other beings do not sin, so don't need that cleansing and forgiveness which maybe just a human need."

"So humans are uniquely bad?"

"It may be so!"

Catherine leant over and switched off the radio. She sat there for a moment surrounded by the silence, pondering the discussion she had heard. These debates were going on all over the world: She could see it now – of course! She wouldn't be the centre of attention for long. The politicians, religious leaders, talk show hosts, celebs, even terrorists; in fact, anybody with some degree of power or influence, would soon be pitching in and Professor Catherine Holmes would fade from the limelight. Before long, few would be interested in what she had to say. The discussion would move on to the *implications* of the discovery, not how, or who, had made it. She only had to ride out a few days or weeks and she'd probably be fine. No one would be the wiser: her past wouldn't catch up with her and she'd be safe. John would never know. With those thoughts, she tossed the duvet aside and leapt out of bed and into the shower. She was ready for what the day may bring.

****

Catherine sat in the cramped studio with headphones clamped to her head, a mike in front of her and a screen with information of the callers' names and questions. A small light indicated if her mike was on and as it flicked red, she took a sip of her much-needed coffee.

"We're delighted to have Professor Holmes here to take your calls, so let's get straight on with it."

Catherine dealt with numerous calls and much to her surprise, found she was enjoying it, the thirty minutes went by fast.

"We've used-up just about all the Prof's time," said the presenter, looking at the studio clock. "We've time for one last question."

Catherine glanced at her screen and froze. *'Bill Ridley from Harlow wants to know about the prof's early life and influences. Keep it brief.'*

"We have Bill on the line, go ahead Bill," said Matt.

"Yes good morning Professor…." Catherine felt her heart racing. A picture flashed in her mind and she instantly knew she couldn't talk to him. Catherine scribbled 'stalker!' on a piece of paper and thrust it across toward Matt. He looked down and immediately made a sign through the glass. The line went dead.

"We seem to have lost our caller, that's a shame. Anyway, it just leaves me to say thanks to Professor……"

Catherine gathered her things and headed to the Ladies and locked herself in. For more than twenty years she'd not heard his voice. Everything she'd feared was going to happen. How could she have thought otherwise? This was the beginning of the end, surely?

"Where have you been?" Asked Sophie as Catherine exited the building. "You disappeared." Without waiting for an answer, she continued as they got into the taxi. "Went well, don't you think?" Getting no response, Sophie added, "You, okay? You look stressed."

"I'm fine," snapped Catherine. After a minute she said, "Actually, I'm not."

"What is it?"

Catherine looked down. "It's a long story. I can't talk about it now."

Sophie looked quizzically at her. "Okay." Then after an awkward silence added, "We have the same again now but a different station. We'll be there in ten." But she got no reply from Catherine who faced the other way, staring out of the car window. Shortly, Catherine leant forward and tapped the taxi driver on the shoulder. "Change of plan, we're not going to the radio station after all. Take us back to the hotel please."

JOHN

CHAPTER 38

Chloe and Ruth sat at the kitchen table listening to their mother being interviewed on the radio as John cooked their tea.

"Are the aliens going to come and find us?" asked Chloe.

John turned around, knife in hand. "I don't think so, they're too far away."

"How far?" asked Ruth.

John turned back to chopping the carrots. "Further than the chip shop."

"Don't be silly Daddy," replied Ruth.

"Granny's then."

"It's light years," said Chloe.

John's phone buzzed on the worktop. "Hello?"

"Hi John, my name's Sophie, I work for Catherine. I'm not sure if she's spoken of me and I apologise, but I can't recall if we've met."

Odd question he thought, she'd remember if we'd met, wouldn't she? Or was he really that insignificant? "Of course, I've heard a lot about you, and no we've not met," he replied as he walked into the dining room, leaving the girls chatting at the table.

"Well, we may be meeting sooner rather than later," she began. "I'm going to need your help with something."

"Go on," he said, sitting down.

"Catherine is leaving the studio now and what she doesn't know is that an impromptu reception is being held at the uni at shortly after six tonight. She'll be on the train in a few minutes."

"At least I'll get to see her tonight."

"I guess so," she replied. There was a momentary silence before she continued. "The event is partly in her honour and partly to host a foreign dignitary who wants to donate a substantial sum to the university. Catherine has no idea it's happening; it'll be a nice surprise. So don't take a call from her and obviously don't call her either."

"All very clandestine! But thanks for letting me know."

"Actually, it's more than that." Sophie hesitated. "We want you there too, it's important."

John ran his hand through his hair and looked toward the girls in the kitchen. "I'd love to Sophie but I'm here with our girls and I can't get a babysitter at this short notice and it's too late to sort with my parents."

"It's my job to sort things, so I've got you covered, don't worry. I can come over and look after them. You'll only need to be there an hour, so it'll be no bother and I've got a five-year-old of my own, so I know what's involved!"

"Aren't you in London with Catherine?" With no answer John wondered if the line had cut. "Hello?"

"I'm here. No, I came back early."

"Don't you need to be at the reception?"

"No."

John thought for a moment. "What time could you get here?"

"The event is at six o'clock, what's that, an hour away. I can be there in thirty minutes?"

"Do I need to wear a suit?"

"Smart casual, it's fine."

John sighed.

"So?" she prompted.

"I guess so," he said wearily. He'd have to get up early to catch up on the marking he'd planned to do this evening, but maybe Catherine could get the girls ready for school to give him time.

"See you soon," she said and hung up.

She seems nice enough, he thought as he drove away. Smartly dressed, cut glass accent, attractive blond medium length hair. The girls took to her and dragged her into the playroom to make a tent. John pulled into the astronomy building car park and was surprised to see only a handful of cars and wondered if this was the right place.

"Mr Holmes," said the porter, "What a pleasant surprise!"

"Thank you," he replied, "I'm here for the reception, can you point me in the right direction?"

"For the…?"

"Reception."

"Not sure I know about this," replied the porter.

"I'm positive it's here," added John feeling slightly irritated.

"What's it for?" he asked.

"Catherine. And a philanthropist. Plus guests, I assume."

"Typical," replied the porter as he picked up the phone. "Nobody tells me anything."

John looked at the large posters of the planets on the wall, each accompanied by a set of incomprehensible graphs, while the porter made at least three calls, each requiring him to hold. The porter tutt-tutted in between and muttered something about being a mushroom. Eventually he slammed the phone down. "Mr Holmes," he called. John returned to the desk. "I'm afraid nobody knows anything about a reception. There's nothing happening here tonight, so maybe you have the wrong building."

John felt his blood pressure rise and wished he'd never agreed to attend in the first place. He looked at his watch and it was already quarter past. He was late, damn it.

"You've no idea where it might be?" he asked.

"None if it's not here. The university's a big place," he said unhelpfully.

"Thanks anyway," replied John as he headed outside. "Damn," he mumbled as he got out his phone. He'd have to call Sophie. He still had her number from when she'd first called him an hour ago. He pressed redial only to be greeted with a solid tone. He tried again. Nothing. It was as if it was disconnected. He could feel the anger rising as he wondered what to do. "Damn it!" he muttered as he walked back to the car. I'm going to be so late it won't have been worth it. After a few minutes sitting in the car and retrying the number and still getting nothing, he decided he had no choice, he'd have to call Catherine.

"Hi!" she said animatedly. "Did you hear the interviews?"

"Of course. Where are you?"

"Is everything okay?" she asked. "You sound cross."

"I'm stressed! I'm late. And….I don't know where you are!"

"Late? For what?"

"The reception!"

"What are you talking about?"

Suddenly he felt bad for giving it away: perhaps she didn't know yet. He looked at his watch. It was already six thirty, so she'd have to know. "Where are you?"

"Now you're worrying me. I'm in the hotel bar."

"Thank goodness, which hotel? I can be there in a few minutes. Hope I haven't missed too much."

There was a moment's silence. "What? You're talking in riddles. I'm in the hotel bar in London with Sophie before we head out to a dinner with a journalist."

John froze. "You're in London? With Sophie?" His heart was pounding. "Can't be. Sophie?! Can you put her on?"

"Hello John, nice to speak with you at last."

"What?... What's going on?"

"Sorry?"

"Oh god!" he shouted. "Who's babysitting then?"

"What do you mean?" asked Sophie. Confused, she handed the phone back to Catherine. John heard Sophie whisper to Catherine, "I think he's angry with me?"

"Hello?" said Catherine. But John had already hung up.

John screamed, "Fuck!" as he started the engine. His heart was racing, thumping in his chest. He hit the steering wheel with the flats of his hands, "Damn! What have I done!" He accelerated as he reversed, sliding on the gravel and spinning the car almost three hundred and sixty degrees. He restarted the engine, took a deep breath, and drove away. The girls, oh my god the girls, they have to be alright, please God they have to be. "Please, please, I'll do anything!" he called, out loud. His phone was ringing, so he glanced at the passenger seat to see it was Catherine again. He dared not answer, so he let it ring out again and again. By the time he reached the edge of town, he knew it was Tina in the house with the girls. Of course, it was her! It was DI Flanders who he'd met in the café but with a blond wig rather than the black hair in a bun, gone was the Newcastle accent, replaced by a cut glass posh one, smarter clothes, high heels to look taller and large glasses. She'd played him so easily. He thought back to her phone call, realising she'd even checked to see if he'd met Sophie. How did she know where Catherine was? Or Sophie? "Fucking Tina!"

Has she kidnapped the girls? Peter the journalist said she would play with his mind. Oh god I hope the girls are okay he thought as he sped across a red light. John immediately saw her car wasn't in the drive as he screeched to a halt. He flung open the car door and rushed to the house, his shaking hand struggling to fit the key in the lock.

"Chloe! Ruth!" he shouted as he stumbled into the hall. The only sound came from a cartoon playing on the sitting room TV. He burst in, to find the room empty. John switched off the TV and stood motionless, listening. An eery silence hung over the house. He ran from room to room, then leapt two stairs at a time, up to their bedroom. He knelt down and looked under the bed, but they weren't there either. John frantically pulled opened the wardrobe doors, almost ripping them off. Then he peered out of the window into the garden, but it was too dark to see. His heart raced as he searched each room upstairs, calling out as he did so. John ran downstairs into the garden. "Chloe! Ruth!" he called. Suddenly the shed door burst open and the girls ran to him, wrapping their arms tightly around him as he knelt down. "Thank God!" he said as he pulled them close, his chest beating fast as he gasped for air.

"We were scared," said Ruth. "We hid inside the shed."

"We know we're not allowed to be alone in the house," said Chloe.

"What happened? My little darlings, you're freezing! Are you okay?" Before they could answer he added, "let's get you inside and warmed up." John sat them in the kitchen. "Now tell me what happened, then I'll make us hot chocolates."

"She left us alone in the house!" cried Ruth.

"How long was she here?" asked John.

"Not very long," replied Ruth. "She said she was going to buy ice cream, but after a while we got scared and got the shed key."

"I told her we already had ice cream," added Chloe. "She said she was only going to be a few minutes."

"Nothing else happened?" asked John.

"No," replied Chloe.

John fell silent as he put the pan on the stove. His hands were shaking and he was still breathing fast. He'd call the police. He blew out his cheeks and almost said 'fuck' but managed to stop himself. The whole thing gave him the creeps. And she'd abandoned the girls: anything could have happened. How could he have fallen for it? Why did she do it? How was he going to explain it to Catherine? Mind you, he had questions for her too. It was time for answers he thought as he felt the anger rising in his chest.

CATHERINE

CHAPTER 39

The moment the call had finished she knew she had to get home fast. Now on the train Catherine tried John once again. She felt sick with fear, wondering what had happened.

"Hi," he answered.

"Thank God I got hold of you," she began, "what's going on?"

"We're okay, but we need to talk, Catherine. Things aren't right."

She ran her hand through her hair. She was frightened by not knowing what he knew. "I'm on the train now, I'll be home within an hour." Should she ask now, she wondered. "What's not right?"

"Just get home and we'll talk," he replied and hung up. She stared at her phone. A tight knot had formed in her stomach. Had Billy contacted John? What was this about a babysitter?

When she walked in, John was sitting at the kitchen table, arms folded with a half-finished bottle of red. Without removing her coat, she slowly sat down opposite him. His eyes didn't leave her face and she felt trapped in the headlights. Tentatively she asked, "What's happened?"

Without answering he picked up the bottle and topped up his wine, watching the red liquid as it flowed into the glass.

He carefully placed the bottle down in front of her. "You'd better take your coat off, this may take a while."

"Are the girls awake?" she asked as she removed her coat.

"Leave them, they're exhausted."

"John, what's happened?" she begged, her heart racing. She pushed back her chair and got herself a glass. "Please John…"

"You know when you said there was something going on and I wasn't telling you?"

Catherine nodded; her mouth too dry to speak. Please God, tell me I'm not losing him.

"Well, there was, and I'm going to tell you now. Hopefully that will prompt you to explain things."

Catherine took a swig of her wine. First, he told her about what had happened this evening, how he'd been tricked by a woman he now guessed to be Tina Evans. At the mention of her name, Catherine's stomach flipped.

"After we've talked, I'll call the police." John banged the table with the palms of his hands. "She just left them here!"

"I must go up and see them!"

"No! We need to finish this first. They're fine."

Her beautiful girls. She couldn't bear to think about what could have happened. Catherine put her head in her hands. "Please don't call the police, John."

"Eh? Why not? The woman's a danger!"

"Can we talk first? Please?" she begged. Catherine stared at him, her heart pounding.

"Okay, but *I'm* asking the questions."

Catherine nodded, defeated.

John continued, now with the story of how he'd met DI Flanders, or as it turned out, Tina Evans. How she had quizzed him on Catherine's background. Catherine remained silent as he moved on to his meeting with the journalist, Peter Leech from the Harlow Chronicle, and the newspaper article of Jimmy's death. She watched his lips as the words left his mouth, wondering if this was the end. Then he hit her with the question she had always dreaded being asked.

"So, what is the connection between you, Tina, Jimmy Evans, Amy and Billy Ridley? I'm sure you knew them, and this is a part of your life you've kept secret from me. Why? Then I need to understand why Tina is freaking us out. As for Billy Ridley, I've spoken to him."

"What?!"

"Yeah, after speaking with the journalist, I tracked Billy down; he lives in Harlow, works at a mental health charity. That's about all I know of him." John pressed a finger against Catherine's arm, then added, "Although he did ask me if my wife had a birthmark on her neck. Like yours. God knows what that was about." John got up, went to the cupboard to retrieve more wine. He turned to her, bottle in hand. "You know we could have lost the girls tonight."

Catherine rested her elbows on the table and put her head in her hands. Her entire world was collapsing around her. She felt him tap her arm.

"I need answers."

Her mind raced. There was no hiding now, he knew too much. She was cornered. Eventually she looked up at him, tears smudged her cheeks. "Let's not do it here," she said, "I want to sit close to you. It's painful, John."

Without answering he picked up both glasses and carried the bottle into the sitting room. She sat next to him and took his hand and held it tightly. "I love you, John," she said. "I always will." She looked into his eyes. "You must believe me."

The look on his face unsettled her and his words "I love you too," sounded hollow. "But I need to know, Catherine."

"I know you do. Give me a moment to gather my thoughts."

He didn't answer and instead looked down at her hand holding his. Catherine took a deep breath then let the words flow. "I was born and grew up in Harlow, not Hertford. My name was Amy Ridley until the age of eighteen and Billy is my younger brother."

"What?!" John abruptly pulled his hand away and stood up. "You were Amy Ridley!?" She watched in silence as he paced the room. Was she about to lose him for good?

"Shit" he hissed. Suddenly he stopped and turned to her. "So, what, you didn't lose your parents in a car crash?"

Catherine looked down and whispered, "There was no car crash."

"Catherine!" he shouted. "What?!"

"Please John," she said wiping her eyes. She couldn't look up at him. "Don't shout at me. Please."

"I can't take this in," he said waving his arms. He was silent for a moment then asked, "No fostering?"

She began to sob, her hands covering her face. Through her crying she heard him ask, "Are your parents still alive?"

She looked up at him, hardly recognising the face staring back at her. "Please John, hear me out." Her heart ached as she pleaded, "come and sit next to me. I'll tell you everything."

John took his hands out of his pockets and slumped down next to her. She took another deep breath before continuing. In the second before speaking, she wondered if she could tell him, but she had no choice now. "Up until my early teens, life was kind of okay. I did well at school, we were a happy family. Billy and I were thick as thieves." Catherine gasped from all her crying, "Then things began to go wrong."

John turned to her, eyes on fire. "What do you mean?"

"Our parents split up was the first thing." Catherine stared at the floor as the events ran through her mind. "I don't want to talk about it, but I witnessed my mother having an affair." She shook her head as if it would shake away the memory. "I think that was the moment my life changed." Catherine sighed again. "I've never been sure if my father knew about that, or other affairs, but not long after that, they split up. Dad moved out and eventually he met another woman, moved to Bristol, taking Billy with him."

"Why was life so terrible though? I mean, many families go through break-ups."

"Well, it was bad for me." She replied. "Mum and I never got on. We simply didn't understand each other. I don't think she had any real interest in me. As soon as she could, she left and emigrated with some guy." Catherine hesitated, then turned to look at John. "But that wasn't it really. The worst thing was the bullying at school."

"What? Why?"

How many nights had she lay awake trying to answer that question. "Why is anyone bullied? I guess because he *could* bully me. I was vulnerable, an easy target. A bit of a swot. He wanted to be top dog academically and couldn't because of me. Then... it seems so silly to say it, but when we were young teenagers, he asked me out and I said 'no'. Anyway, I don't know why he bullied me and it could have been for any number of reasons. But what I do know is that it was relentless."

"What did he do?"

"I don't want to talk about the things he said and did, but I was mentally damaged by it. It dominated my life, to be honest."

Maybe Catherine noticed a flicker of sympathy in his voice? "How did it stop?" Asked John.

Catherine turned to him. "John." She watched him as he thought and saw the horror and flicker of realisation on his face. "The bully... it was... it was... Jimmy Evans, wasn't it!?"

Catherine nodded.

"*The* Jimmy Evans. Oh god, the bullying ended with his death." Suddenly John leapt up and walked around the room, his hands on his head. Then he turned to her, shock written across his face. "Of course!... you're the one who went up the tree!"

"Trying to save him, yes."

"I can't believe it." He stared at her and put his hands on his hips. "Tina and her mum didn't believe your account though. They believed he fell *because* of you. Was that because they knew he bullied you, so you had a reason to do it?"

"No of course not! That's completely crazy. It was an accident! Anyway, they didn't know he was a bully. Nobody did. Nothing would stop them waging a vendetta against me. They made my life hell."

John flopped back on the settee putting his hands behind his head. She turned to him, desperate for sympathy. "Tina wrote spiteful letters, went to the police."

John thought for a moment. "Mr Leech said the police interviewed you a number of times."

"Twice, that was it. They had no evidence I'd done anything other than try to save him."

John looked directly at her. "And that's the case, is it?"

Now she stood up and turned to him. "What do you mean?!"

John shook his head. "Well, let's be honest, there has been a lot of lying going on all this time. You've lied to me since the day we met."

"That's not fair," she replied as she sat back down.

"So many secrets, Catherine, you can hardly blame me. You really didn't cause it?"

"No!"

John shook his head, then asked, "and why did you change your name?"

Catherine scrunched up her tissue. "I needed to start again: to escape my life as it was - the name change was part of my plan. And I needed to hide from Tina: from everything that had happened." Catherine grabbed another tissue and wiped her eyes. "I hated myself and thought I could be someone new. It wasn't just a name change either. I told everybody I'd accepted a place at Manchester uni, to help in my disappearance."

"Parents? School?"

"Everyone. I went to Oxford of course, met you, fell in love, immersed myself in studying. My life and everything changed for the better."

"Didn't your parents try to contact you at uni?"

"Of course, but I did things to keep my new identity hidden. In the first year, or so, I called Dad regularly and still used the name Amy on the phone. I gave Mum a PO Box in Manchester and told her this was the college postal address. I had the post forwarded to me. I got letters from her in South Africa and I went to Manchester once a term to post letters back. Do you remember my trips?"

"I thought you were visiting an old school friend."

"I know, that's what I said. Then over time I took longer to reply and so did she. By the end of my second year our contact had dried up."

John grimaced. "And I thought you always had vacation jobs in Oxford because you had no family to return to."

"I didn't really. Anyway, just prior to uni was when I changed my name to Catherine Motson. I left to go up to Oxford a day early, checked into a hostel and went to the hairdresser and had my long hair cut short, dyed it and bought different clothes. I didn't take any clothes with me from my old life, other than those I travelled in. Even they went in the bin. Then you'll remember I was pretty much alone in wearing make-up at uni. That was all part of my reinvention."

John put his head back and closed his eyes. They sat in silence for what seemed to Catherine as minutes. She dare not say more.

John turned to her, anger in his eyes. "It's a pity you felt you could never tell me any of this."

Can I ever truly explain it to him, she wondered. "Honestly, it wasn't a case of telling you or not. I was Catherine from the day I changed my name. From then on, in my head there was nothing to tell. Amy was dead and buried." Catherine hesitated as she had to explain more. "But the truth is, I banished Amy from my mind some time prior to the name change."

"I've got no idea what you're talking about," said John angrily.

Catherine sighed. "It's going to sound ridiculous and I've never told anybody this. From about the age of fourteen, just as my parents' relationship began to fall apart, I found a friend, someone who stayed with me throughout all the horrible teenage years. She loved the same things as me, we never argued, she understood me, she was kind, she listened, we laughed, and I told her everything and she confided in me too. The only difference between us was she had things I could never have: a happy family; she was pretty; had close friends and… confidence. I wanted to be her, really."

"She sounds too good to be true."

"In a way you're right, as she was my *imaginary* friend. The best friend I've ever had." Catherine began to cry; she hadn't thought of her in years.

His comment felt cold to her. "I thought only young kids had imaginary friends."

"Not at all."

"What was her name?"

"I think you can guess, can't you?"

John turned to look at her. He hesitated, thinking. "Catherine… Motson?"

"Catherine, yes. Strangely she never needed a surname when we were friends. The Motson was a spur of the moment thing when I filled in the Deed Poll forms. It seems crazy now, but Catherine got me through so much. Then when I was seventeen it ended."

"Not sure how much of this I believe. Sounds like another invention, similar to the car crash."

"Don't be like that. Please. I'm telling you everything and it's not easy for me to face my past."

"Go on then. So you fell out with your imaginary friend."

"Don't take the piss."

"Sorry, carry on."

"At seventeen I became Catherine in my head, just to survive. I had so wanted to be her. From then on, I thought of myself as her – someone with confidence. As I walked out of the house, I was her. As I walked into a shop, the school, throughout my time in the sixth form, anywhere, I was her in my head. I was still called Amy at that point but not in my head. It gave me a new strength to face up to the horrible things that had happened and to Tina and her mother's vendetta. Its's the only way I survived until I went to uni and escaped my old life completely. I arrived at Oxford as Catherine in name and spirit. Amy really did die one day and was replaced by Catherine."

"She became your alter ego."

"Precisely."

"And then you sort of morphed into her permanently."

"Yes. My dearest imaginary friend, then my alter ego, then well, I was her, yes. Amy had died. In fact on the day I got my uni offer letter, in the February prior to going to uni, I already knew I was going to change my name before going to Oxford. I'd worked out how to do it with Deed Poll. I took the offer letter with me and went by myself to the tree in the woods where Jimmy had died. It was my own ceremony, my way of saying goodbye to Amy and my old life. I've never spoken of it to anybody, and it's faded into the past: something that happened a long time ago. I'm Catherine and I can't remember much of this girl called Amy."

John sighed. "There's so much in that head of yours that I've never known. I remember telling Tina the whole 'parents in a car crash story' and she was quizzing me, knowing you had been Amy. You made me look so stupid."

Catherine sat up. "I'm sorry. She's evil though. I wonder how she tracked me down and recognised me after all this time? Her contacting you as a police officer pre-dated the exo-planet announcement."

John didn't say anything.

"What do you think?" she prompted.

"That's down to me."

"How come?"

"Do you remember the journalist, Martin Mitchell, who came to your talk at the school? You may recall the article he subsequently wrote in The Times Educational Supplement. Well, I learnt from Peter Leech that Tina is a teacher so I reckon she read the article and recognised you."

"You're probably right."

"And now I know why you were so shirty with Martin when we were at the school, saying you were going to Copenhagen. You never wanted a profile that could expose you."

Catherine sighed. "Yup." They sat in silence for a while before John asked. "There is still one thing I don't understand."

"Go on."

"When I spoke with Billy, he said it had taken 'years to get over it.' What did he mean?"

Catherine stiffened. "Maybe Jimmy's death traumatised him long term? I mean it was me in the woods, not him, but he was very young and it probably shocked him more than any of us realised." Catherine thought, then added. "Thinking about it now, if I have regrets over my disappearance, then it's cutting my ties with Billy." Catherine looked at John who sat there passively listening. She was quiet for a moment before continuing. "I recall that after Jimmy's death, Billy became difficult to live with and disruptive at school. Not so much the cute little boy he had been. But I still loved him." Catherine fell silent again, before adding, "Billy wouldn't be alone in blaming me for Jimmy's death though, would he? Even though Jimmy was drugged up to the eyeballs and climbed up a tree to some crazy height. But there you go."

John didn't comment and she wondered if he doubted her account. "What are we going to do about Tina?" she said changing the subject away from Jimmy's death.

"What do you think she'll do? Out you?"

"I don't know. Tina seems to want to create a rift between us."

John didn't react and instead asked. "And Billy?"

"I don't know what he wants. I didn't tell you, but he called into the radio show yesterday and planned to asked me a question about what inspired me when I was young. The interviewer cut him off at my request. It was simply to let me know he had found me. I hadn't heard his voice in so long, it shocked me."

"Not surprised. Maybe he won't bother you anymore."

"I'm not sure." She hesitated before saying what she had really been thinking. "I guess he only found me because you contacted him, right?" Immediately, she regretted saying it. But to her relief John didn't react to her accusation.

"I know I know, both Tina and Billy caught up with you not because of your sudden fame but because of me poking my nose around. But you can hardly blame me for trying to find out who my wife is. Anyway, what are we going to do?"

"I don't know, John."

Suddenly he turned to her. "Is there anything else you want to tell me?"

Should she tell him about the rape? No, she thought, that would definitely make him think she had killed Jimmy. Or that she had been on the same branch? No, she couldn't tell him that either. Not now. Not ever. She could lose him if she did. "No. Now you know everything," she replied.

"It took you a while to answer," he said.

"I was trying to think," she replied. Catherine's heart raced as she wondered what he would say.

"I don't judge you for what happened in your past or how you tried your best to cope. What really hurts though is your lying to me for all these years. How could you?"

Catherine sighed. "I don't know. As I said, it's long been buried in my own head. The idea that I should suddenly resurrect it, made no sense." She reached out to take his hand but he pulled away.

"Thanks for finally telling me anyway." He shifted as if about to stand up. "Listen, I'm exhausted and need to go to bed. I'll be sleeping in the spare room," he added as he stood up.

"John?" said Catherine, crestfallen. But he didn't answer or turn around.

CATHERINE

CHAPTER 40

10th January 2019

"Mummy!" The girls jumped on the bed. "You're home!" She'd hardly slept but must have finally fallen asleep in the early hours. "Come here my little darlings," she said, wrapping her arms around them both.

"Where's Daddy?" asked Ruth. The question brought back last night with a thud. She gathered them close and gave them a squeeze. "He didn't feel well so slept in the spare room. I think Daddy's getting a cold... What time is it?"

"Seven o'clock," replied Chloe, jumping up and down on the bed.

"What? Mummy needs to get a wiggle on!" she replied, throwing back the covers. Should she knock on his door? How would he be feeling? She wondered if he really believed her story about what she did and didn't do on that branch with Jimmy. The journalist might have told John more than he was letting on. Catherine gently tapped on his door. "John?"

A moment's silence, then, "I'll be down soon."

"How are you this morning?" she said brightly as he appeared in the kitchen. She handed him a mug of coffee. John took it without replying and sat at the kitchen table.

"Are you sick, Daddy?" asked Chloe.

"Sweetheart, I'm fine," he replied. Suddenly he stood up and turned to Catherine. "I need a word."

Catherine stiffened. "One minute," she replied, but he already had his back to her as he left the room.

"Is Daddy cross?" asked Ruth.

"Finish your breakfasts," she replied, glancing at her phone. She had a long list of missed calls from Sophie. She'd have to wait. Her head thumped from everything that had happened yesterday and last night. And now John was as cold as ice. What did he want to say? John was staring out of the window, hands in his pockets and his back to her as she entered the room.

"John?" she began. Her heart was racing. As he turned around, she hardly recognised the expression on his face.

"I thought more about what you said last night," he began. He looked down at the floor, then back up at her.

"What is it?" she asked, her voice trembling.

"I'm leaving. Taking the girls and we'll be staying with my parents… for the time being."

"John, please, no!" she stepped forward, her arms outstretched. "Don't do this!"

John stepped back, avoiding her advance. "Just stop it! You've lied to me all these years. And you've been acting strange for months."

Catherine put her hands on her head, "No!" she pleaded.

"No, you didn't lie, or no, you've not been acting strange?"

"I was worried about being found out."

"Well, now you have. Maybe it's the lying, maybe the fear of being found out, or the obsession with work, or maybe it's just you. But whatever it is you need to sort it out. And tell me the whole truth."

"I have told you the truth! Please! I'll do anything. Please!"

"It's too late Catherine. I've been living with someone I thought I knew, but it turns out I didn't."

"No! That's not true!"

"Keep your voice down," he hissed.

Catherine felt sick as she cast around for the right words. She reached out and touched his arm, but he pulled away again. "I love you," she said. "You *do* know me. I'm the same person as I was yesterday, last week, last year… you're the only person in my life who really knows me."

"That's what *I* thought… until recently."

Suddenly Chloe appeared in the doorway.

"Go and finish your breakfast," called John.

"We've finished," replied Chloe. "Are you having an argument?"

"No! Go and get ready for school. We'll be leaving in fifteen minutes."

"Ruth can't find her spelling book."

"I'll help look for it in a minute. Now off you go," said John.

Chloe stared at him before turning around and marching off. Both heard her say to her sister, "they're fighting."

John put his hands on his hips. "Now see what you've done!"

Catherine felt her anger rising. "What?!"

"Look, I need to get a move on… I'll grab the girls' things now. Tonight, I'll take them straight from school to my parents. I've already packed my stuff," he added.

Catherine felt faint as she slowly sat on the arm of the chair. She felt beaten. Looking down at her hands she whispered, "Please don't go, John."

"I need to," he replied.

"I can't go on without you and the girls." Catherine looked up at him pleading. "You're everything to me."

"You've got your work. That's all you really need."

"You know that's not fair!"

"Whatever. I need to get my head together. Listen, I've got to go," he said, as he moved toward the door. Suddenly he stopped and turned, "We'll talk." He hesitated, then added, "When I'm ready. So please don't keep calling me."

"John!" she called. "Please?" Catherine hardly recognised him. How could he be so cruel? But then it was all her fault, wasn't it? Catherine put her head in her hands and sobbed, steadying herself so as not to fall off the arm of the chair. Minutes later, she heard the girls' excited chatter as they came downstairs. She frantically wiped her eyes and blew her nose as they bounced into the room.

Chloe frowned. "Why are you crying?"

"I'm not," replied Catherine, immediately regretting it.

"What's wrong, Mummy?" asked Ruth as both girls stood close.

"I'm going to miss you, that's all," she said, wiping her eyes.

"Why don't you come too!?" asked Chloe.

Catherine sighed. "Come here," she said, wrapping her arms around the girls' waists. She pulled them closer still. "Poor Mummy has to work hard at the moment. And I'm going to America for a week." Catherine kissed them both in turn. "But I'll see you as soon as I'm back."

"How long are we staying at Granny's?" asked Ruth.

Catherine let go of them and blew her nose again. "You'll have to ask Dad," she said, as John entered the room. "He's planned your trip to Granny's," she added, looking up at him. She smiled through her tears, hoping he may respond in kind, but there was no sign. He didn't answer the question and instead said matter-of-factly, "Come on girls. Say goodbye to Mum."

"I love you both so much," she said, squeezing them close.

"You're crying again, Mummy," said Chloe. "We won't be gone for long!"

Catherine smiled and kissed them both. "You're beautiful," she said. "My treasures!" Catherine looked up at John, then back to the girls. "Why don't you take your things out to the car. I need a quick word with Dad." She looked back at John who grimaced.

When they had left the room, she took a deep breath and said, "John, please don't be so hard on me. I love you! Can't you see? I'm pleading with you."

John looked down and nodded his head. "I need this time away… we'll talk, when I'm ready," he said softly. Then his voice hardened. "But it *will* be when *I'm* ready, Catherine. Please don't come round or keep calling."

"You remember I'm going to the USA soon?"

"Of course," he replied. There was a moments silence as Catherine's mobile rang. John shook his head and turned to leave.

"Bye," she called after him, but he was gone. Catherine killed the call and sat in silence, listening to the car whisk away the three people she loved, leaving her in an empty soulless house. Suddenly her phone rang again, making her jump.

"Hi."

"What happened? I've been worried sick," began Sophie.

Catherine was momentarily confused. "Oh, you mean about last night. The babysitting thing. Sorry, yes. It was a misunderstanding, that's all. No harm done." She hesitated, then added, "And John apologises for getting angry."

"No problem. Glad it was nothing serious," replied Sophie. "Have you got a cold?"

"No."

"Sounds like it. Good. Now, you've got the morning off."

"Oh?"

"Remember the journalist we were supposed to be meeting last night? Well I tried rearranging for this morning, but her number was unattainable. I also called the magazine, but nobody had heard of her, bizarre. So the upshot is, you're off the hook for this morning."

That's Tina, thought Catherine, playing more games. "Okay," she said. "But can we meet this morning at the uni? I've got things we need to discuss."

"Sounds ominous."

"Ten o'clock?"

"See you then," said Sophie.

****

"You look terrible," said Sophie as she shut the door of Catherine's office. "What's happened?"

"Sit down," replied Catherine. "There's a lot to go through."

"Now I am worried," said Sophie, removing her jacket.

Catherine rubbed her eyes with her hand, then put her head back and looked up at the ceiling. She sighed, holding back the tears.

"Are you okay?" asked Sophie.

Catherine took a deep breath. "No… Give me time to gather my thoughts." After a moment she looked at Sophie. "John has left with the girls. Gone to stay with his parents."

"Oh. I'm so sorry. Why?"

Catherine hesitated. "The intrusions on our lives. The press. Me never being around. Everything."

"I'm sorry," repeated Sophie. "Anything I can do?"

Catherine shook her head.

"How long will they be away?"

Catherine stared at the wall, hardly listening. "Err… don't know. It's my problem and I'll deal with it." They sat in silence until Catherine suddenly sat up straight. "But I didn't get you here to discuss my marital issues." She took a deep breath. "I'm going to tell you something that's just between us, okay?"

"Everything is."

"Somebody phoned in to the radio show yesterday, you probably don't remember as he was cut off before he said anything. His name was Bill, actually, Billy Ridley."

"No, I don't remember."

"Doesn't matter. The point is, it's likely he, and maybe one other person, are going to cause me trouble."

"Trouble?"

"Trouble, yes… I don't want to go into the details."

"Listen Catherine, I've handled most things for clients. So, if you've had affairs, I need to know now: you need to be straight with me and we can handle it?"

"Ha! No!" she replied, "nothing like that!"

"O… kay."

"I can't explain. Let's say for now they're stalkers."

"Sounds like a police matter to me."

"Absolutely not! Let's say stalkers are our working hypothesis. I need something on him and the other person, a woman called Tina Evans. Things which I could use to push back."

"Sounds like your mind is made up. But I don't understand what you want from me?"

"I'd like you to find a private detective and have Billy Ridley and Tina Evans investigated. Behind the scenes, if you know what I mean."

"Seriously?"

"Absolutely."

Sophie shook her head. "Catherine, I run a marketing and PR agency, not some secret…"

Catherine held up her hand. "Stop! It has to be you." She reached over and put a hand on Sophie's arm. "This is important, and it can't be arranged by me. If the press got hold of it then it would be a disaster."

"This is crazy. Plus I'm being asked to investigate something I know nothing about."

Catherine stood up and looked out of the window thinking, as Sophie sat there in silence. The snow was settling. She turned back to her. "Crazy it may seem, but I'm you're most important client and if things go the way they could, you may not have a 'most important client' anymore. I'm at breaking point."

Sophie sat back and breathed out heavily. First, she looked up at the ceiling then directly at Catherine. "Do you at least know where they live?"

"Not precise addresses but they both live in Harlow."

"Together?"

"God no…. I assume not anyway… No they can't!"

"Okay, I'm just asking." Sophie fixed Catherine with her gaze as if trying to read her mind. "When we secured the uni account it really made a difference to my company," she began. "If I'm honest, we were close to going under? Then when the VC presented you, it transformed the business. So, no surprise, you're the best client anybody could have and without you, I don't know, things would be very different." Sophie hesitated then added, "so the fact is, if you want a private detective, then you'll have a private detective. I'll sort it."

Catherine felt some of the tension drain as she sat down. "Thank you," she replied. "And just between us obviously."

"Obviously. Anything else?"

"Nope, that's it," replied Catherine.

"Okay then. Now back to normal stuff; it's the meeting with my recommended literary agent here at two o'clock. Let's see what she has to say on a possible book deal. See you later," Sophie said as she stood up to leave.

Catherine only muttered a goodbye: she was staring at an email from Billy. "Hold on," she called, "I will need the Billy Ridley information fast, real fast."

Sophie picked up her bag and smiled. "I get it."

No you don't thought Catherine. You have no idea.

Amey

After all these years. Now I have found you I think it's time for you to help me. All I'm asking for is some money – I expect you'll be making some from your discovery, so this is not much to ask. Let's say £10,000 will stop me telling the world what happened.

I'll be in touch to make the arrangements.

Billy

Odd he's spelled her name wrong was her first thought. But as she read the message it made her blood run cold. He didn't seem to mind putting his bribery in writing, but then she could hardly go to the police herself. Ten thousand pounds. And would that even be the end of it? That's most of their savings, she thought. And John would soon find out. "Oh God," she said out loud. Catherine decided not to reply.

****

"We'll need a synopsis first," replied the agent. "But if it's along the lines we've discussed, then that'll be fine."

"When do you need it? I'm in the US next week," replied Catherine.

"Five hundred words will be enough and asap," she answered.

"What are we talking about as an advance?" asked Sophie.

"This is super-hot right now and I'll orchestrate a bidding war between publishers. I think we should secure around a million as an advance, plus say two fifty on publication. Then we'll see on the royalties. I estimate it'll be worth more than a couple of million over time. Then depending on how the story develops, and that will partly depend on further research I guess, we could be looking at a second book."

"Crikey," said Catherine.

The agent smiled. "There'll be global interest, so you're sitting on a gold mine."

"Okay," said Catherine, "you'll have your words by close of play tomorrow. Now I apologise I have meetings; the normal work still has to be done."

As they gathered up their things Catherine stood up, "one thing," she said, "if it all goes to plan, when do you think I could see the advance money?"

The agent stopped and looked at her. "Let's say I reach an agreement within a week, which is possible, then another week for a contract to be drawn up, hmmm, let's say within four weeks. Then the actual cash, that will come in stages as the book develops." She hesitated then added, "I think you can reasonably expect two hundred and fifty thousand quid within four weeks."

Catherine sat alone in her office staring at Billy's email. What should she do? Would it work? In the overall scheme of things, ten grand wasn't going to make much difference now. But then, would he keep his word? No, screw him, I'm not replying she decided.

****

It was Saturday morning 20th January and Catherine was back in the UK from her USA trip. John had rarely taken her calls and when he had, he told her not to call again. She'd pleaded with him but had got nowhere. In her heart, she had hoped he would be back home on her return. She'd imagined the girls rushing to greet her, feeling their arms around her. As Catherine opened the front door, she knew the house was empty. Her texts after landing, *'can I see you? Can I come and see the girls?' will you be home?* had gone unanswered.

Catherine slumped onto a kitchen chair and kicked off her shoes. "John, please, no," she whispered. "I can't take it." She rubbed her temples, stood up, took a glass from the cupboard, and drank as much water as she could bear. Then she pushed past her case in the hallway, went upstairs and flopped on the bed, still in her coat. The house wasn't just empty, it was soulless.

She tried his number again but it went straight to voicemail. On the third try she thought she would leave a message but didn't. On the sixth she left a message. "Please John, talk to me. I miss you. I need you. Please call or come home. I love you. Please."

She wondered what he had told his parents. Surely not that they'd had a falling out in some way. She wondered if she should go and collect the girls but felt in no fit state to look after them. It was after midday when she awoke, still lying on the bed, her head spinning. She tried his number again and texted. *'when are you coming home?'* No replies. Catherine left her phone on the side of the bath just in case he rang as she had a long soak. After some hot food, she began to feel human at last. What was going through his mind? It was no good, she couldn't do anything, she was exhausted, so went back to bed.

Catherine was awoken by the girls running into the room and jumping on the bed. "Mummy! You're back! We've had a holiday at Granny and Grandpa's!" enthused Chloe. Catherine gathered both girls into her arms and cuddled them close. Her immediate thought was, 'where is John'? Then she heard him shout from downstairs.

"Catherine!"

"Mind out girls," she said as she leapt out of bed. "John, you're back!" she called as she raced to the stairs. Before she had taken the first step he had turned to go.

"I'm going back to my parents," and the door slammed.

For a moment she stood there in silence, hardly able to believe what had happened. She was half minded to race downstairs and catch him, but she could already hear the car reversing out of the drive. Catherine ran her hand through her hair as she slowly went back into the bedroom.

"Daddy had to go back to Granny's," she began.

"Granny's not well," said Ruth.

"Oh dear. What's wrong with her?" asked Catherine, getting back into bed.

"I don't know," replied Chloe. "Daddy told us in the car."

That evening, when the girls were in bed, she lit a candle and slumped in a chair in the semi darkness of the sitting room, her phone in her lap. She tried again and to her surprise he answered. "John…" she began. "Is you Mum okay?"

He didn't reply at first, then said. "She's fine… I just have to tell it to you straight."

Catherine's mind raced and her head spun. Oh God, he's leaving me, she thought as she tried to speak, but no words came out.

"You being away gave me time to think about what you told me," he began.

"And?" she whispered, her voice trembling.

"I understand how you wanted to put things behind you. I get that. But since the day we first met you've made stuff up. Lied to me. You should have trusted me."

"I don't think I can make you understand what it was like. I don't know what to do, honestly."

"I need the truth, Catherine."

"You've got it… Although I should have told you before. I can see that now."

"But have I got the whole truth?"

Catherine sat upright. "What do you mean?" The phone felt hot against her ear.

"I'm being fed just part of the story. Maybe Tina is right. There's more to it."

Catherine felt the blood rush to her head as she killed the call. "Damn him." Then she regretted it and called him back, relieved when he answered. "Please come home, John. I can't do this on the phone."

"I've told my parents I'm finding the press intrusion too much and need this time away. I'll be back later in the week, and we can talk when my head is straight."

"I miss you. Please don't be cold."

"I'll be back and we can talk. I've gotta go," he said and the line cut. The phone dropped from her hand to the floor.

****

Sitting at her desk on Monday morning she opened her emails to find one from Billy. Maybe if she ignored his mails he would go away? Catherine stood up and paced her office, her heart racing, contemplating what to do. Two minutes later she was back behind her desk.

Amey

You're ignoring me, not a good idea.

Billy

Catherine checked the savings account. Would John check it? He rarely did as far as she knew. It was her job. It could be replenished within a few weeks and if he asked why ten thousand went out, then came back in, she'd think of something. An error. The balance would be in the hundreds of thousands by then so would he notice or care?

Billy

How do I know you will keep your word and not just keep asking for more?

Within minutes he replied:

I've kept my word for over 20 years. That's why. You'll have to trust me again.

She sat there thinking. Perhaps she should wait? No, I need to get this behind me or I'll never sleep, she thought. Suddenly she felt herself begin to sweat and her heart race. She looked down at her shaking hands. Slowly but surely her whole body began to shake uncontrollably. Catherine stood up, holding on to the arms of the chair, then steadied herself against the desk as she tentatively tried to walk. Fresh air, give me fresh air, that's all I need, she thought as she left the safety of her desk. Catherine never made it to the window as she collapsed, hitting her head on the side of the desk on the way down.

"Catherine, wake up, wake up." Slowly she opened her eyes to see Sophie kneeling over her. The pain shot across her forehead. "Ouch." she said as she struggled up onto one arm. "What time is it?"

"It doesn't matter what the time is." Sophie helped her to a chair. "Here, have this," she said taking a tissue from a box, "you've grazed your forehead."

Catherine dabbed her head. "Ouch! Does it look bad?"

"It's small. What happened?"

"Exhaustion that's all. I fainted. Not recovered from the crazy schedule of last week and the flight I guess."

Sophie sat down opposite her. "Shall I go?"

"No, no, stay, I'm fine, it's nothing."

"There's not much time for resting," Sophie replied. "But at least you're here all week."

"Thank God." Catherine closed her eyes. "Give me fifteen minutes then we'll talk," she said breathing deeply. "I'll be alright."

Sophie let her be for an hour before returning. "I've got information on both Mr Ridley and Ms Evans," she began.

Catherine sat upright. "That was quick. Hope I'm going to like what I hear."

"It cost you four thousand quid, is the first thing. But don't worry, I won't invoice you until you've got your book advance."

Catherine sighed. She was in no position to argue. "Thanks. Okay let's hear it then."

Sophie opened a file. "Let's start with Ms Evans, as this is the most interesting. Born in Harlow, 10th April 1974, making her, what, getting on for forty-five. She has, or should I say, had two brothers, one died when he was mid-teens in an accident. The other older brother we couldn't find anything." Sophie ran her finger down the page, "She still lives in Harlow, got her address here and mobile number for you, works as a primary school teacher at Greenway Primary School for the past seven years, made deputy head last year, blah blah blah, there's a few more details about that." She looked up to see if Catherine was still listening to find she was staring at her with an intense look she had never seen before. Sophie returned to the page. "She's into amateur dramatics and has appeared at the local theatre. Her mother lives in the same town and she visits her every Sunday. Father… No idea. She has no children but is married to a guy called Graham Blake who owns a garage, does bodywork repairs… She kept her original surname by the looks of it."

"You said this was the most interesting one."

"I'm getting there, hold on. So here it is," she said, handing over an A4 photograph of an attractive well-dressed woman kissing a man in a dark corner of a bar. Catherine couldn't see a likeness to the girl she had once known. "Is that her and Graham?"

"It's her, but it's not Graham," replied Sophie. "She regularly meets this guy. They're clearly having an affair."

Catherine looked up. "Ah now, that is interesting. Do you have more photos?"

"As many as you'll need," replied Sophie. She slid another envelope across the desk. "They're all in there. Our detective did a good job."

"Indeed, he did," replied Catherine, as she flicked through the photos. "I'll send her some of these marked for her attention. Any more games from her and it'll be *Graham* receiving the photos instead. That should do the job." She was distracted a while until she rested her chin on her hands and looked directly at Sophie. "It's all very grubby, isn't it?"

"I guess so. They meet at least once a week. Sometimes in an hotel," replied Sophie.

Catherine smiled. "No, no, I mean what *we are* doing is grubby."

Sophie grimaced. "Maybe."

Catherine pushed the file aside. "Okay what about Billy Ridley?"

"Not so exciting I'm afraid. Not at all." Sophie delved into her bag and retrieved another file. "Also born in Harlow. He's thirty-six. He has an older sister called Amy, but our detective couldn't find anything about her beyond school age. Ah yes, parents split up when Billy was young and the father and he went to live in Bristol. Not sure what happened to the mother. But he now lives back in Harlow. His father is unwell in a home, also in Harlow and he visits him regularly." She went quiet for a moment, reading. "And takes him out in a wheelchair every Sunday. Here," she said handing Catherine a photo. Catherine didn't take it and shook her head. "Keep it for now."

"Alright. William works at a mental health charity in Harlow called FirstStep. The detective said Mr Ridley got involved in the charity in the first place as a volunteer as he's had several breakdowns himself and was even homeless for a short while. Sounds like he's had a tough time but looks like he's back on his feet."

Catherine swallowed hard and glanced at the email from him still there on her computer.

"And he has a partner, her name is Joy, think they've been together a long time, she works in a shop in the town centre. Here's a picture…"

Catherine shook her head again. "No thanks."

"Nothing bad on him I'm afraid. Cleaner than you or I."

"It seems so," added Catherine. She could see him back then, in his pyjamas cuddling up to her, wanting to play, to be with just her. And now, this email? It was her fault and she'd have to fix it. Ignoring Sophie, she picked up her mobile to see if there were messages from John. Nothing. She looked up. "Anything else for me?"

"I don't think so. You know your interview schedule for this week, so I think we're done."

Catherine picked up the file. "Thanks. Good work."

Sophie stood up. "I hope it works for you. Let me know if you require more and … be careful how you use the information."

Catherine nodded as she studied her phone again. Still no message from John. Without looking up she replied, "will do."

****

Catherine quickly gathered up her things and ran to the car. She had just enough time to buy food at the supermarket before picking up the girls from school. Her mind was in a whirl.

"What's happened to your head?" asked Chloe as they got into the car. It was after eight before she had them tucked up in bed and their story read. She flopped into a chair with a full glass of red wine and took a large slug before checking her phone. Nothing. She tried John's number but it went straight to voicemail. "Please John call. Please." She rested her head back and must have fallen asleep as it was nine before she realised the time. Opening her laptop, she checked for more emails. Nothing from Billy. Catherine finished her wine, topped it up and started typing.

Ok Billy. Where when and how?

She watched her screen as she finished her second glass. Her heart leapt as the new email pinged into her inbox.

This Thursday evening 8. You know where to leave it

She sat back and stared at the screen. What did he mean, 'you know where'?

She emailed back.

Even before the answer came, it hit her. She gasped at the thought. Please God no, don't say it, but he did.

The Witch's Tree. Leave it by the trunk. I'll be in the woods watching. Send me your phone number I'll text your instructions on the night.

Catherine immediately replied, *not there. I can't – no*

No choice - be there

Ok she replied. Her heart raced. She'd have to get ten thousand pounds in cash by Thursday afternoon.

CATHERINE

CHAPTER 41

Thursday 24th January 2019

The house in Harlow where she'd grown up looked different from when she'd last visited more than two decades ago: a scrappy front garden, peeling paint and cars parked on the pavement. She switched off the engine so as not to draw attention to herself but left the wipers swishing so she could look at the house. Catherine stared through the driving rain; she was being pulled back to her past life against her will. As she glanced at the bulging rucksack on the passenger seat, her mind drifted back to the last time she used it; the lovely family holiday in Devon when she'd first received the call from Lucy and Neil about the discovery. So much had happened since then. Suddenly her phone rang, jolting her to the present. Glancing down, she was shocked to see it was John calling. She hesitated before answering, wondering what she'd say if he asked her where she was. Quickly she switched off the windscreen wipers.

"Hi."

"Hi," he replied. "I've just returned to the house to find a babysitter. Where are you?"

"You didn't tell me you were coming home. I've had to meet up with someone… work thing… are you coming home, John?"

He didn't reply immediately, then said, "It's always work, isn't it. Are you ready to talk?"

He sounded so cold it chilled her heart. "Yes… "

"Where are you?" he asked again.

"I'll be back in a couple of hours," she replied. "… I'll head home as soon as I can."

"We'll talk when you have time then," he replied.

"I'm so pleased you…" But he had gone.

Catherine put her head back and watched the rain splatter on the windscreen. There were things from her past she could never tell him. Things that had been buried with Amy: the rape; what really happened with Jimmy. But she'd have to tell him something more, than she already had.

Catherine looked at her watch. It was already seven thirty and she needed to walk to the woods and find the tree. As she opened the door the wind and rain hit her. Should've parked closer, she thought. "Damn it," she muttered as she adjusted the straps of the heavy rucksack over her raincoat. The water trickled down her neck as she marched toward the woods, constantly looking to see if there was someone that could be Billy, loitering or sitting in a parked car. A man walking a dog came toward her and she stared at him as he passed but he was too old to be Billy. At the edge of the wood, she stopped and shivered with cold and fright. The woods were pitch black. The idea of being back at the tree where Jimmy had died gave her the creeps. His ghost was everywhere. Could she do it? She had an instinct to run, but instead pressed on into the wood.

The branches swayed in the wind and the rain clattered onto the leaves on the ground. She looked down at her shoes, realising she hadn't even thought to change into boots; she'd turn up at home soaked and muddy and how would she explain that?

Catherine knew the route precisely, muscle memory from years playing there and climbing trees. She didn't need her torch and as her eyes adjusted she could make out the path toward the clearing and riverbank where the Witch's Tree stood. At one point she stopped, her body shaking, wondering if she dared go on. She could take flight now and be out of the woods in two minutes. Then call him, saying; 'you'll have to come to the car if you want it'. Perhaps he would be by the tree, wanting her to hand it over in person? She wondered about switching on the torch and scanning around, but the thought of spotting a person, or a pair of eyes behind a bush, petrified her. Tentatively she walked toward the Witch's Tree, glancing around, before taking off the rucksack. Could she hear someone? Was that a branch snapping? No, she told herself, it was just the rain splattering all around her.

Catherine carefully placed the rucksack up against the trunk. Her heart was racing. "Billy!" she called. She looked around, still no sign. She shouted even louder, "I've left it where you said!" She put her hands in her raincoat pockets and swivelled around sensing somebody behind her, but there were only more trees. "Billy!" she called. Catherine hesitated, wondering if he would appear but with no sign, she took out her phone, the screen dazzling her eyes. No new messages so she stuffed it back in her pocket and made her way toward the path, stumbling over a root on the way. Once on the path she felt a tightening in her chest. Oh god, I can't have a panic attack here, not now. She broke into a run and within minutes she was back at her car, leaning against the side, her chest rapidly rising and falling as she tried to get her breath back. A thought flashed through her head – had she lost the car keys in her mad dash? With relief she wrapped her fingers around the keys, still there in her pocket and within seconds was sitting inside, engine running, doors locked, heater on full, white knuckles tightly gripping the steering wheel. There she remained thinking, 'What next'? Shall I wait to see if someone arrives or leaves? But what for? It was an agonising half an hour before her phone pinged.

Thank you have rucksack and left

Without replying, Catherine drove off into the night.

****

As she approached the house, she was relieved to see John's car in the drive. How would he be? Would she be able to say the right things to keep him? She switched off the engine and stared ahead, lost in her thoughts. Taking a deep breath, she slowly got out of the car. Her hand was shaking as she unlocked the front door.

John was sitting in the kitchen, a glass of wine in front of him. He looked up as she entered. "Looks like you've been through a hedge backwards."

Catherine sighed and looked down at her coat. It still had wet patches. She ran her hands through her knotted hair. "I got caught in that storm," she replied. Catherine smiled at him, hoping to illicit the same, but to no avail. There was an awkward silence as she removed her coat and threw it across a chair. "I've been desperate to see you. I've missed you." She sat down and reached across the table, hoping he would take her hand. But when he didn't, she quickly retracted it. She wasn't sure if she felt stupid, hurt, or angry. Without saying a word, John got up and got her a glass and poured her some wine.

"Thanks," she said, "I need this." Catherine took a large gulp and thumped the glass down harder than she meant, nearly breaking the stem.

John folded his arms. "I've given it a lot of thought," he began. He hesitated then added, "You should know that I love you."

"Oh John, you've no idea what…"

"But," he interrupted. "Finding out you were not the person I thought you were, really hurt me. It knocked me sideways."

"I know. I'm sorry. So sorry. The truth is, I'd blocked out that life and talking about it would have brought back the horrors. But I know now that doesn't make it easier for you."

John sighed. "In a way I understand, even if it hurts that you never said." He picked up his wine and sipped. "You've always been, how can I put it, detached. Emotionally detached, that's it. I now see why, as you've been hiding so much."

"I don't know what you mean. I love you and the children unconditionally."

"I know, I know," he replied. "But now I can see more clearly that there's another side to you and that's why you're often distant." He thought for a second. "No, I don't mean distant, I mean it's as if you're here but not totally here, if you see what I mean. I thought it was that you were wrapped up in your job all these years but it's not that, is it? It was the burden of what you've been carrying."

"I can't analyse it, honestly. I've never meant to be distant and until recently I'd hardly thought about that other girl, Amy. I'm Catherine with the life I've, we've, created." She looked at him. "I do know I want us to be a family again."

"I know," he replied. "So do I. But I'm still not convinced you've told me everything. And you need to."

Catherine hung her head and whispered, "you're right." She looked back at him.

"Go on," he prompted.

Catherine took a deep breath. "That afternoon in the woods. It's true. I was on the same branch as Jimmy. Tina's suspicions were correct." She looked pleadingly at John. "But I swear I never caused him to fall."

"Are you sure?"

"Yes!"

"Why did you never tell the truth to anybody, then. Most of all me!?"

Catherine wiped her eyes. "I couldn't admit to it: nobody would have believed that I hadn't accidently or deliberately killed him. Can't you see?"

John thought for a moment. "Maybe. But what about me?"

Catherine wiped away her tears with the palms of her hands and looked at John. "I should have. I'm sorry. I'm so sorry. I just wanted to be believed. I guess I was worried you wouldn't believe me."

John shook his head. "Anything else I should know?"

Catherine tensed. It was now or never, she thought. "That's it," she replied and glanced away, then added, "there's no more to know."

John stared at her without saying a word, then nodded his head. "Okay," he answered, matter of factly. "I hope not."

Catherine reached her arms across the table. Her heart melted when he took her hands and gave them a squeeze. "Let's start again," he began. "But with no more secrets."

"No more secrets," she repeated.

Still holding her hands, John leant forward. "There's a couple of other things we should talk about."

Catherine tensed. "Go on."

"What are you going to do about Billy and Tina? We can't have her playing any more games. She's upping the ante. And there's no telling what Billy might do."

"I'll sort it," replied Catherine.

"How?"

"I don't know. I'll think of something."

"Let me know what you plan."

Catherine nodded, although she'd never be able to tell him. There was an awkward silence before she asked, "you said there were a *couple* of things."

John picked up the wine bottle and topped up her glass. Now it was his turn to take a deep breath. "I hope, one day, you'll be able to be more part of this family. Your job, this discovery, the cost to this family… I… just didn't realise how much it would rip you away from us."

Catherine suppressed the tinge of anger that welled up. What did he expect? "Things are going to change for the better," she began.

"How so?"

"I'm going to cut down the speaking engagements. The fact is, I think the intense interest in me will fade. So, I'll spend more time working from home, taking the girls to school. Everything."

John half smiled as he topped up his wine. "Let's see," he replied. "Let's see."

****

The next morning Catherine hadn't been in her office for more than five minutes when Sophie knocked on the door.

"Didn't know we had a meeting," said Catherine as Sophie came in.

"We don't," she replied. "Hey, you look better!" she added.

Catherine smiled. "John's back," she said.

"All good?"

"Getting there," replied Catherine.

Sophie sat down without replying. "Right. Are you ready?"

Catherine tensed. Why was it every time somebody said something unclear, she assumed the worst? She shut her laptop and looked up at Sophie. "For what?"

"You have a book deal! The advance is one million and you'll get half of that immediately you sign the contract. The remainder on submission of the manuscript."

Catherine sat back and blew out her cheeks. "Wow, that's unbelievable!"

"Not bad, eh? If it wasn't nine in the morning, we'd be opening the champagne."

"Thanks Sophie," she said. "I've no idea how I would have handled any of this without you. Well, it's more than that, it would have been a complete mess."

"My pleasure and as I said, you pretty much saved my company so it's a two-way thing." Sophie hesitated. "I'll go to the canteen and get us two coffees; you wait here and then we can discuss next week's schedule and contract signing? Oh, and while I think of it, the publisher got ahead of themselves and put out a press release. Here, you're on page two of The Times announcing a multimillion pound book deal. Not what we wanted, but hey," she said, tossing the newspaper onto Catherine's desk. "Back in a minute."

Catherine picked up the paper and with horror read the story. More publicity was exactly what she didn't want and she felt the anger rising. No more than a few seconds later her phone pinged.

Just seen the book money -I've been stupid not realising how much ya gonna be earning - asking for ten was ridiculous - I think another fifty is fair don't you? then we're done forever I'll give you time so shall we say three weeks today same place? You don't want to ruin everything now do you?

billy

Her first thought was to text back something obscene but instead she threw the phone onto her desk, knocking over a glass of water. This could go on and on, she thought.

"Seen a ghost?" said Sophie as she carefully placed the hot coffee on Catherine's desk. Deep in thought Catherine didn't reply.

"Okay?" Sophie pressed.

Catherine looked straight at Sophie. "No," she replied. "I'm not."

"Nothing I've done I hope."

Catherine sipped her coffee. "Of course not. I need more help from you though."

Sophie smiled. "Oh god, go on, what now?!"

"This is serious," said Catherine. She blew on the surface of her coffee, giving her time to think. "Listen, I'll deal with Tina using the information you've given me. But I need at least something more on Billy."

"What's happened?" asked Sophie placing her cup on the desk.

"He's threatening me and it's getting, well, difficult."

"Difficult? Give me some idea."

Catherine wondered whether she should say. "Put it like this, he's blackmailing me, wants tens of thousands of pounds and I doubt giving him money will end it there."

"Christ. He must have something on you. Still won't tell me? It could help."

"It's complicated."

"Have you tried reasoning with him?"

"No, not sure that would do any good."

Sophie thought for a moment. "Okay, leave it with me, let's see what I can come up with."

"Thanks, but we'll need to move fast."

Sophie nodded again, "I get the message. Now about the schedule for next week…" They worked through until lunch time when Catherine said, "Oh one thing before you go." She pulled out the photo of Tina with her secret lover. "Can you write on the back of this," she said handing it over. "Write, 'I'm sure Graham won't want to see this.'"

Sophie wrote as asked and handed it back. "Speak soon and good luck with the TV show?" she said as she opened the door.

"Thanks – I hope to get back to doing my real job sometime – science!"

Catherine sat back and studied the photo of Tina and her lover. At least Tina shouldn't be a problem, she thought. She'd pop it in an envelope marked 'confidential' and post it on the way home. As for Billy, was there anymore that Sophie could find out? It would have to be soon if she was going to head-off the demand for the fifty thousand pounds. Maybe she should try calling him? Catherine twiddled her pen around between her fingers, contemplating what to do next. She couldn't decide and thought the best thing was to get on with her engagements, spend as much time as possible with John and the girls and get her next research project on the go. Oh, and start the book. Christ, she thought, there's no time to think.

Catherine stared at her phone and the last text from Billy. She decided she needed to reply, so tapped out, *don't believe all you read in the newspapers -I can't get that sort of money plus we had a deal.* She hesitated, wondering if she should send or change it. In the end she pressed send.

A message came straight back, *of course you can and this is the end of it*

Catherine couldn't think of anything else that would help, so decided to leave it for now. She wanted everything to go away; craved for her normal life; not being famous and no ghosts from her past life. And John, he was right of course and she knew it. She had always felt detached, creating a cocoon around herself, protecting herself from Amy.

CATHERINE

CHAPTER 42

February 2019

As Catherine's taxi drew up outside the Salford TV studio, her heart sunk. Protesters lined the street waving placards and shouting. Only a handful of police and a flimsy barrier separated her from this angry bunch. Thank God John and the girls had been taken to a different entrance, she thought.

"You'd better get inside," said a Policeman, as he took her arm and guided her toward the building. But Catherine stopped in her tracks and turned, curious as to the nature of their protests. As she took one step toward the crowd, a man leant over the barrier and shouted right into her face. "You're an agent of the devil!"

Catherine recoiled at the stink of his breath and the anger written across his scarlet face. She went to speak but couldn't find the words.

"Ma'am," said the Policeman, as he tightly grabbed her arm. "This way!"

Catherine was taken to the green room with little time to recover from her ordeal. Her hands shook as she held her coffee, which she had no desire to drink. A few minutes passed before a young man popped his head around the door. "I'll take you up in three minutes," he said. "You, okay?" he asked.

Catherine nodded and smiled the best she could. How had it come to this?

"Lots of people get nervous prior to going on TV. You'll be fine," he added, smiling.

Catherine carefully put down her mug. "I know, thanks. I'm already an old hand at this."

As the door closed, she leant back in the chair and tried to bring her breathing under control.

The studio was hot and the lights bright. Catherine was ushered to the settee while a video played from the previous item.

"You ready Professor?" asked the presenter.

She was about to answer when a woman rushed over and ran a makeup brush over her cheeks and dabbed her forehead. "Quick last-minute touch-up. You're ready."

"Three, two, one," and they were live.

"We're so fortunate to have Professor Holmes here today. Good morning, Professor."

Throughout the interview Catherine could feel her phone vibrating in her pocket. Thank God, she'd put it on silent. Usually, the floor manager would take it away but it had been missed in the rush. Catherine could see John and the girls in the darkness off-camera, Chloe and Ruth under strict instructions to remain silent.

Now the presenter turned to Catherine who was aware of a camera moving, presumably zooming in on her. "You've made a discovery of a lifetime," she began. Catherine's phone buzzed again. "What's next for you?"

Catherine smiled as she began to explain all the exciting avenues of research now open to her. "Also," she added, "I want to inspire a younger generation, particularly girls, to take up science. I'm worried that in the frenzy of the talk of aliens, it will be forgotten how important rigorous science is, and how an exciting a career it can be."

"I'm sure you'll do a wonderful job at that!" The interviewer hesitated and Catherine just knew what was coming next. "But there's some considerable anger at this discovery. I believe you experienced this as you arrived here today," added the presenter. "Can you explain the nature of this and your reaction?"

Catherine's voice quivered as she answered, "Yes. Outside the building there are a few tens of protesters, some who appear to be extremely angry. It's difficult for me to comprehend."

"What's making them so angry?" asked the presenter.

"One placard seemed to suggest I am an agent of the devil. Not sure I can expand on that. Another seemed to suggest I am in cahoots with the government and this is a plot to distract the nation from what is really going on. Then I saw another which suggested we have known about this alien lifeform for decades and it's been a conspiracy of silence."

"And how do you react to this?"

Catherine straightened her shoulders. "I take little notice. All you can do to counter conspiracy theories is to present the facts as they are. From there, some people will believe what they want, I guess."

"And what about the chatter on social media?" asked the presenter.

"This is more concerning," replied Catherine. "I have death threats from people who have decided, for whatever reason, that this discovery is entirely fictitious. I have one group on social media who believe I'm an alien." Catherine forced a smile. "Mostly, I don't see these posts as somebody handles the social media for me. You'd be shocked at what some people, holed up in their bedrooms, safe from scrutiny, can say to another human being, without being held to account."

"I didn't appreciate you would be targeted like this."

"I guess all people in the public eye have to put up with this. It's remarkable that wild conspiracy theories can carry more weight than serious considered scientific research – that evidence based reasoning can be trumped by ridiculous baseless ideas, ungrounded in reality. It's a mystery to me."

"Let's hope the social media platforms get a grip of it."

Catherine grimaced. "I doubt that will happen without regulation. It's so important that we follow the science. We have found evidence that there *may* be life, but we cannot say with one hundred percent certainty that there is life on that planet."

"Fascinating," replied the presenter. "When will we know with more certainty?"

"Not yet. In a couple of years, we should see the launch of the James Webb Space Telescope. This will transform our understanding of the cosmos and that includes that of exo planets and their atmospheres. Even their moons. Until then, I think we'll have to wait."

The interview continued and so did the vibration of her phone. Twenty minutes later she was back with the family, being bundled into a taxi.

John leant over close to Catherine and whispered, "didn't know about the death threats."

"Don't worry, it comes with the territory. As I said, everyone in the public eye gets it. And I don't look at it, that's Sophie's job." To change the subject, she turned to Chloe and Ruth, "Breakfast time, girls!"

"Sausages for me!" replied Chloe.

"And me!" added Ruth.

John smiled at Catherine and reached his hand out across the taxi. She took it and gave his hand a gentle squeeze.

"Good to have you back," he whispered.

"It's good to be back," she replied and sighed. She felt better now than she had for a long time. Catherine pulled her phone out of her pocket. Ten missed calls and a long string of texts.

John leant over and put his hand on her phone. "It's Saturday."

"One second," she replied without looking up. The text read:

This is joy, billy's partner, call me urgently - what have you done?

"Okay?" asked John.

Catherine glanced out of the window wondering how to answer. "Sort of, I'll need to make a call."

"Want to share anything?" he asked.

"I'm hungry," piped-up Chloe.

"Me too," replied Ruth. "Are we nearly there?"

The taxi stopped outside the hotel and as they got out Catherine didn't follow. "I'll join you in a minute."

John held hands with both girls. "Then switch your phone off?"

"Sure," she mumbled. The girls went inside with John as Catherine walked away from the hotel entrance for somewhere more private. Is this thing ever going to go away? What did Joy mean, 'what have you done?' Catherine wondered if Joy knew Billy had extracted ten thousand pounds from her.

"You bastard!" greeted Catherine's connection. "How could you do that! You've got no idea what you've done!"

Catherine's heart raced. "Joy, what are you talking about?"

"Doing that to Billy, how could you!"

"Stop, stop, I've no idea what you're talking about."

"Yeah right! It'll be your fault if he kills himself!"

"Joy, please tell me what's happened."

"On his way home from the pub last night he was accosted by your henchmen. They took him into an alleyway and threatened him with his life. One even punched him in the stomach just to make sure he got the message. When he got home, he was totally distraught, screaming, petrified. Said they had threatened to kill him if he made any further contact with you or said anything. It was all under control until you did this."

"Joy, I have no idea what you're talking about, honestly. I've got no henchmen, I'm a uni professor!"

"You sent them. Who else would have?!"

Catherine was silent as the dread of what must have happened hit her in the stomach. Her shoulders dropped as if in defeat as she realised it must have been Sophie. Or rather her connections to the criminal world through her old boyfriend Jack. He could probably make one phone call and rustle up a few unpleasant individuals to scare the hell out of someone. "Oh God!" she exclaimed.

"And it's worse than you can imagine," continued Joy, "he's disappeared. He had no sleep last night and I couldn't console him this morning so he left the house, took the car and I don't know where he's gone. He's fragile. He's tried to commit suicide once before."

"Oh God Joy, please, I've had nothing to do with this. You have to believe me. Have you any idea where he may have gone?"

"Last time he went to a train station, planned to kill himself that way. You need to fucking do something!"

"I'll come right now. It'll take four hours to be with you, but I'm coming."

"I'm going out looking for him. You'll need our address?"

"Got it thanks," replied Catherine.

There was a moment's silence. "How come?"

"See you as soon as," she replied and hung up. Now she needed to deal with John and the girls. How was she going to do that?

Orange juices had arrived and the girls were already looking at the buffet. "Mummy!" called Chloe, "they've got chocolate things!"

"Lovely!" she called back as she sat down next to John.

"And?" he began.

She reached out and put her hand on his arm. "Listen, Billy's in trouble. He may be about to take his own life. I need to help him."

John sat back and folded his arms. "Christ! What's happened?"

"He's missing. I need to go to Harlow right now, help look for him, reason with him if I can."

John's face fell. "But that's hours away and you'll need the car. Are you sure you'll be able to help? You might make it worse."

"John, I need to go."

"Are we ever going to have you to ourselves?"

"John, please. This is life or death of my brother. I must."

"How do we get home without the car?"

"Train I guess, and the girls will find it exciting."

"See what I've got," said Chloe, putting a plate full of food on the table.

Catherine looked across. "How lovely! Toast, jam, sausage, baked beans and pain au chocolate, all on one plate!"

She glanced at John before continuing. "Listen girls, unfortunately Mummy has to go. No breakfast for me!"

"Oh, where are you going?" asked Ruth as she munched on her breakfast.

"Mummy's got to sort something, but I'll be back tonight in time to read you a bedtime story. Promise," she added as she stood up.

"You'll be needing these," he said, holding up the car keys.

"Thanks," she said and bent over and kissed him on the cheek. "Love you." Catherine left, taking time to grab two sausages, a slice of bread and a paper napkin on the way. Five minutes in the car and she called Sophie. "What the hell did you do to Billy?"

There was a silence from the other end, then, "You asked me to sort it. It's okay, isn't it? They planned to scare him, rough him up a bit. I heard that's what happened and he walked home pretty much uninjured, but with a clear message. What is he doing now?"

"I didn't ask you to set the heavies on him!"

"I'm sorry," she replied. "I thought it would work. What choice did I have?"

Catherine shook her head and banged the steering wheel. "Hell!... Alright, it's partly my fault. I didn't expect you to do that and now he might be trying to commit suicide."

"Oh God no!"

"I'm on my way to try and find him."

"I'm so sorry Catherine. Is he missing?"

"He is. His partner Joy called me, clearly overwhelmed with fear and not surprisingly extremely angry as she assumed I had instigated it."

Sophie thought for a moment. "They'll never connect anything. These guys will have been careful and they are good."

"Good?"

"You know what I mean. Good at what they do."

"I can't believe we're having this conversation. I've got to go. I'll let you know what happens."

"Ple…" was all she heard as she finished the call. The journey to Harlow took nearly five hours and she was exhausted and tense as she rounded the corner and finally found the house. She stared at the terraced property; to think Billy lives here, my lost brother. Or rather I'm the lost sister she thought. Catherine knocked on the door but there was no reply. She looked again at her phone - she had a text.

amey I've been to the parks been to the police station they're not interested as he's only been gone hours and now on my way to the railway station - you'd better start looking for him when you get here let me know -it's your fault

Catherine texted back, *I'm here*

She sat in the car not knowing where to start. She had his number, perhaps she should try ringing? Her call went straight to voicemail where she left a message. *Billy it's me, Amy, Catherine. I'm sorry, really sorry. Please don't do anything. I so need to talk to you. I'm sure we can work something out. Please Billy. Please.*

For a while she remained in the car, paralysed by indecision. She put her head back on the headrest and closed her eyes. What would he do? Where would he go? She stared at her phone - nothing. Then it hit her – no, please, not there. Catherine instinctively started the engine and the tyres squealed as she pulled away. She knew exactly where he would be and she needed to get there fast.

CATHERINE

CHAPTER 43

Catherine parked on a lane which ran along the edge of the woods. The light had dropped and a damp muggy fog had descended. Grabbing her torch, she leapt out of the car, slammed the door and ran into the woods, following the path she knew so well. Close to the clearing she called out, "Billy! It's me! Billy!"

She entered the clearing, her feet soaked and clothes damp from the water dripping from the trees. Suddenly she slowed, almost creeping toward the Witch's Tree, careful step by step by step. As she approached, she couldn't see anybody: she'd wasted precious time. Catherine walked close to the trunk and looked up. There on the broomstick branch, the one on which she had read her books and watched her little brother whizz around on his bike, was Billy, sitting motionless. She felt her flesh creep and she shivered as she took in the scene: One end of a rope was tied around his neck and the other dangled down and looped back up, tightly tied around the branch on which he was sitting. One leap or slip and he'd be killed instantly.

"Billy," she whispered, "it's me, Amy. I want to help." No reply and he didn't even look down. She stared up at him, hardly able to believe this tubby bald man was the little brother she had once known.

"Speak to me, Billy. Please. I want to help you." A picture flashed through her mind of him slipping off the branch and hanging in front of her. Her stomach flipped as she grabbed the lower branch and hauled herself up. Quickly she was on the broomstick branch and slowly sat down next to him. She was sitting no more than two feet away. Without warning, he turned and in a monotone voice said, "I didn't recognise you."

Catherine smiled. "Think we may both have changed, Billy."

He continued to stare at her although she noticed he didn't return her smile. "I can't take this life anymore." Billy then fell silent, before adding, "Don't try and change my mind."

Catherine had no idea how to handle such a fragile mind. What should she say? She said the first thing that came into her head. "I'm not here to persuade you; you must make your own decisions. But I'd never forgive myself if I lost my little brother."

Billy began to cry, eventually wiping his eyes on his sleeve. He turned to her. "You should have thought about that, a long time ago."

"Oh, Billy I know, I'm so sorry. But will you hear me out, at least? Give me a chance? Then decide and judge me?"

He didn't reply, so she continued. "Is it about what you witnessed here?"

He wiped his eyes again. "What do you think? I was never the same after that afternoon and have struggled in one way or another, ever since." He fell silent again and she wondered if she should say more. She was about to fill the void when he said, "But it's an illness, Amy. If it hadn't been *that* shock that triggered it, it would have been something else. A ticking time bomb, that's me." He turned to her, "although the way you silenced me was cruel."

Catherine winced. "I know Billy. I'm so, so sorry."

"And now, you walking back into my life brings it all back. The stuff I'd tried to bury. Then being beaten up by those men last night. I can't take it. I've become worthless and I hate my life. And myself. There's nothing you can do now, it's too late; the damage is done." They sat in silence for a moment, before he said, "Joy said it was you who sent those thugs. Why would you do that?"

Catherine shuffled closer, hoping she might be able to grab hold of him.

"Stay there!" he shouted, his aggression surprising and unnerving her. She carefully shuffled back sideways. "Okay, okay, sorry." After a moment she continued. "You'll have to believe me when I say I had no idea that was going to happen. Somebody I know decided to do it, without consulting me."

"But *why* for godsake!?"

"After I'd delivered the first ten thousand pounds, I hoped you'd keep your word: that it would be over. Then when you came back and asked for another fifty thousand, I asked a colleague what I should do and she said she would help… but you have to believe me, I had no idea what she was planning. Had I known I would have stopped her."

"What are you talking about?"

"Your emails and ransom demands."

"What are you talking about?" he repeated.

She thought for a moment, confused by the conversation. What game was he playing? Or was his brain muddled? "You wrote to me and demanded ten thousand pounds, remember?! But honestly, I forgive you!"

He turned to her, his face angry. "I've absolutely no idea what you're talking about. Why are you saying this?"

At that instant she wondered if he was going to jump and she tensed. "You didn't email me?"

"Why would I do that?"

"You did phone into the show though?"

"That was me. I wanted you to know I'd worked out who you were. Or I thought I had and I wanted to make sure. When the presenter cut me off, I knew it was you. Plus of course your husband contacted me at work. I'd guessed he knew nothing of your past."

"And what about the emails?"

"I've already said, I don't know what you're talking about."

"You didn't send emails asking for money?"

"What do you take me for? No!"

Catherine was dumbfounded. "Oh God, Billy. I'm sorry. Somebody has been pretending to be you and blackmailing me."

"I don't know how you think I could do such a thing. I've kept quiet for decades and it will always be between you and me, you know that."

She so wanted to move closer and hug him but dared not. "I'm sorry Billy. I was tricked. Somebody has that money and well, more importantly, contributed to where we are now. Please, please forgive me."

He didn't reply and they sat in silence for what seemed like minutes. "Billy," she eventually began, "can I tell you something I've never told anyone?"

Billy shrugged his shoulders.

"It doesn't excuse what I did to Jimmy, I know nothing can ever change that, but something happened the night before Jimmy's death, which contributed to my reaction."

"Reaction? Is that what you call it?"

"Action, I mean." She hesitated. "Billy. He raped me at the party." Catherine watched him and could see him processing what she had just told him. Before he said anything, she spoke again. "I know it doesn't excuse what happened. But maybe you could have some sympathy? I had been attacked, violated; I wasn't in my right mind when I met them here the next day. What I did on the branch was impulsive. It wasn't planned; it wasn't deliberate. I was scaring him, getting my own back the best I could in that moment and it just escalated. Then suddenly the branch broke and to my horror… he fell." She wiped away her tears. "You've got to believe me."

After a moment he said. "I didn't know."

"I've told no one until this moment. Not even my husband."

"You didn't tell Mum that he raped you?"

"Especially not Mum."

"I get that," he replied. Then added, "I'm sorry. I had no idea."

Catherine began to cry. "I know, that's why I disappeared, became someone else, to leave my life behind."

"Perhaps that's what I should have done," said Billy.

"Who knows. But… I know nothing of your life." She reached out a hand, but he didn't take it. "I'd like to know more. I want us to be close again. Can we?"

After a moment he said, "do you remember when we used to come here? I'd ride my bike and you'd sit up here reading?"

Before she could answer he said, "of course you do, that's why you came to find me here. You knew."

She dared again to reach out and touch his arm and this time he didn't pull away. "Those memories are etched in my mind. Happier times Billy, before all the homelife shit started."

"You looked after me, didn't you?"

"In my way, yes. And I loved you, Billy. You were my little brother. You always will be. I still love you."

"But everything changed right here, in this tree, the day Jimmy died. And now?" Billy turned to her. "It's the end for me, Amy. At least we have had this talk."

Catherine tensed and said the first thing that came into her head. "What about Dad? I just heard he was ill." She immediately regretted bringing up such a bleak subject and worried that it might take him over the edge. "I mean, don't talk about it if you don't want to."

Billy stared ahead. "He and Janice were involved in a car accident. She died and the accident was Dad's fault. He was badly injured. He recovered, although he needs physical and mental support. He's in a flat which has some care and I visit him every day. He's with it, it's just he goes vacant from time to time and forgets things."

The tragedy and irony of it all, thought Catherine. "God, that's horrible."

"They loved each other dearly and looked after me, that's despite me being a nightmare kid. Janice was lovely."

"Billy."

He turned to her and she saw that face she had loved so dearly. "What?"

"Can we go and visit him?"

He was quiet for a moment. "Maybe."

"I couldn't do it without you. Please?"

"You're a big celebrity now, you don't need me."

"Only *we* know what we've been through and it's only us that can get through this… together."

"Maybe," he repeated.

"Can we get to know each other again?" She reached out and touched his arm. "I love you Billy, remember that. Shall I untie this rope from the branch? Then we can carefully climb down and get you home. Joy is worried sick." Her heart raced as he sat there in silence. Then suddenly he twisted slightly and she yelped, thinking he was going to jump or fall but instead he began to untie the rope, then he took the noose from around his neck and let the rope fall to the ground.

Before she could say anything, he shuffled across and wrapped his arms around her and sobbed. "I've missed you," he whispered through his tears. "So has Dad."

"I've missed you too, Billy," she said holding him tightly. They embraced in silence for what seemed like minutes before she gently moved away and smiled at him. "Come on Billy, let's get you down. You okay to do this?"

"I think so" he replied. "I was taught by the best."

For a moment she worried about his dramatic change of mood. Perhaps this is how it is, one minute high, the next rock bottom. She'd need to be careful. Soon they were standing on the soft damp leaves. She put her arm around his waist, almost guiding him through the woods to the car. She started the engine to get them warmed up. "You'd better call Joy," she began, "I've had ten missed calls and goodness knows how many you've had."

Billy touched his pockets. "Didn't bring my phone. Didn't think I'd be needing it."

"Hi Joy," began Catherine. "Billy's fine, he's with me and we'll be home in five minutes."

"Oh, thank God!" she replied. "Where was he?"

"Doesn't matter, he's safe." She replied and hung up.

Joy was at the door when they arrived and ran out to greet Billy, hugging him tightly. Catherine watched as they went inside, arms entwined, both with tears in their eyes. She stood outside for a while, neither Billy nor Joy realising she hadn't come in. She needed to let them be. A minute later Billy came out, "come on sister, you'll be needing a cuppa." The three of them sat at a small kitchen table with mugs of tea. Joy had said nothing to Catherine and avoided eye contact. Billy chatted about when he and Catherine had been young. Neither could stop him or change the subject. Then he moved on to apologising profusely for the terrible angst he'd caused.

Joy leant over and hugged him. "It's not your fault," she whispered. "You're ill and need more help."

He looked from one to the other. "My mood can change in a flash. It's like walking down the street and somebody coming up behind you and whacking you across the back of the knees with a bat."

He began to cry again and Catherine put her hand on his. "We'll help you get through this."

He nodded and sniffed. "Thank you. I need to get better, otherwise I'll lose you Joy, I know."

As he started to cry again Joy hugged him. "Of course you won't. Don't talk nonsense."

Catherine thought she had better leave them for a moment. "May I use your bathroom?" She asked.

"It's that door in the hallway," said Joy, tears still running down her cheeks. Catherine stood up, left the kitchen, and opened the first door she came to in the hall. But it was a small cupboard with an ironing board, coats and shoes scattered across the floor. And then she saw it, stuffed in a corner: her green rucksack. She picked it up and looked inside: empty of cash. Her first thought was Billy had lied so convincingly. Then it dawned on her. It had been Joy, of course it had! She had pretended to be Billy in her emails. Her mind raced. That meant she must know something about what happened in the woods all those years ago to even know that she could blackmail her. How much did she know? And Billy, had he any idea about the money Joy had stolen? She had to be careful: she couldn't risk upsetting him. But then she couldn't let this go, she had to find out. As she walked back into the kitchen she said, "oh I found this on the bathroom floor, I guess it wasn't supposed to be there," and dumped the rucksack on the table. She looked at them both to see the reaction and it was clear.

"Weird, never seen it," replied Billy. He turned to Joy. "Is it yours?"

The frightened look on Joy's face said it all. "I guess so. Not sure how it got there. Not used it in years," she said as she grabbed the bag. She avoided eye contact as she collected the mugs and placed them carefully in the sink. But Catherine could see her face was scarlet.

"Oh well, no matter," replied Catherine nonchalantly, "didn't want to trip over it, that was all." She'd sent a clear message to Joy and she'd received it. Better still, Billy had no idea.

"I'd better be going," said Catherine. She put her hand on Billy's arm. "Can I come and see you soon?"

He smiled. "Of course. Anytime. But…" his voice trailed away. "Will you come with me now?"

"Where?" asked Catherine.

"I go and see Dad most days and always early Saturday afternoons. He'll be wondering where I am. I don't want to worry him so I've got to go."

Could she cope with it, after everything that had happened today and not least the lost years? How would her father react? She glanced at her watch. And it would mean not getting home on time as she'd promised. Then again Billy had asked and she needed to support him.

"Hadn't you better warn him first? Then we do it another day?"

"We could, but let's just do it."

In the silence Catherine looked at Joy, then back at Billy. "Okay," she said. "Hope it doesn't give him a heart attack!"

In the car, Catherine plucked up the courage to ask. "Does Joy know about what happened at the Witch's Tree with Jimmy?"

Billy was silent for a moment and she wondered if he'd heard. Then he replied. "Sort of, not everything. She came with me once on a visit to my therapist, to support me. There she heard about the shock I experienced back then when Jimmy died. But I didn't say everything, although she thinks you must have caused it by being on the branch." He turned to Catherine. "But she really doesn't know the whole story."

Catherine felt her shoulders relax. "Thanks Billy. And what about your therapy, do you still have someone helping you?"

"It's difficult. It's been sporadic with the NHS. Joy said I should go private, but it was so expensive. The charity I work for helps people get back on their feet but doesn't help with long term therapy. In the end, Joy said she would pay from her savings. She has two jobs and works like crazy. But she's used her savings to help pay for Dad's care and now there's nothing left. But the other day she said to me she'd managed to borrow some money, which really worried me. She said we can now afford to get the right treatment and help Dad. Joy has been an absolute angel. Living with me has cleaned her out, not sure why she sticks by me, I'm hardly a catch."

Catherine nodded as if not really paying attention. Now she knew why Joy had blackmailed her. Joy knew just enough about her and Jimmy and at the same time desperately needed money. It all fitted. Could she blame her?

Catherine parked the car and turned off the engine. "Before we go in, you should know that I can afford to help you. This discovery has brought me wealth I didn't expect and to support you and Dad would be something I would love to do. I'll give you the money for whatever treatment you need and for however long."

She saw Billy begin to cry which set her off too.

"Thank you. You'll need to speak with Joy about the money, she handles everything."

Catherine smiled. "Of course she does. We'll sort it in no time."

"It's good to have you back, Amy."

"It's good to be back Billy, it really is… one thing though… will you call me Catherine, not Amy? I let Amy go and became this different person, Catherine. It was my way of escaping. It hurts to hear her name."

Billy nodded and smiled to himself. "Of course," he replied. Then added, "in some ways you've not changed."

"How do you mean?" she said as they got out of the car.

"Well look," he said pointing into the car, "it's spotless!"

"Very funny! Now," she added, "I hope I'm ready for this," as they headed to their father's flat. "And that he is too."

CATHERINE

CHAPTER 44

10 months later December 2019

Catherine stepped out of the stretched black Mercedes; John close behind. They'd come straight from The Dorchester Hotel where the publisher had put them and the girls up for two days. She was in the most expensive dress she'd ever bought. The fact that she had no idea if she would wear it again didn't bother her. This was going to be a big night.

"Catherine!" called Sophie. "How are you feeling?"

Catherine smiled and gave her a hug. "Anxious, but no surprise there. Excited too!"

"You look, like, amazing?" enthused Sophie.

"She does, doesn't she?" answered John as he put an arm around Catherine's waist.

Cameras clicked from every direction as the team from her publisher ushered her toward the magnificent entrance to The Natural History Museum. Over the past ten months she had never worked harder: research, TV, radio, travelling, conferences and of course, the book. Fortunately, she had been able to write most of it from home; she'd cherished taking the girls to school and seeing more of John.

"This way, Professor." Immediately they were at the stunning Romanesque entrance to the Hintze Hall. "Wow," enthused Catherine. The magnificent blue-whale skeleton hung over their heads. The hall had been beautifully laid-out for a banquet.

"Gosh, how many people are coming?" asked Catherine.

"About seven hundred?" replied Sophie. "This is an *international* book launch! I've heard the numbers. Around fourteen million hardback copies will roll off the presses. The US is getting nine million and Britain three. Advance orders have been huge: Amazon has sold over one million worldwide already."

"That must rival The Goblet of Fire!"

"It might well, yes!" replied Sophie.

Catherine took in the hall, the grand staircase at one end leading up to the statue of Charles Darwin. Above the statue was a huge screen, with an image of her book cover. Above them, the intricately hand-painted ceiling with relief carvings of plants and animals. "It's just stunning. And the lighting, oh my," she added. "The whole hall is bathed in blue and purple light."

****

Catherine stood at the lectern as the applause died down. "Thank you, Vice Chancellor, for the introduction and thank you all for coming tonight."

"It's only fifteen months since I was lying on a beach with my family, enjoying a much-needed holiday; oblivious to what was about to unfold. Discovering we are not alone in this vast cosmos has shaken the world.

The knowledge we are not a uniquely intelligent species has led us to question our beliefs and to re-examine our place in the universe. Humankind can never be the same again. I am often asked, what is next? What is the research that follows this discovery? Of course, there are many exciting avenues of research, whether that's learning more about this new lifeform or looking for life on other planets. But for me, the real question is, how will humankind use this new knowledge? How will we behave as a species now we know? Will it bring us together? As we examine ourselves in this new reality, will it help us better understand the true nature of life and how precious it is? I'm an optimist, so I believe this to be the catalyst we need to find a new peace; to take care of each other and to treasure our fragile and beautiful planet.

Catherine picked up a book and held it aloft. *"This book takes the reader on a journey. A journey through key scientific breakthroughs and initiatives upon which our discovery is built. And don't worry, it's digestible! But it puts the discovery into context and, as Sir Isaac Newton so eloquently put it, 'If I have seen further, it is by standing on the shoulders of giants.'*

But it's not exclusively a view of the science. For me that would not have expressed the essence, meaning or significance of the discovery. It's also a book about my life; how a nerdy, difficult, and uncommunicative young woman; one who had, in her mid-teens, experienced first-hand the death of a friend; one who hid her past from herself and those she loved: How she came to where I stand before you today. And like the achievements of us scientists, it's so often the encouragement, brilliance and devotion of others that inspire and enable progress, redemption, and in my case, atonement. I'll forever be grateful for the love of my husband, my gorgeous twin girls, my brother Billy and my father.

I sincerely hope that those who read the book will see that this discovery holds a mirror up to us as a species and individually. Laying bare the challenges of life and how we react and behave to not being alone; not being at the centre, not being the exclusive product of our gods.

It's about life, here and on planets far away – those we are just glimpsing and those yet to be discovered.

Thank you.

Catherine would not normally drink Brandy, but tonight was different. She studied the golden liquid as she swirled it around her glass, smiling to herself. She'd spent an hour circulating, guided from table to table by Sophie. Now the evening was catching up with her. The girls had been whisked away straight after the meal and prior to her speech. Everything was taken care of in this new world she occupied. Now she was sitting with her father, Billy, Joy and John, enjoying a final drink. In the weeks that had followed her saving Billy, she'd met with Joy and told her she could keep the money. In the end they'd gone to a local pub and had too much to drink and laughed until they were thrown out.

In the distance she saw Professor Morehouse. "I must go and see Stuart," she said, touching John's arm. "Back in a moment." Catherine felt the effects of the alcohol as she walked over to greet him. She hugged him and they talked about the evening and were quickly joined by an animated Neil and Lucy. After a few minutes he put his arm around her shoulder and steered her away from the group. "What's your thinking?" he asked.

"About what?" she replied, feeling giddy.

"You know, the offer from the University of California: you returning to the USA."

"I'm probably going to accept," she whispered. Catherine put her hand on the back of a chair to steady herself. "Who wouldn't want to live in sunny California for a while!"

"I thought you might say that. You'll be a huge loss, you know that."

Catherine touched his arm. "Thank you." She smiled, "let's discuss how we might collaborate."

He nodded and put his hands in his pockets. "Have you told them you're accepting?"

Catherine shook her head. "Nope. I'd thought I'd get this out of the way first. But I'll do it shortly. Then somehow, I'll have to tell the VC."

"Indeed," he replied. She noticed his expression change as he asked. "And John, he must be excited I guess."

Catherine hesitated. Professor Morehouse looked her in the eye. "Catherine. No, surely."

She bit her lip. "I know I know, I must, it's ridiculous. I should have already of course, but with everything going on and being scared he'll say no; I've not managed to find the right opportunity. But I will," she added. "Tomorrow. Soon. I promise."

"You're a very determined individual Catherine. You let nothing get in your way it would seem."

"You're right," she replied wistfully. "Someone once told me I'm emotionally detached." Catherine glanced around then back to Stuart. "I guess I am."

****

She slumped in the back of the limousine, her head resting on John's shoulder as they headed to the hotel.

"What a night!" said John. He thought for a moment. "You know, as you were writing the book, I was really surprised you delved into your past. You opened your heart in a way I thought you never would." He turned to her and saw she was looking at him intensely. "It helps make the whole thing more of a human story," he said, "connects the person to the discovery."

Catherine thought about what he had said. He was right. The book had been cathartic. But wasn't it time to tell him what had really happened in the Witch's Tree? The rape and the true nature of Jimmy's death? Would she ever be completely free until she had told the one person she truly loved? Before she knew it, she was saying what she thought she never would. "What happened that day wasn't an accident," she whispered.

John said nothing and she wondered if her speech was too slurred for him to understand.

"You know that don't you?" she added.

"What day?"

She had to concentrate to speak. "The day of Jimmy's death."

He took hold of her hand. "Oh, you mean being on the same branch, I kind of guessed it had caused the branch to snap, despite what you said." He turned to her and gently kissed her on her forehead. "Who wouldn't have kept quiet about that?" he continued. "I would, I'm sure. It was still an accident. I mean, he was high on drugs for a start."

She was quiet for a moment, then said. "I don't mean that." She looked out of the window at the brightly lit shops, windows full of Christmas. "It wasn't an accident," she whispered." Suddenly she felt dizzy and nauseous as the car navigated the heavy late-night traffic. Her eyes felt so heavy she couldn't keep them open. Catherine put her arms around his chest and pulled him closer. "I've always wanted to tell you," She mumbled, as John stroked her hair. "Exactly what happened that day."

He smiled at her. "You already did, don't you remember? You said, you were on the branch." He smiled again and put his arm around her shoulders. "You're a bit drunk. Rest here and we'll be at the hotel in no time."

She heard herself mumble, "I need to tell…" but couldn't finish and instead, through her tears whispered, "I love you."

"I love you too," he replied. "A day in London with the girls tomorrow," he added brightly. But she was already asleep.

CATHERINE

CHAPTER 45

It was a week since the book launch and Catherine had been on tenterhooks, waiting for John to ask what she had meant by 'it wasn't an accident'. How could she have been so stupid? She had been drunk, but still, she should never have said it. Through the alcoholic haze, he must have misunderstood. God, she hoped so. All week Catherine found herself analysing his facial expressions, his moods, bracing herself each time he looked serious and began to speak.

To her relief, he was happier than he had been for a long time. John was excited about Christmas and she had promised faithfully she wouldn't let it be disrupted, as it had been last year.

But her loose tongue hadn't been her only source of worry. She still hadn't raised the subject of the new job and she'd known of the possibility for nearly a month. Soon she would receive a formal offer. Her tummy flipped each time she thought of telling him. What if he said he didn't want to go? What would she do? But then she told herself, of course he would love to go. It would probably only be for a few years anyway.

As she drove into the restaurant carpark, she saw his car already there. Catherine checked her watch: she was on time for once. John had phoned her at work with the news he had booked their favourite restaurant. It was the last day of his term and they often celebrated with a dinner out. Now they could afford the very best, but still preferred their old favourites.

The waiter pulled out her chair.

"Hi, you've started without me," she exclaimed, smiling. The waiter took the champagne bottle out of the cooler and filled Catherine's glass.

"Sorry, couldn't resist it," he replied.

"Cheers," she said as they chinked glasses. "Here's to a peaceful family Christmas."

"I'll drink to that!" said John, taking another gulp.

As the alcohol hit her stomach she immediately relaxed and decided tonight, right here, was the moment to tell him. It couldn't wait and he was obviously relaxed.

Before she could speak, John leant forward, as if wanting to confide in her. "I've got some good news," he whispered. He tilted his glass forward, as if to emphasise his point.

Catherine put her hand on his. "Gosh, that makes two of us! You go first," she added.

"Okay. Ready?"

Catherine laughed and clapped her hands. "Don't tease me!"

"I've been offered a new job!" he announced. "At last! Some recognition."

Catherine gasped and sat back. "What!?" She hesitated then said, "Oh sorry, that came out all wrong." Her heart sunk;

she could hardly believe what he had said. "Exciting…Tell me more."

He hadn't seemed to notice her shock as he took another gulp of Champagne. "The Head of English quit today. She'll work her notice and finish at Easter. The Head called me in and asked if I would like the job. I'd have to be part of an interview process but she made it clear: I was the only qualified internal candidate and she didn't want an 'outsider' as she called it."

Catherine stared at him, then did her best to smile. "That's…" She finished her glass in one, then added "Amazing. Congratulations, darling." An awkward silence followed as she picked up the bottle and topped up his glass and then her own.

"If you're worried about me going full time, we can easily afford help with the girls," he said.

"It's fine," she replied. "I'm so pleased. You… deserve it."

John frowned. "What's wrong, then?"

Catherine took his hand in hers. "Nothing's wrong, as such," she began. "But. Well. I've also had a job offer."

John squeezed her hand. "That's good, isn't it?" he said. "Both of us in the same week! What is it?"

Catherine let go of his hand and leant back, folding her arms. She was about to speak when the waiter came over to take their order. She waved him away, "Five minutes," she said.

Catherine turned back to John. "It's less of what the job is and more about where. It's at the University of California, Irvine, UCI… but I don't have to take it," she added without thinking. Her heart was thumping as she watched John intensely.

John nodded and his expression was one of defeat. "I see."

After all they had been through, she couldn't bear to make him unhappy again. But this job...

"What is the job?" he asked.

"Another Professorship. A lot more money. Even greater funding. No teaching and...

"Perfect, then," he interrupted.

"I guess so." Would it be emotional blackmail to tell him more? She had to, she thought. "I've had other offers too this week. I met with Sophie yesterday who told me offers have come in for TV appearances; a trial to host my own science program; a contract to advise on a sci-fi movie. And all these are in LA. And that's just the start of it." Catherine reached across the table again and took his hand. "You could get a super teaching job out there and it would be amazing for the girls. Just think what an experience it would be!"

John looked away, then back at her. "I thought our lives were getting back to some sort of normality. Some stability at least."

Catherine sighed. "I know. It's not ideal timing."

"Bit of an understatement," he replied.

She hated this conversation. "We don't have to go, John. It's a joint decision. You know that."

"Is it?" he asked.

"Of course."

"How long would it be for?"

Catherine had no idea. "As long as we wanted. Three, four years, I guess."

John folded his arms and nodded, thinking. After a moment he said. "I love it here." He hesitated then added, "don't get me wrong, our time in the US was fun. But our life now, here, in Cambridge, living in this beautiful village, my parents close by, the girls' school, my job… *Your* job, even… The money. It couldn't be better, could it? Can't we just enjoy what we have, rather than shooting off in search of something better?"

Catherine put her head in her hands, then looked back at John. Her heart ached. She was torn. "You're right. It is lovely here." Catherine sighed. "It's just that opportunities, they come and go."

John shook his head. "Not for you. Be realistic. There'll always be something exciting after what you've done. You don't have to take the first bunch of things that come along."

He had a point, she thought. But this was so prestigious, exciting and they could live in California.

"Have you had a formal offer from UCI?" he asked.

Catherine shook her head. "No. I only heard about it in the last few days."

"When do you have to give them an answer?"

"They want to know asap. And I owe it to the uni to let them know I'm going… *if* I am going."

"Who else knows about it?"

"I mentioned it to Stuart today," she replied. "I needed his view. He thinks it's a smart move, although he says I'll be sorely missed."

John sighed again.

Catherine positioned her elbows on the table and rested her chin on her hands. "I'm sorry, John. I really thought it would be exciting news."

John smiled ruefully. "I thought mine would be too."

"Shall we talk about it another time?" asked Catherine.

"Good idea," he replied. "Let's eat."

Later that night Catherine got out of bed and sat in the kitchen. She couldn't sleep with her stomach cramps. John had hardly touched his food and they had left early and driven home in silence.

Opening her laptop, she emailed her contact at the University of California asking if she and John could visit for two days, early in the new year. If she could get John there, she was sure he would change his mind. Within an hour, she had a reply: 'of course - would be delighted to host you and your husband'.

****

"I've got to go into work first," said Catherine jumping out of bed. "We'll have to go to the airport separately," she added.

John, still half asleep, turned over. "What time is it?"

"Five thirty," replied Catherine.

John rubbed his eyes. "We are leaving for the airport at, what, eleven?" John sat up. "You'll be back well in time, right?"

Catherine had had to work hard to persuade him to visit. The whole subject had lingered over Christmas, festering in the background. He'd made it pretty clear he didn't want to up-sticks and go abroad, but at least he was now coming to check it out.

"My meeting is in London, so I'll take my bag now and get the train out to Heathrow. I'll see you there. It's Business Class so we can meet in the lounge."

John slumped back down on his pillow. "Whatever."

"What do you mean?" Catherine sat down on the bed next to him and stroked his face. "The car's coming for you at 11 and the flight's not until 2. You'll be fine. We'll have fun!" She looked at him but his eyes were closed. "John? Please? Try and at least appear enthusiastic."

John rolled over onto his side facing away. "I'm getting some more shut-eye."

Catherine went into the bathroom and stared at herself in the mirror. Am I really doing the right thing, she wondered. Could he be right, our lives are sorted, why mess with it? She suddenly realised she was gripping the sink tightly and let go. No, it's the right thing. It'll be amazing. Catherine brushed her hair and went back into the bedroom. Trying to lighten the mood she said, "Love you! Wish I was in there with you. I'm jealous." But she wasn't jealous in the slightest. She was excited by what the next few days may bring.

****

Catherine checked-in for her flight and decided to wait for John before going through security. She got herself a coffee and then called his mobile. Her heart was racing she was so excited. Seeing it was after 12, she knew he would be well on his way. The call went straight through to voicemail so she left a message: *'Hi it's me – I'm sitting in Pret just opposite the check-in desk - see you soon. Love you.'* Catherine then sent the same message as a text. After fifteen minutes she had finished her coffee and had checked her phone a dozen times. She tried his number again with no luck. She texted, *'call me when you can- I'm going through to the lounge. See you soon! Luv's ya!*

    Catherine grabbed a salad and a glass of Chardonnay and found a table in the corner of the lounge. It was close to 1 now and with the flight an hour away she took a sip of wine and called John. Straight to voicemail. She called his mother's mobile.

    "Hi, it's me!" She began.

    "Hi Catherine. Where are you?"

    "Still at the airport." She hesitated then asked. "Girls okay?"

    "Happy as can be!" she replied.

    There was an awkward silence before Catherine explained that she and John had travelled separately. "Did you hear from him before he set off?"

    "No. Why?"

"No reason. I was just wondering what time he set off as he's leaving it a bit late."

"No idea."

"Okay, see you when we get back," replied Catherine. Now she felt a flutter in her tummy. Why was he late? She checked the traffic reports on her phone: Nothing. She went over to the desk and glancing at the woman's badge asked, "Hello Elaine, I'm Professor Holmes, can you tell me if my husband, John Holmes, has checked in yet?"

Elaine tapped on her computer, then looked up and smiled. "No, not yet."

Catherine checked her watch, it was 1:10 and they'd be boarding at any moment. "Can you let me know when he does?" she asked.

"Of course, my pleasure," replied Elaine.

As Catherine fetched another glass of wine the announcement came over to board. She got up and went to look at the screen, as if she needed confirmation. Her flight number was flashing and the word 'boarding' was clear. Catherine sat down and tried his number again, only to find it went to voicemail. *"I'm still in the lounge,"* she said. *"It's one fifteen and we're about to board. Where are you? Let me know. I'm worried."*

Catherine pushed her salad plate aside, checked her watch and took another sip of wine. Had she told the driver the wrong terminal? She checked her emails. No. Perhaps he had gone to the wrong terminal anyway? Or the wrong airport? Surely not? But then he would have phoned her, wouldn't he?

Then she heard her name being called over the Tanoy, requesting she went to the desk. "Thank God," she whispered as she hurried over.

"It's time for you to board, Professor Holmes," said Elaine. "You're almost the last person."

Her stomach flipped as she looked at the clock. One thirty. "Has Mr Holmes checked in?" she asked. Her mouth was dry and she could feel sweat under her armpits.

"I'm afraid not. He'd probably miss the flight now, even if he checked-in in the next five minutes."

Catherine looked at her phone. No messages. She looked back at Elaine. "I'll wait a few more minutes." She took a deep breath and did her best to smile. "Until I'm actually the *last* person to board. Come and get me then."

"I…" began Elaine, but Catherine had already turned to go back to her seat.

Catherine sat and put her head in her hands. "Oh God," she whispered. She slouched back in the chair. She knew then he wasn't coming. Perhaps he'd had no intention of coming? Or had she upset him by travelling here separately? No, she thought. One way or another he was going to disappear at the last minute. What have I done? Why didn't he simply say?

"Professor Holmes?"

Startled, Catherine looked up at Elaine. "Is it time?"

"I'm afraid so." She smiled adding, "You're officially the last passenger to board."

At that moment, a memory flashed into Catherine's mind: heartfelt words and a promise, written in a diary, over twenty years ago by a naïve teenager. She stood up and handed her ticket to Elaine. "I'm not flying," she announced. "Apologies," she said, picking up her bag, "But I need to go and mend something very precious to me." And with that, she was gone.

Acknowledgements

I am indebted to the many people who have helped me write this novel.

My wife Fiona has been with me on this journey since the beginning. She has read every line countless times, listened patiently to numerous plot ideas, (some better than others) and encouraged me when it got tough. Without her hard work and endeavour there would be no book.

I am profoundly grateful to Katy Regan, author of How to Find Your Way Home, Little Big Lies, The Story of You, and many more, who mentored me from the outset. Her guidance, encouragement and insights were invaluable. Thank you!

I am also indebted to my trusted readers: those dear friends who diligently ploughed through the manuscript, spotting errors, and making insightful suggestions to improve my story. Thank you to Olivia Baker, Wendy Blanton, Christine Anderson, Hani Edwards, Simon Church, Lisa Price, and Karen Thew.

Thank you to Dr Ed Gillan who guided me on the exo planet science and the life of a University Professor, James Tunley on the structure and language of a Coroner's report and Janice McClean on police interview and forensic procedures. Any errors are entirely mine.

A special mention must go to Emma Parkes-McQueen for the stunning book cover design - another super job done with a lot of hard work and creativity.

Finally, to Catherine Holt for the loan of her Christian name!

The Science

Do exo planets exist?

Yes. As Catherine describes in her talk at John's school, the existence of the first exo planet was confirmed in 1995. Since then, many thousands of exo planets have been discovered, revealing planetary systems around thousands of stars in the night sky. As the technology has improved, astronomers have detected ever smaller planets, even those similar in size to the Earth.

Does the star Proxima Centauri exist?

Yes. And it has its own exo planets. Proxima Centauri is the nearest star to the Sun, at around 4.2 light years away. At the time of writing, in late 2023, there are two known exo planets orbiting the star: Proxima Centauri b and Proxima Centauri d, plus one candidate exo planet, Proxima Centauri c, which requires additional data to be sure of its existence. The exo planet Proxima Centauri b, is a rocky planet of comparable size to earth.

So what about Catherine's exo planet, Proxima Centauri e? Astronomers do not yet know if such a planet exists. But it may well be just a matter of time before another exo planet is discovered orbiting Proxima Centauri.

Can we detect the constituents of exo planet atmospheres?

Yes. It is true that astronomers are now able to detect the composition of exo planet atmospheres. A key discovery by Catherine is the detection of CFCs in the atmosphere of the exo planet. CFCs are yet to be detected in any exo planet atmospheres. But the technology and methods exist to achieve this and should they be discovered, then it would be as exciting and shocking as in the novel!

It is true that there are no known mechanisms for CFCs to occur naturally.

Printed in Great Britain
by Amazon